A CHALLENGE TO HONOR!

"Falc of Risskor," Altmer said, "how can we accept your word?"

After a few moments of silence Falc said, "Once, in over two hundred years of the Order's existence, one man of the Order Most Old swore falsely; *once*. You know that. All know it. That forsworn Son of Ashah was slain *by members of the Order*. We swear, and we fear only ourselves. And the penalty for even minor transgression of our oath is removal of the Sath-scar."

Falc shot forth his right arm. "Here is the scar, on the right wrist. Its removal means taking off hand and wrist, above the scar. You know this, Prefect Altmer. Your stance and tongue and that suggestion insult both you and your master. I will pass now. Stand aside."

DEATHKNIGHT

ANDREW J. OFFUTT

ACE BOOKS, NEW YORK

This book is an Ace original edition,
and has never been previously published.

DEATHKNIGHT

An Ace Book/published by arrangement with
the author

PRINTING HISTORY
Ace edition/March 1990

ISBN: 0-441-14159-5

Ace Books are published by The Berkley Publishing Group,
200 Madison Avenue, New York, New York 10016.
The name ''ACE'' and the ''A'' logo are trademarks
belonging to Charter Communications, Inc.

PRINTED IN THE UNITED STATES OF AMERICA

10 9 8 7 6 5 4 3 2 1

DRAMATIS PERSONÆ

The Order Most Old

the Master
the High Brother
Sir Ashalc
Sir Ashamal of Mersarl
Sir Ashax
Chernis   *monk at the High Temple*
Sir Chondaven of Ryar
Sir (Pryor) Coineval
Sir Falc of Risskor
Sir Kaherevan
Sir Parneris
Sir Relashah the Gasser
Sir Sench of Southradd
Sir Senithal
Sir Sijamal of Missentia
Sir Vennashah

Holders

Arisan of Secter
Barakor of Missentia
Chasmal of Lango
Chazar, *his son*
Daviloran of Cragview
Daviloran, *his nephew*
Faradox of Lango
Mellil, *his daughter*
Hanliven of Ryar
Havenden of Kem
Kaladen of Missentia
Kinneven of Lock
Kinnemil, *his daughter*
Minndeven of Ryar
Stavishen of Lock
Synaven, Arlord of Zain

Historical

Bazarga Redstar
Jalan   *a soldier*
Sai MaSarlis   *Emperor*
Sar Sarlis   *Conqueror*
Sath Firedrake   *Liberator*
Shardanis   *Emperor*
Sharsarlis   *Emperor*

Others

Alazhar   *Housechief of Chasmal Holding*
Altmer   *Prefect of Chasmal Holding*
Arle   *agent of Chasmal*
Baysh   *Housechief of Faradox Holding*
Sir Bellenevin, Morazain
Chalan   *peacekeeper at Daviloran Holding*
Colax   *an innkeeper*
Corunden   *an innkeeper*
Ezalil   *an ajmil*
Garsh   *peacekeeper at Kinneven Holding*
Jinnery   *a farmer of Zain*
Jorgen   *Prefect of Kinneven Holding*
Mandehal
Parshann   *a farmer of Juliara*
Querry   *a farmer of Zain*
Querryson Chalis   *his son*
Sak   *rejected by the O.M.O.*
Shalderanis   *"Emperor"*
Salih   *an ajmil*
Sarminen   *peacekeeper at Daviloran Holding*
Sendaven   *rejected by the O.M.O.*
Sereah   *an ajmil*
Shar   *Prefect of Faradox Holding*
Simayil   *an ajmil*
Sulah   *an ajmil*

to Christopher John Offutt, firstborn and writer

"In each ending there is a beginning"
—*ancient Sijese saying*

"In the beginning is the seed of the end."
—*Sath Firedrake's addition*

DEATHKNIGHT

FALC

He drew rein when his mount topped the final rise on the Old Road and he had first sight of the walls of Lango-by-the-Sea. While he sat gazing down at the city, he stripped off soiled tan gloves and the long, white derlin. Cut full, almost voluminous, the hooded sun-robe buttoned down the front. The sleeves were long and full and the hood designed as protection from dust- and sandstorms: it ran to a point and could be drawn over the head so as to cover the wearer's face completely.

He drew it off over his head without disturbing the buttons. He bundled and folded it while his mount, Harr, stood patiently. His rider, having uncovered clothing of unrelieved black, felt no movement. With meticulous neatness he packed the derlin away in a knapsack of black leather, one of three hung on his mount. Knapsacks, bedroll, harness and canteen were all of black with the merest touches of maroon. He drew on gauntlets of leather black as the wings of a crawk, with a narrow border of maroon.

He rode down to rose-walled Lango with his eyes of dark, dark blue slitted against those mites called *anjoni* that danced

1

before his face. The sun was low over the ocean to the east and its late afternoon rays painted buildings gold and orange amid pools of purple shadow. With the scent of the sea in his nostrils he began the "Song of the Omo," in the singsong murmur that was as close as he could come to singing:

> Oh how I love the open road!
> The sky above sunlit with gold!
> Honor lies ahead on this long ribbon of dust—
> O let me but ride the open road!
>
> Oh how I hate the falling rain,
> For I am not a field of grain!
> Weary buttocks tonight and ever more mistrust;
> Oh you may have this rearward pain!
>
> Oh how I love my slith'ry st—

Nearing the city walls, he broke off and slid into a repetition of the second verse of "Destiny Wears a Black Cloak," in the same muttery singsong:

> Pitfalls and treachery and call of lechery!
>   How these conspire to firm my desire
> To seek a different road!
> Ashah accept me!
> Ashah guide me!
> Ashah deliver me;
> Sath inspire me!

The gatekeepers heard. At sight of his clothing and gear, they opened for him without question or comment. The black-clad man rode past just as silently so that they fancied they heard even the faint creak of his leather mailcoat. His mount rolled yellow eyes at them. They saw him send forth his tongue to take an insect out of the air.

Harr paced through the city, noisy as any city and all cities, and as full of color and brightness, bustle, and occasional beauty amid ugliness. He did see evidences of damage from the quake a couple of weeks ago, which had been more severe than usual. Here and there work parties labored at repairs. People glanced at Harr's rider and stayed out of his way. Most looked away as well, although a few stared. The traveler's face—all of him that was unclothed, though it was bearded and mustached—was unusually dark even on Sij, but that was not the reason people stared or looked affectedly away. He was abundantly accustomed to it by now and it was easy for him to appear not to notice. Almost, he did not.

He had been to this eastern coastal city before, and knew his way to the House of Chasmal. He directed Harr there at the plod, with care for others in the streets. Harr knew every whim and knee-pressure and rein-twitch of his master, as well as six vocal commands, two whistles, and his own name— which his master had chosen because in time of trouble it could be bellowed out in one breath.

They paced carefully around workmen repairing a ragged crack in the street. The result of a smallish afterquake, Falc assumed, seeing no damage to the buildings here.

A little deeper into Lango he halted without a sound or the sign of a smile while a panicky mother hustled her child from his path. Like nearly every woman of Lango, she had sur-rounded her deep blue eyes with a busy design in red-brown cvarm, the same dye that so darkened her nails. Harr availed himself of that opportunity to take six or eight ants off a drainpipe, with one whip of his tongue.

Another time the traveler drew up rather sharply because of the cart emerging from a blind cross-street. The driver was having trouble with his dray-beast. He showed nervousness, and made some obeisance, and looked quite helplessly apolo-getic in his faded, dusty clothing. All the while, he jiggled and slapped his reins and said nasty things to the recalcitrant beast. It, meanwhile, showed interest in Harr.

The interest was not mutual. Harr was a war-darg, and a consummately well-trained one at that. Harr was a rather austere and ascetic beast, if such attributes could be said to be possessed by a darg.

A party of three peacemen—watchmen or police employed by the city's ruling Council of Holders—drew up on the far side of the troubled carter. They made faces and stood in such ways as to show contempt while making an elaborate display of patience. Their uniforms were bright green with blue; their metal was polished to high gleam. The traveler said nothing and showed nothing, recognizing in this uniformed trio the attitude of the hired help of the powerful. That provided opportunity and suggested action.

He did not resist the temptation. With a quiet word to Harr, he swung down onto the cobbles.

The cart's driver looked fearful as the dark man paced toward him, full black cloak a live thing about him. The buckle of his weapons belt provided the only color in his somber garments. A carnelian the size of his palm without the digits was intagliated with the snarling head of a writh.

Keeping his gaze fixed on that buckle, the carter made no move to defend or to flee. He did make a sign, pressing the first and middle finger of one hand together and drawing them up the center of his tunicked chest. On dull old quiet boots of black, the traveler turned so as to come up alongside the dray-darg's blinkered head from the rear. He muttered a word or three just before he slid all three fingers under the beast's halter, immediately back of the blinder. A slight tug of the black-gloved hand brought a complaining hiss from the darg before it allowed itself to be set in motion. The cart, piled with speckled melons, clatter-rumbled across the intersection. Its driver appeared to be in a semi-shock of relief.

At the last moment he thought to make the offer: "Do have yourself a melon, good Sir Knight of the Order!"

"Wi' thanks," the traveler said in a good voice, and released the darg's halter.

The cart rumbled by. As its tailgate passed, the traveler easily plucked out a melon, without choosing. They all looked good, head-sized red-orange fruits speckled with yellow. He stepped away holding it against his chest with his left hand. The cart rolled on down the narrower side street. The traveler's long cloak, cut so that its hem was concavely arched between two points, swirled like the wings of a gigantic crawk as he turned. He strode back to his mount, hardly pausing to direct an abbreviated bow to the three peacemen.

They stood staring in open-mouthed silence. This, from a Deathknight!

The dark man swung into Harr's saddle one-handed, getting his cloak's skirt out of the way with a gesture made unconscious by long repetition. None of the three peacemen or the two Langomen who had come along and paused to watch saw him move his legs or gauntleted hands or heard him speak, but the charcoal-and-maroon-equipped darg started forward the instant his master's buttocks touched the saddle.

"Sir Omo," the leader of the police trio said in greeting, and his hand was nowhere near the neck of his holstered electric pistol.

The traveler, having accorded them that brief bow previously, took the words as acknowledgment only and said nothing. Harr paced on.

His dark rider would far rather be called omo than Deathknight. Over two hundred years had passed since the founding of the Order Most Old. O.M.O. had become OMO and its black-swathed servants, the Knights of Ashah, were often called by those initials. This omo rode on through the city's noise, and was stared at and avoided. He saw only three others who were mounted, and none others who appeared to be from outside Lango's walls. The sun was riding the eastern horizon with the dull glow of old gold when he reached another wall and high gate.

This wall was stuccoed in an off-white now gilded by the setting sun. Pale green paint divided the wall into wedge-shaped panels pointing alternately up and down. The points of the green-painted sections were upward. Black wood and black iron barred the red gate, which was visibly thick. While the tower to the right of the gate appeared empty, the traveler knew that it was not. He sat his darg, looking up at the tower. A man stepped from it into view atop the wall. He wore green and green and brass, with brown leathers. A soft, side-flopping cap of green leather rode his shoulder-length hair, rather than a helmet. The hair was of such a dark blue that it appeared almost black. His crossbow was not wound. He said nothing, but only stood gazing down, waiting for the dark man to speak.

He did: "I am Falc of Risskor, member of the Order Most Old and years-long Contracted with Holder Kinneven of Lock in Juliara. He sends by me a message to your lord, whose blood I hope is swift and warm."

"Sir Omo," the sentry acknowledged with a little inclining of his head, and gestured to someone below him. "Open for Falc of Risskor, Deathknight of the Order and bearing message for Holder Chasmal."

His "Deathknight of the Order" was both pretentious and redundant, but the traveler said and showed nothing. He was sure that no insult was intended. People did like to say the words! That did not dissuade the Sons of Ashah from wishing uncharitable things to him who had first uttered the unfortunate word "Deathknight."

The gate opened. Falc of Risskor, O. M. O., rode into the courtyard of the House of Chasmal of Lango. Soon one of Chasmal's green-collared, green-headbanded slaves, delighted with the melon presented him and charmed with the information that Harr would appreciate the seeds and rind, was prepared to lead Harr away to good care. The youth turned back.

"Wi' respectful abjections, S'r Deathknight . . . might one ask why such a noble war-darg bears the name of a blossom?"

"Ah," Falc said, "you are from over around Morazain and Shoe Lake, then. But hush; he does not know his name is also a small shadeflower. Perhaps his master has a sense of humor, and perhaps it is a word chosen because it is easy for a dutiful darg to recognize."

"Ahhh!" The young man smiled. "He knows his name and responds to it, then!"

To that the dark man said nothing, and Harr was led away by a "boy" who wondered if it were true that this shivery, midnight-clad man from the farthest south never smiled. That could not be asked, with or without "respectful abjections." And how had he known where the groom was from?

Falc stood looking after them, wearing a whimsical expression as he watched Harr's lazily carried tail. He and the darg had been together for years, and trusted each other. Never mind that a harr was a lovely little blossom of spring, in shades of pink or nursery fulve with its stamen centered in black. Harr did not know the meaning of his name, or his master's strange sense of humor. To the darg the sound "Harr" meant "This Self," and he responded instanter. Further, Harr had no compunctions about charging and chewing men and other living things including dargs ridden by enemies of his master; indeed, like his master, Harr enjoyed it.

As for the boy; no matter where they moved or were moved and no matter how long they remained there, people from the Morazain/Shoe Lake area never quite lost that odd lengthening of the short *a* sound.

Falc, carrying one fold-top knapsack battened with thong, entered the House of Chasmal. Patiently he awaited the fetching of Chasmal's Housechief.

The Housechief came. His medallion of office shifted importantly on the chest of his green robe with his movements. No big man at all was this Alazhar, and with a bit more hair at cheeks and chin than above, where his dome shone like a copper skullcap before the receding line of still-blue hair. He wore three rings, one on each finger of his left hand. The gold signet was ostentatiously huge and shiny.

"Falc of the Order Most Old greets the honorable Housechief Alazhar. My Contractor, Holder Kinneven of Lock in Juliara, has sent me with a message to your lord, whose blood I hope is swift and warm."

Alazhar, who was familiar with Falc from three previous visits over several years, heard out the formality and nodded. "And yours, Sir Falc of Risskor. Holder Chasmal will be occupied for some hours, and then will surely be glad to welcome and hear Sir Falc. Holder Kinneven's blood is swift and warm?"

"He had no complaint when I departed Lock."

"Good, good. What may we supply? Wine or beer; a snack, perhap? Bathwater, a companion?"

"Nothing of food or wine. I would not reject a horn of beer and a bath in private, if you could arrange, and perhaps a companion after—depending on your lord's pleasure and availability."

"I fear it may be a matter of some hours, Sir Omo. Do come."

Soon servants had been importantly dispatched to fetch beer and hot water, and Falc was remarking that he had not previously seen this chamber to which Alazhar led him.

"Your memory impresses," the Housechief said. "It is best for the bath in private your honored Order requires."

"M'thanks, Alazhar."

He accepted a carved rhyton from the whisper-footed ajmil who had fetched it, but politely did not drink while she and Alazhar were present. With a querying look Alazhar indicated the young slave who, undismissed, stood gazing at the floor before her toes; Falc shrugged, signifying an unvehement negative. Alazhar nodded his understanding.

"Get hence," he said, and the ajmil departed without a glance at the men.

"A good girl," Falc said to the Housechief, to mitigate his semi-rejection of her. "I do like her attitude and carriage. From Kem?"

"Yes. You have seen her aforenow?"

"No. The Kem-trained do have a way of holding their heads."

Alazhar gave his own balding head a little twitch to show that he was impressed. "She has also just come into heat— œstrus, in the event you wish to reconsider."

Falc shook his head.

"Might one ask what it is about her that displeased you?"

"Nothing, I assure you."

"You have a practice of not accepting the first offered?"

"I have done so," Falc said, batting aside a question both stupid and wasteful of breath and time.

"No prying was meant, Knight of the Order—Oh! My great apology! Do be at home in this House."

Falc's nod was brief. He saw no reason to say anything more. Having been welcomed, belatedly, to partake of House Chasmal's hospitality, he hefted the horn carved into the likeness of a legless darg. He drew the plug from the tip of the tail and took the thin stream of amber liquid expertly and easily at a distance equal to the length of his forearm. His head easing forward as his thumb eased over the snout, he took the last of the stream without spilling so much as a drop.

At that moment an ajmil and two boyslaves came into the room. They bore four steaming buckets and one that did not steam. The four were poured into the wedge-shaped tub, which was of brass-banded marble the color of a cow's cream a week after the birth of her first calf. Falc watched the girl's grace as she set down her bucket. To Alazhar he turned a dark face with eyebrows raised; the Housechief nodded.

"I shall see to it, Sir Falc."

"I have four-fifths of an hour?"

"I fear so. Sereah! Go and sit by the waterclock and think carnal thoughts. When four points have elapsed, return to this chamber."

"And knock," the omo said.

The mildly pretty slave glanced up at him, a tall lean hawk-faced man all in bulky black that did not lessen the darkness of his face. Eyes on the man so dark they looked black, too; like a pool of water in an old and abandoned quarry. She nodded, and left her head down.

"Get hence," Alazhar said, and she was gone, with neither man having seen aught of apprehension or anticipation in the attractive face with its pointed chin and cvarmed eyelids. She was neither girl nor small, Sereah. Alazhar turned back to the guest. "Do be at home in this house," he said and, the slaves having left, he too departed the company of the omo Falc of Risskor.

Never forgetting his thumbtip over the pouring hole in the horn he held, Falc waited until the door had closed before he went to it. Quietly he eased the bolt across. He lifted the horn and drank deeply from the large end. Lowered it while he swirled the beer in his mouth. Spat it into the bathwater, and poured in the rest of the rhyton's contents. Wisps of steam rose lazily from the big basin. Into it Falc upended the fifth bucket, the tepid water. He saved back only a little. The rhyton he rested on a low table carven of selwood and fitted with iron feet.

Falc lifted his hands to the vicinity of his collarbones. With two little *snik* sounds the clasps of his cloak came free of the metal receptacles in his leathern shirt. They differed from its ninety-seven thumbprint-sized studs of iron only by being not convex, but hollowed to receive the cloak's clasps. In his hands the hook on the carnelian buckle's back came free of the leather. He laid aside the unenhanced weapons belt, which bore two holes only. A knight of the Order might smuggle this or that, but he did not fatten. With the gemstone buckle, the sheathed sword and knife, and the belt's width that matched the length of his forefinger in front and nearly twice that in back, he had divested himself of four kilograms of weight.

Falc paused, eyes closed. Slowly he lifted his arms and seemed trying to stretch up to overtake his extended fingertips. As slowly, he came down again onto his feet. His lips were moving.

He drew up the hem of his surcoat of black, which fell to mid-calf. Ritually rolled upward, it came off over his head to be laid on the table with care, rolled. He freed the three laces on the left side of his half-sleeved mailshirt of leather, then loosened the six under his right arm. The shirt peeled all the way across to the left, revealing another layer of leather. On the left side, the coat parted with the overfold. The three laces drew through their holes; they were attached to the under-layer, which was dull and smooth. It swung loosely outward and Falc doffed the undershirt with its added protection of another strip sewn across the back.

He laid aside over seventeen kilograms of iron-bossed black leather with a little clunk of its throwing knives and, on his knees, ritually arranged the mailshirt so that it could be got into swiftly.

His quilted under-jerkin clasped in back. Rising, he pulled it, with its studded crotch-protecting pendant, over his head. Under it he wore the cap-sleeved, double layered shirt of Rissman cotton, this from the area of his native Risskor. It was gray with age and much sweat, except for the long sleeves. Those were black because they showed, down to his gauntlets of black suede reinforced with stiffer bands of the same.

Falc extended his arms straight before him, fists balled, and stood very straight with his head high. His crawk-head beard, trimmed short, seemed to bristle outward from his chin. He dropped his arms to his sides before removing the left gauntlet, and the right. He was careful to lay them on the low table so that they were palm to palm, left on top. Straightening, he stood with his head bowed a long moment before he drew the cotton shirt straight up over his head. An omo in such a position was vulnerable; Falc whipped both arms swiftly down and let the shirt fall.

Strangely, for a man who wore such a bulk of clothing above the waist, he looked little smaller without it; only tauter. The clothing was dull black and the omo, while lean, was no small man. His chest was divided into distinct plates. Muscles moved visibly in it, and in his arms and back, with the movements of those thick-wristed arms. Rangy rather than bulky, he was nevertheless a man of obvious strength and condition, with a stomach in which the musculature was visible.

His body was marked by more scars than one.

A knight-Son of Ashah did not sit to remove his boots. Lifting his left leg across the right on which he stood, he drew off the soft boot without a waver or a hop. That stockinged foot he planted, and removed the other boot of old black suede, soft with the rintseed oil that lent it some odor other than that of feet. The stockings were kept up by being folded over the boot-tops. That foot planted, he removed the left stocking, and then the right. First arranging the toe of each stocking in the boot and the rest dangling, he stood the boots between tub and door, pointed doorward.

"A knight of the Order Most Old is ever ready to go forth on behalf of the Order, honor, or his Contractor," he murmured, and added other quiet formula-words memorized long ago.

His leggings were leather with the rough side faced out, for a dull appearance. Under them, gauzy cotton tights had been white and were now gray. Falc skinned out of them and stood nude but for his crotch-protector. A tall man and dark, lean of hip and small of buttocks; wiry of calf and tight-skinned in the thigh. The hip strap of the snug, reinforced pouch for his genitals was a hairy and visibly rough length of rope about half the thickness of his least finger. Almost as oddly, the stonepouch itself was white.

Having disrobed in the ritual Way of the Order that left a man ever ready for swift defense and vulnerable for one instant only, Falc arranged his discarded clothing. He patted the knife of unrusting obsidian in the slender sheath attached to his stonepouch. With his arms folded over his chest he performed thirty-three slow squat-to-heels and rise-on-toes. The last ended with his seeming to strain toward the sky, his lips moving, his body a taut line from the toes on which he balanced to the upward straining fingertips. His lips were moving. He relaxed and breathed deeply, diaphragmatically, for ninety-nine beats. The number of a man's fingers and its multiples, without the thumb, formed the mystic number sacred to Ashah.

Falc stepped into the tub and sat. Immediately his eyes closed. His lips moved while he washed the pouch for his stones, wrung it, and laid it on the floor well away. The obsidian knife remained with him in the tub.

Once he had bathed, swiftly and in a businesslike manner,

he drew his shirt and under-leggings or tights into the water with him. He murmured the poem of the Way, sloshing the garments gently. Then Falc of Risskor rose and stepped naked from the tub to turn and, on his knees, wash his own under-garments in the way of all knights of the Order Most Old.

2

The ajmil Sereah returned full of the widespread curiosity about these men. What did Deathknights wear under all that crawk-colored clothing, and what were they like naked? Could they truly be as other men, these strange traveling monks who were so sinister and were known to do death as part of their work, their Order? Were they more than other men as some said, smiling? Were they less, as others sneered, perhaps hopefully?

Naturally Sereah concealed her disappointment at finding this knight O. M. O. dressed, at least partially.

Fresh-washed tights and shirt of cotton hung on a cord stretched before the window. From the same knapsack that had produced that cord, along with comb, toothbrush, razor and scissors, Falc wore snug black leggings of wool, low boots of wine-red felt, and a long-sleeved, long-tailed shirt of mossweave the color of glittery jet. Its collar was ascetically high; its chest was blazoned with the Order's stylized closed fist and enough of a forearm to show the scar of Sath. This was in deep scarlet picked out with nothing, so that at times it hardly showed against the black. She saw that he had no sideburns, and no hair was visible because of his coif or skullcap. No, Sereah saw, he did not wear an earring. So much for that myth of these grim monkish messengers and super-warriors!

"Do not stare at your betters, ajmil."

"Abjections, my lord! I did not expect my lord to be clothed."

"You have no experience with knights of the Order, Sereah of Lock?"

"No, my lord." She regarded the floor, wondering how he knew whence she had been sold, when she was eleven.

"We choose who sees our skin, ajmil. I am like other men in few respects, and I am cruel as well."

"My lord has but to command his slave."

"I see that you have brought beer. Drink."

"My lord . . . I may not."

"Your lord has but to command, you said? Is this your obeisance, your abjection? Drink."

She went to her knees. "My lord, I may not. It is not permitted."

"And if I beat you?"

To the floor Sereah said, "It is not permitted that an ajmil of this household drink beer, Master. To beat me would be cruelty without need or provocation."

"You provoke me by lecturing me, Sereah."

When much later another green-jerkined ajmil came, she noted that neither Sereah's clothing nor the Deathknight's had been unlaced, but that Sereah had been physically chastised. Further, he was fully dressed even to mailcoat and that big cloak like a sail, and held his belt of weapons. What was not visible were the scores of questions he had asked of Sereah, and the knowledge of Langese affairs he would take away with him and bear home to Kinneven. Carefully not looking at Sereah, the new ajmil addressed Falc's chest.

"I am bidden to guide Sir Falc to my master the lord Chasmal," she said.

"An odd house," he commented, "in which ajmini begin speech with the personal pronoun. Outside, both of you, and wait."

The slave opened her mouth to speak and thought better of it. She stepped outside the door. The mildly whipped Sereah accompanied her.

Falc closed the door.

In private, he performed the Rite and Words of the Blades, buckled on the belt, drew sword and renewed the approved shorter version of his vow. Sword sheathed, he went out to be led, unnecessarily, to the anteroom of Holder Chasmal's audience chamber. His guide did not go in but closed the melt-bossed door behind him. He stood soft-booted on a refulgent floor of tiny multicolored stones that formed a mosaic landscape.

Across the large, empty chamber another door opened. In

to face him filed three men in helmet, cuirass and greaves.
They were sword-armed but empty of hand. The man in the
middle wore one of those silly little electric pistols that
(sometimes) launched a jolt for seven or ten meters. He also
wore a ring with a large green stone. An aventurine with
intaglio, Falc saw, just as he saw that the leftward household
peacekeeper wore his sword on his right hip and the rightward
man was just past his youth.

Seven or nine other things Falc noticed then as well,
though that was wholly automatic. He had no expectation of
having need of the observations and knowledge gained; his
was the eye of an omo. Since they were helmeted, he too
covered his ever-present coif with helmet. That came automatic, to a knight of the Order.

"And what does a Deathknight seek here?" That from the
man in the middle, he who wore the ring of authority and
cuirass of shingled placks. His eyes were strange, the pupils
large and almost round.

Falc had been taken aback by three armed and armored
men, household peacekeepers, but he had not showed it. He
deemed it best now to let them see him taken aback by the
question and tone, and he did.

"Passage," he said, "to Holder Chasmal."

"Who are you, Deathknight?"

"I am Falc, of Risskor—"

"Risskor!"

"—Contracted with Holder Kinneven of Lock, with a message for your lord." Only control kept him from adding
"your master," as reminder.

"Pass in to our lord an armed Deathknight in mailcoat?
Not likely!"

This time Falc met the ringed man's gaze without showing
anything of reaction or emotion. He felt both. He was accustomed to respect, and an omo had to grow accustomed to
unreasoning fear that came from lack of knowledge. He was
not accustomed to challenges. His expression was as bland as
was possible on a large but lean face of unusual darkness,
with prominent brow and cheekbones and hawklike nose. The
three Langomen saw blue eyes nearly as dark as his black
mustache and sidewhiskers and the kempt beard that left most
of his chin bared. His brows were not fierce in that fierce

hawkish face, but straight, even tending to a slight upward tilt where they approached each other above his nose. A dark, black-bearded and -mustached man with midnight eyes, all in black broken only by the deep red gemstone of his belt buckle. Even the hilts of his weapons were of crawk-hued horn. Masters of effect, these servants of Ashah.

"I am just now called to audience, to deliver my message to your lord."

"We know what sort of message your kind delivers, Deathknight. Have you the scar on your wrist?"

"Remember my purpose here, weapon-man. You overstep your authority and your master's hospitality. The words of hospitable welcome have been spoken to me, twice. And you know I bear the scar."

"A *Death*knight, though!" The man with the ring wagged his helmeted head. "We serve Holder Chasmal, Sir *Death*knight, and surely we serve him best by keeping you from him."

"Lock is no enemy of Lango. I am the same Falc who visited your lord Chasmal on behalf of Holder Kinneven less than a year ago, when I met you. Altmer, is it not? Prefect of the House?"

The other two shot surprised glances at their leader; Altmer tightened his lips and stared. "And do you observe the ninth day of the month Sarloj?"

Falc bade himself cease seething. "You know that I do. Are you unable to hear, or understand? I am here on an entirely peaceful mission. I am merely a messenger to your master from a fellow Holder and friend." (The left-handed man snorted but Falc continued without pause or glance.) "Your lord has nothing to fear from mine, for they are friends. Holder Chasmal has nothing to fear from me, who am Contracted with Aron Kinneven, Holder of Lock—in Juliara."

"Nothing to fear, you say. Peaceful mission, you avow. Hand over your weapons for safekeeping, then, whilst you visit our lord Holder."

"You know I cannot. I have taken the oath of the Order Most Old, and bear the scar. We of the Order hand weapons to no one. We use them or we break them ourselves."

"Break your blades, then. It is as one to us."

"What soars in you, Prefect Altmer? I will break my

weapons when they have dishonored, or when I yield me. In fewer words, I'll not break them ever."

"Yield, then."

"*What*!"

Incredibly, Altmer dared repeat the incredible.

All of this was quite outside Falc's experience. A man grew accustomed to certain aspects of being of the Order; aspects both good and bad. Respect might be fear, but that was familiar and tolerable. This scornful challenging, however, was unprecedented. Altmer's purpose and goal seemed apparent, but that did not make it acceptable to Falc. Or believable.

"I do not want to say this, Altmer of House Chasmal, but I am forced: I will not yield me or my weapons or my mission. Three of you are not enough to make me consider that. This is hard for me, but I wish no trouble here. Already I have accepted enough from you to put my honor in question. You will not call your master to confirm that he has just caused me to be escorted here?"

In reply to that most earnest and even demeaning effort, Falc received three sneers. Consciously lowering his shoulders in a relaxing exercise, he swiftly reviewed the words of the Way of Sallenar the Calm; the so-called Calm Psalm. Only then did he speak.

"I go far and far with you then, Altmer. I walk the desert for you: Falc of Risskor, of the Order Most Old, swears by his scar and the events of the ninth Sarloj, and by the First Knight of the Order, Sath Firedrake, and finally by Ashah patron of the order: I am here to deliver a verbal message to Holder Chasmal, and that only."

Their eyes and their silence told him that they were aware of what he had done, and impressed. None could be so insolent or so stupid as to reject or gainsay such a mighty oath from a Son of Ashah. The younger peacekeepers looked with visible nervousness to their leader, seeking guidance. It was he who spoke, again.

"We know what you are, Falc of Risskor," Altmer said. "How can we accept your word?"

This time Falc was shocked and showed it. "Man, man, I see that your purpose is to provoke me, but *why*?"

After a few moments of silence he said, "Once, in over

two hundred years of the Order's existence, one man of the Order Most Old swore falsely; *once*, since Sath Firedrake ended the rein of the tyrant Sai MaSarlis and dedicated his own battle scar and the tyrant's head to Ashah. You know that. All know it. Only one man of the Order has sworn falsely, ever. That forsworn Son of Ashah was slain, *slain by members of the Order*; and his weapons, clothing, and scar removed before he was hurled into the sea where no god or man could find him. We swear, and we fear only ourselves. And the penalty for even minor transgression of our oath is removal of the Sath-scar.''

Falc shot forth his right arm with a susurrant flutter of black sleeve and watched the instant tensing of three men of weapons. He showed them an empty fist; no open hand to these three daggertongues!

''Here is the scar, on the right wrist. How can it be removed? A scar cannot. Its removal means taking off hand and wrist, above the scar. You know this, Prefect Altmer. Your stance and tongue and that suggestion insult both you and your master. I will pass now. Stand aside.''

''No.''

O Ashah, is this a test of Thine? Falc slid his left hand and wrist through the broad sheathing strap inside his cloak's lining. *Can these men want me to act, as ever, in Thy name?*

Yet Falc walked farther on the desert, for those of the Order were taught control, and reinforced it daily to keep it sharp as their blades: ''Shall I go then to another Holder of great Lango, and have word sent to Holder Chasmal that his hirelings have insulted Kinneven and the Order by insulting the emissary of both?''

''No. You will not pass, darkling, and you will not leave this chamber either.''

''Ah.'' Falc understood, and saw no reason to say anything more.

The three had begun drifting apart, and the omo felt something akin to joy come upon him. At last this tense exercise of his ever tenuous control was ended. At last he was sure as to what was expected of him; what they wanted. Now he knew that these three ''peacekeepers'' were here to kill him. They had meant all along to kill him. They merely had hoped to

gain his weapons first and thus have the ease of slaying an
unarmed man!

Sath Firedrake had said it long and long ago: *"He who
seeks advantage only to slay is not worthy of life."*

Falc murmured the rite-words *"For Ashah, honor, and
Sij,"* while the three achieved a distance of more than a meter
between each, and set hands to hilts. Altmer's went to the
handle of his pistol. When they began to draw their weapons,
Falc moved.

While his left hand thrust the cloak to that side and began
wrapping it over the arm, his right hand rushed straight up to
his right shoulder and the sheath behind it. That hand snapped
straight forward toward Altmer and without pause continued
the same motion down and across Falc's belt to his hilt. He
was charging the prefect before he had the sword out. That
drew the man on Altmer's left to turn that way, blade sweeping out. The automatic reaction of the left-handed peacekeeper presented his left side, as Falc had intended. (Altmer
had jerked into stiffness and begun to shiver.) Falc ended the
feinting charge by swerving at the man he had intended all
along to attack. The fellow did not turn quite fast enough to
bring his blade into line and the omo's chopping slash took
him just behind the left shoulder, deep.

Falc had to pause long enough to twist the blade free before
he raced leftward. He passed behind Altmer, who was just
sinking to his knees, shaking all over as if with a severe chill.

The third keeper was badly shaken by the sudden attack
and its awful effectiveness. Still he readied himself and met
Falc's rush with a broad slash timed to intersect the dark
man's charge. Falc did not duck; he preferred the shock of a
fall to a tendon-pulling dodge that might not save him anyhow. Instead he aborted the charge by slinging himself to the
floor. Even then his arm swept out. His sword was a horizontal blur a hand's breadth above the beautiful mosaic. The
blade entered the guardsman's ankle just below the greave
and cut well into the bone.

In that instant of agony the young keeper was rendered
ineffectual now and, as a weapon-man, forever. He did not
grunt; he screamed. Falc was up by the time the fellow's
collapse was completed.

"I'll give you the gift we of the Order pray Ashah for," he said: "a swift death. But you can wait for it."

Falc turned from the man in time to see Altmer complete his fall. The prefect lay twitching. Less than a minute had elapsed since Falc had begun moving. Nor yet did he pause, but pounced to the sprawled Altmer. He wiped his blade on the prefect's skirt before turning him over. He had to grip the light hilt tightly and slap Altmer's forehead with the heel of his other hand to get the throwing knife out of his eye. Prefect Altmer had died on his feet, instantly or almost.

While he wiped that blade in the prefect's hair, Falc looked beyond the corpse to the youthful left-hander. On his knees, the fellow had tucked his left hand into his belt. He clutched his sword with his right, and Falc respected such persistence.

"Forget that," the omo said as he rose. "You know you cannot win. Cling to the sword and you discard your life. Discard the sword and clutch that shoulder, man, and you may avoid bleeding to death."

He knew there was no danger of that if the Langoman would just be still, but Falc did not wait to see whether he was heeded. He swung back to the downed man he had left in agony, and kept his promise to him. Even as he drew his sword out of the young Langoman, his lips moving in rite-words, Falc was on the move.

He sped, cloak a great swooping bat some would have seen as a dark shadow of death, to the door through which the trio had entered to challenge and murder him. In Chasmal's name? He doubted it. As he ran, he slipped the throwing knife back into its mailcoat sheath behind his right shoulder and shook folds of shielding cloak off his left arm. Beyond the door lay Chasmal's audience chamber. As Falc had expected, Chasmal was not in it. Nor was anyone else—almost.

Across the impressive room, some seven meters away, a man in a robe of House Chasmal green was just rushing through a doorway. The door was set for Chasmal's convenience: it opened out of the audience chamber, not inward.

He watched his three bravoes until he was certain they had failed, then he fled, the omo thought, and knew the motherless cack would close and bar that door against him.

Falc did not try to reach it first. He was a fighter who never paused until a combat was done with, but he was not the

speediest of runners. Instead he began his charge by whirling
up a side-chair and letting fly at the door with both chair and
sword. They hit the floor and then the door with a frightful
series of bangs, thuds, and clangs. The door was arrested in
its closing, and forcefully knocked open as well.

The dark man ran on. He slowed briefly to snatch up his
sword and left-hand the chair out of his way. His shoulder-
ramming the door wide apprised him that the robed man had
not got away; Falc felt resistance and heard a groan. He
pounced within the small third room and looked down at the
sprawling man struck twice by the door.

Sheathing his sword, Falc grasped Alazhar by the back of
his robe's neckband. The short man made a gagged noise
when he was jerked to his feet. Two fingers drove into the
back of his hand, hard, and the little electric pistol fell with a
clatter. Falc gave it a good kick as he drew his dagger and
showed its dauntingly broad blade to the Housechief.

"It is over. Where is your master?"

"Listen . . . name a price . . . gems, melts . . . land—a
title!"

"Thoroughly rotten alley-rat!" Falc shook him. "How
could a Son of Ashah be bought so? Nine of us could take
Lango if we were so minded! Speak or I will begin with a
small but very painful cut: your left nostril."

"We will give you this entire house, Falc! Think; you
cannot continue this wanderous life forever! What, when you
are older and are slowly d—*uhhh*!"

Falc had not sliced Alazhar's nostril. Instead he gave him
the other end of the dagger, in a jerk, just below the center
arch of his chest. The dagger's hilt was char-hued horn;
pommel and hilt were of iron. Alazhar was instantly bereft of
breath.

"Where, I asked, is Holder Chasmal?"

"He . . . guests this . . . evening with an . . . the Holder
Brostaval."

"Oh does he. And was he here when I arrived? *Speak.*"

"Uh-oww! No, he was not here—don't break my arm!"

"Alazhar, I am going to stand beside you with my arm
behind you. Feel the point at your back? Try to bolt or say a
wrong word and I will stick you. Now summon a slave. Ask
for the ajmil you sent to fetch me. Her name?"

"I . . . I will not tell you."

"Do you fancy that to be bravery? Alazhar, traitor, I will not kill you. We both know that I prefer you alive for a time. Yet I am a cruel man. I enjoy it; hasn't Sereah told you? I will open the back of your right upper arm. Then an incision, carefully under the bicep, if you have one. Then—"

"Simayil! Her name is Simayil!"

"Do as I said."

They were in Chasmal's office, a warmly paneled room in which Holder Chasmal saw to his Holding, transacted business, and prepared for audiences in the adjoining chamber. A few feet away stood a statue of the demigod Markcun. He wielded both sword and sickle, for weapon-man and farmer, against the creature whose talons clung to his chest: a vulture, symbol of death. All around them the walls of wood veneer were set with brass sconces bearing the lichen lights from Drearmist. The Housechief indicated the bell-pull adangle beneath one of the amber-hued pillars. Falc accompanied him to it. The bell chimed beautifully, in a sustained middle C.

The ajmil tapped and entered before the two men were back in the center of the room, boots silent on the richly patterned carpets and smaller rugs from Morazain. She showed some small surprise at sight of the large, dark and darkly clad man standing so close on Alazhar's left hand.

At the last instant the omo stole the initiative: "Where is Simayil?"

Slave looked at Housechief, who experienced a little nudge at his back and knew it was sharp. He nodded.

"She waits in your apartment, Master Alazhar. She—"

"Send her to us," Falc said.

"Bid her come hither," Alazhar swiftly said.

"Do not tell her that the Housechief is not alone," Falc went on, "only that he wants her here." When the ajmil had made standing obeisance and departed at speed, he continued to Alazhar: "She will knock before she enters?"

"No."

"Then I shall stand just beside the door, and you right here, in the center of the room. Observe, Alazhar: the door-jamb."

Housechief Alazhar felt the movement, heard the sound of

impact, and saw the doorjamb sprout a slim knife. The message was clear.

"Tell Simayil to submit, Alazhar, and then come and bind her wrists behind her, or you will surely be sore hurt. You must have been peeking at a door not quite closed when I put that knife into Altmer's right eye."

"Is . . . is *that* what killed him!"

Falc did not waste breath on unnecessary replies. Cloak and surcoat rustled. Alazhar had a vision of what seemed a great black bird, a crawk sweeping from him. Then the dark man, sinisterly slender throwing knife poised in upraised hand, was facing him from beside the door that led out into the corridor. His face was composed, his midnight eyes staring, his mouth dour.

"Do remember, Alazhar. And try to give her orders firmly, just as if you were a man."

Alazhar stood considering. Weighing the possibilities. By the time Simayil entered, he had decided. Sternly he bade her submit. She showed her surprise even as she went to her knees, head bowed in the demanded posture. A moment later he was behind her, demanding her hands. She did not question the command. Alazhar bound her wrists.

Within a minute the Housechief also wore his wrists behind him, secured. Soft boots kicked the door shut. Soft boots paced past the kneeling, bowed Simayil from behind, and the pointed hem of a crawk-wing cloak brushed her arm. That put goose flesh on her arm and brought her head up sharply.

"Wak!" After that involuntary ejaculation poor Simayil could only stare and shudder when she saw that she and the Housechief were captives of the Deathknight she had guided into a trap.

Beside the statue of Markcun Deathslayer, he wheeled.

"Both of you turn, on your knees, and face the door. You need not have to look at ugly Falc." When they had done so, he added, "Nicely done, Simayil. Now straighten up on your knees and try to imitate a woman."

She did, teeth chattering. Falc stood still. He folded his arms with his cloak drawn about him, and closed his eyes to breathe himself into relaxation and calm. Alazhar offered, then threatened, then offered again. His captor seemed not to hear. The three waited, the napes and armpits of two of them all aprickle.

After many minutes the door to the audience chamber opened and a household peacekeeper staggered in. He was very pale and clutching his left arm, which was soaked with red-brown. It dripped.

"Hou—Housechiefff . . ." he said, and collapsed.

"This man I respect," Falc of Risskor said, and soon the left-handed keeper, unconscious from shock and loss of blood, had his arm bound up with a strip of green from the shuddering Alazhar's robe.

Several minutes later Alazhar suggested, "The House physician," in a small and tentative voice.

Falc's voice sounded surprised: "I do not respect this fellow that much."

They wondered at the rustling of his clothing and the creak of leather. Wondered, and feared. Well-trained, Simayil knelt erect and stared at the door. The Housechief could not stand it. He had to twist around and look. Their captor was exercising, slowly and with seeming calm.

3

Much time had passed and all three were more than ready for him when the door opened to admit a portly, homely man in a rich robe of woods-green piped with gold. He entered the office chamber that was his. He halted abruptly to stare.

"Alazh—S'r Falc . . . ?"

"Holder Kinneven of Lock sends a greeting and best of portents to his friend the lord Chasmal," Falc said formally, quietly. "With Holder Chasmal's indulgence I will hold my lord's message while I present my own."

Again Chasmal glanced at the others. "Excellent idea."

"This swine considered me fool enough to believe that my lord Chasmal was here in his House, and sent *this* to fetch me to the anteroom where Prefect Altmer and two others waited to slay me. I much regret their blood on the floor of Lord Chasmal's anteroom, but I make no apology for their deaths. This one is only unconscious. I bound his arm with some cloth Alazhar kindly provided. To my knowledge, my lord, no one else in your House knows of these happenings.''

That was a good deal of compressed information to be assimilated by a man who had been out drinking with friends. Falc was impressed by the fact that Holder Chasmal's face showed surprisingly little in the way of change, aside from a widening of the slits of his pupils. Chasmal stood in quiet rumination for some time before turning and calling for a cold basin. Then he addressed the omo across the two bound and kneeling members of his household.

"Between us kneels a worthless bit of flunderpuff known as Simayil," he said in the rather high-pitched voice he controlled by speaking softly. "Kindly pare off one of her breasts. Your pref'rence as to which, excellent Falc.''

Simayil's lungs, mouth and memory were instantly vitalized. Wailing and pleading, she assured that she knew only what Alazhar told her. It was Chasmal's desire that he capture this omo, whom, the Housechief had said, Chasmal suspected; and Alazhar sent her to fetch him. What choice did a poor girl have when so ordered, and warned to say naught to the dread Deathknight?

"*Barga!*" Alazhar snarled, and if looks could have killed, Simayil would have toppled over.

Chasmal said only, "Alazhar?"

Alazhar neither spoke nor met the eyes of his lord employer.

Chasmal nodded with a sigh. "All is true, then. I see that I owe you much, esteemed Falc.''

"Might I suggest that we allow this worthless creature of Silkevare to retain her uninteresting dugs—if not, as Lord Chasmal sees fit, her life—and question the user, rather than the tool.''

"An excellent suggestion," Chasmal said. He paused then, to bathe face, wrists, and the back of his neck in the basin brought him by a visibly pregnant ajmil. "Ezalil: what does my son?"

"My lord Master, he has spent the evening in his own quarters, with—"

"Ne'mind who accompanies him, Ezalil. Take this to him and say only these words: 'His chamber,' and nothing more. Then send the physician here, wi' knowledge that yon former *guardsman* is to be *guarded* while he is tended. Next, send the chief ajmil here. Tell her that Simayil is t'be gagged to wide distention and kept so, while she is punished. And Ezalil: if your lips are not sealed and your eyes not blind, you could accompany Simayil to Dreamist.''

"Ezalil is deaf and mute, my good lord Master," Ezalil said, while Simayil fell into renewed gulp-weeping and shuddering. Ezalil, with the basin and the ring Chasmal had handed her, departed at a swift pace.

"Simayil," Chasmal said in that soft yet still rather high-pitched voice, "kindly shut up. I cannot keep you here, wi' your knowledge. Can you write?"

She shook her low-bowed head, gulp-weeping and unable to speak.

"Hm, well then, I suppose we could merely cut out your tongue. Try to decide whether you prefer that t'the lichen mines of Dreamist. Sir Falc, I am sure she and that boy will excuse us while we *escort* my former Housechief to my privy quarters." When Falc started toward him, Chasmal added, "I now find m'self 'thout the services of both Housechief and Prefect of the House; a straining position. Have you another of your excellent suggestions, excellent Falc?"

"If my lord will pardon my forwardness," Falc said, hoisting Alazhar to his feet by the back of his collarband. "Might I suggest that you send your son to fetch the ring off Prefect Altmer's finger, while you and I very privately question this source of sausage." He glanced back. "If Simayil is to make the journey to Dreamist, perhaps that one should . . . accompany her."

Chasmal glanced at the unconscious keeper. "You are too gentle, Son of Ashah. Better I think—come along, Alazhar, and do enjoy wearing that medallion for another minute or so—better I think, S'r Falc, to have my physician earn his board by r'storing that fellow to a condition suitable for him to be p'suaded to talk. That way we can learn whether his story agrees with what Alazhar is about, most kindly, to tell us. After which . . . best he join Altmer."

They were soon in Chasmal's private suite. Both rooms were surprisingly small, but after all he also had his office and audience chamber. Too, he had never remarried after a fever carried off his wife, several years ago.

"Did you mean t'suggest that my son be made Prefect of the House, S'r Falc?"

"Perhap I should not speak," Falc wisely said, whereupon he was urged, as he had expected and intended. He was meanwhile binding Alazhar in an interesting position. "Yes, Lord Chasmal, I would. Your son is no happy young man, and so has taken to the flesh and drink you disapprove of—"

"When it is every day and every night—yes, I disapprove!"

"Your pardon, my lord," Falc said, and stepped back. Alazhar rolled his upside-down eyes, which were dark and almost purple. The pupils were huge in fear, approaching roundness. Falc drew his dagger. And waited, seemingly in complete calm.

After a long silence Chasmal spoke, and his voice lofted high. "Ah, plague on you, omo! Your intelligence and judgment are known across the continent. Speak, speak! I will listen—you say that Chazar is unhappy?"

"As Holder Chasmal or I would be, were we sole heir two years past twenty, and unwed, and allowed no responsibilities. Responsibility and a chance to serve and prove himself to the father he is angry with but does love and respect. These would surely be the greatest thing that could happen to your young lord. And to his father, who loves him. Surely a respected servant could advise and temper his youthful judgment. If not, my lord Chasmal might consider asking the Order whether a . . . retired Son of Ashah might serve as his adviser."

Chasmal was staring, shaking his head. "And if that prove inadequate?"

Falc shrugged. "Both father and son will have learned something, and my good lord will be in the same position as now, but with new knowledge: in need of a Prefect of the House!"

"Gugh-hunnh," Alazhar commented, upside-downly.

"I sh'd think you'd be in no hurry for our attention, source of sausage," Chasmal said, and in spite of himself he laughed at Falc's picturesque way of calling the small, thin man a swine. "Oh, Falc . . . by the by . . . how did you know that Simayil is of Silkevare?"

"I stood behind her while she knelt," Falc said, aware that Chasmal was filling time while he considered his son. "When they kneel, those women of Silkevare do have a way all their own of turning their feet.''

Holder Chasmal was giving him a look, almost smiling, when the urgent knock sounded on the big paneled door behind him. He glanced at Alazhar. ''Falc: do stand before him, will you, and hold out your cloak or something?''

Falc understood instantly, and did. He pretended to be examining the arm-loop in the left inside of his cloak while Chasmal opened the door. Here was Chazar, strangely, almost weirdly gray-blue-brown of eye—hence his name—and wearing a short robe of gold mossweave tied with a cloth-of-gold rope. His boots were oddly out of place. Falc assumed they made the poor youth feel more the stern man to those ajmini with whom he disported himself.

''Chazar, I need your help,'' Chasmal shockingly said, and beginning sobriety came into the son's eyes as swiftly as it had the father's at sight of what had awaited him in his office. ''In my absence tonight, Altmer deliberately sought to murder Sir Falc of Risskor here, who you will remember is eminently trusted and beloved by m'Lockese friend, Kinneven. Please go to the Boot Room and fetch the House Prefect's ring which Altmer dishonored.''

''Altmer . . . *dead*?''

''He challenged an omo, son. Worse, he challenged Falc of Risskor, and 'ith only two men to back him.''

''*Only* t—''

Chazar's gaze leaped again to the dark man standing well back of his father, for some reason examining the interior of his sail-sized black cloak with eyes like a pool of water in an old quarry. Then Chazar seemed to jerk himself together, a nice enough looking young man with rumpled hair, a skimpy beard, and too much meat at his middle for one of his years.

''Yes, my lord! I shall bring it to you at once, Father.''

Chazar hurried away. His father closed the door and went at once to Alazhar.

''Sir Falc is of a religious order, and p'suasion is surely b'neath him,'' he told his former Housechief, in an amiable tone. '' 's b'neath me, too, but we are in a hurry, and you know that I have not always been so wealthed. And you do know how I got my start.''

Falc did not, but soon judged that it must have been as

someone's Discipliner of Slaves; Dungeoner, perhaps. Alazhar was swiftly persuaded both to weep and to urge upon his lord the intelligence that he was also employed by another Holder of Lango, Faradox. Faradox was prime rival and no friend to Chasmal, who would not agree to the betrothal of Chazar to Faradox's daughter (an unpretty girl devoted to her music-making, whom Chazar abominated with reason). Alazhar's purpose was to rouse the ire of the powerful Kinneven against Chasmal by murdering his beloved Falc.

All this astonished and horrified the questioners, though Chasmal showed little and the omo almost nothing. Chasmal ruined another tooth. That brought forth the information that Faradox had both paid much and promised much, which had made it easier for Alazhar to subvert the ambitious Altmer to this night's deeds. Weeping, Alazhar assured his master that he would serve him as a groveling slave, whereupon Chasmal disappointed Falc by ruining that traitorous tongue in addition to several front teeth.

Falc sighed. He would have asked a bit more, and cross-checked as well. It was a strange tale, and a strangely circu-itous, even bizarrely complicated one.

He said nothing, but wrapped Alazhar's face in a couple of towels while Chasmal went again to answer a knock at the door. Past his father, Chazar stared at the horrifying sight of that vulturine man cutting a towel-muffled, bloody, and quak-ing Alazhar free of two chairs. He was using an immoderately large black-handled knife with a hilt of jet.

"Don' be staring at him, son. Alazhar is traitor and it was your father, not S'r Falc, who persuaded him to speak. Sir Falc of far *Risskor*, acting for a powerful Holder of far *Juliara*, has saved us much grief this night, if not our lives. Do just be buckling on that weapons belt."

Chasmal accepted the ring from his son and waited while the young man buckled on the sheathed blades and pistol over his bright chamber-robe. Worn, Falc mused, as a disrespect-ful gesture to the father who held him in leash as a pet dog, and summoned him so urgently from his bed-sports.

Be a hound, Falc mentally urged, staring at Chazar of Lango. *Be a hound, Chazar!*

"Father—"

"A moment, Chazar. P'r'ap you will wish to change out of that chamber-robe, which does not wear a sword well. You'll not bear that dishonored blade for long, son; we will equip you with a man's sword. Gi' me y'r left hand.''

Chazar swallowed and his mouth forgot to close while his father weighted his extended hand with a large gold band, set with a caged aventurine cut flat and etched with a vigilant eye. The ring slid up the middle finger, just a bit loose. That was remediable, and besides it would be even looser on either of Chazar's other two fingers.

"Be thou my perfect Prefect of the House, Chazar Chasmalangoson, and my eye, and see thou to the interests of this Holding, that they may be our mutual interests.''

At the words of the formula the astonished Chazar started to babble "Father—'' Instead he remembered himself and, awkwardly clasping his ringed left hand to the sword-hilt on his left hip, went to one knee. "I shall serve my lord Holder to our mutual interest with honor, and to the death!''

Still Chasmal spoke as employer rather than father. "Your first duty, Prefect, is no pleasant one. Convey this traitor, without benefit of physician, to the Pit. There leave him.'' And Chasmal stepped back out of the young man's way.

His new Prefect of the House rose, gnawing at his lower lip. He gazed upon the bloody man who had been second in this House only to his own father.

"Your father,'' Falc said dourly, "has need of a *man*, now; a man he can trust.''

Chazar swallowed. Then, left hand on sword, the new Prefect of the House advanced into the room. This brought him into close-face proximity with the grim Deathknight. Chazar was unable not to stare.

"Prefect,'' Falc said quietly, with a bow of his head. "Would you do me the favor of handing me the dagger you wear?''

The youth swallowed. Again he recovered. He started to reach across himself for the weapon, reconsidered, and instead unsheathed the knife with his left hand. He laid the blade into his right, and proffered it to Falc.

"I am emboldened to offer advice to the prefect: that he never again hand his dagger to another, even a Son of Ashah. Here it is back, with thanks.'' Into the young man's hand Falc laid an evilly broad, long blade whose guard was dark iron and whose hilt was black horn. Falc dropped Altmer's knife into the sheath he had just emptied. "I fear that sheath of Altmer's will not accommodate your dagger, Prefect, but this Holding's leatherworker can swiftly make one."

"A . . . *Deathknight*'s . . . *dagger*?" Chazar stared at the weapon in his hand.

Falc shrugged a gentle negative. "No; the dagger of the prefect of the House of the foremost Holder in Lango. Whom I presume to advise even further: never never depend on that silly little 'lectric pistol! Now, far from me to tell such a man his duties, but Holder Chasmal does want this swine out of his bedchamber."

Chasmal said, "And never never call an omo a Deathknight, either, Prefect"

The source of sausage was soon removed by a young man who walked tall. It was not Holder Chasmal but a father who gazed at Falc.

"That was a . . . a fine, fine gesture, most excellent Falc."

Falc bowed. "I saw a different Chazar, and gave a *man* his first gift."

"I hope you're right. If so, we'll both be much in your debt . . . Lifeknight."

Again Falc bowed. Then he spoke formally, at last delivering his messsage. "Holder Kinneven sends greeting and best of portents to his friend Holder Chasmal, and advises me say to him as follows:

" 'Here is something no one knows about the purple
    shume.
Not only does it stand tall and its main stem grow
    ever
thicker, but it puts forth aerial roots.' "

Chasmal blinked his receipt of that cryptic message. Falc had tried not to question it, although the flowering plant called shume did not grow tall! Then his nod and totally bland expression told Falc that the Holder must understand and, good or bad news, would show nothing.

"Also: Holders Minndeven and Hanliven of Ryar made a hunting-area trade, for variety. Perhaps you will be interested in certain slaves in Darsin, four months hence. They will be the first from the Halatatsy area below Drearmist ever to be trained in Lock.''

Chasmal's face showed mild horror: "I never even heard of Halatatat Sea . . . but *Drear*mist!"

"The area *below* Drearmist, to the south, is perfectly safe, Holder. Halatatsy is part of Hanliven's territory, of Ryar: his vineyards. My employer believes that you will be interested in the Darsin Fair, four months hence. Holder Hanliven has also advised my lord of an outstanding harvest that has yielded a superb vintage.''

"Ah, that alone sounds reason for going," Chasmal said, nodding, "though Darsin is a long, long way to travel. I sh'll have to be giving cautious thought to the enmity and plotting of m'fellow Holder of Lango, and too I must be finding and trusting a new Housechief. I don' suppose you have another'f your excellent s'ggestions, S'r Falc?''

"Holder Chasmal might send word to the Master of the Order with thought of Contracting with one of my brethen in Ashah, for his protection from Faradox. Pardon: the lord Holder Faradox.''

"I like the oversight," Chasmal said, tight-lipped. "Treacherous bastard Faradox', I'd say."

Falc remained stiff. "It might also be amusing for Lord Chasmal to let word wend its way, through third-hand sources, to the Fardox Holding: that the lord Chasmal would double that Housechief's benefits were he to consider change of allegiance.''

"I'd never take on anyone of that Holding! I've just learned that I can trust nothing and no one of Faradox!''

"Nor will my lord Kinneven, once I am back in Lock," Falc assured him. "I used the word 'amusing' apurpose, Holder. The suggestion was not a serious one. Consider how it would upset Holder Faradox, and perhap create some dissension in that Holding! This is if you think he might need something else to think about . . . just to keep his plotsome mind busy?''

"Aha!''

With only a nod, Falc said, "Holder Kinneven believes that Housechiefs are best brought in from outside the Holding. I might manage to stop in Secter, on my way to Lock, and see whether Holder Arisan and his excellent Housechief still find each other . . . difficult."

"Hmm." Chasmal half turned to regard the dark man. "Arisan and his superb Baysh? But they have a problem? Why?"

"One must not tell all that one knows or surmises, my lord, else who would entrust me with knowledge? The problem of Holder Arisan and Baysh is no result of sloth or wrongdoing on Baysh's part. As for the apparent main reason— does my lord Chasmal know Holder Arisan of Secter?"

Chasmal nodded, grinned, nodded, chuckled, bobbed his head. "I understand."

"I will leave on the morrow," Falc said. "The lord Chasmal might consider waiting one day, and then dispatching a public contractor to Secter. That man might consider stopping at the White Horn and there merely dally, in the event that Baysh happened by. *If* so, it would be within two days."

"Hmm. Oh, and is that the extent of your message from my fellow Holder and friend, excellent Falc who has done so much for me this night?"

"I but defended this life and honor, lord." Then Falc shook his head and came as close to smiling as he ever did; the person who avowed to have seen Falc of Risskor smile placed his own credibility in question. "No, Holder; the message I bear is twofold. My lord your friend sent word too that he does not wish to create dissension in Lango, or embarrass his most esteemed friend, or alarm him unduly . . . but that he has certain intelligence that Holder Faradox plots against you."

There was nothing pretty or mirthful about Chasmal's short burst of laughter. "You may advise him on y'r return, twice-excellent Falc—after your brief stop in Secter—that I believe my friend Kinneven! And that I wish Falc of Risskor were in my service!"

Falc bowed, and said nothing. Lord Chasmal was well aware of the code of the Order Most Old, if not its true purpose in linking and guiding the citystates and their greed-ily mistrustful Holders against a unity that could bring the abhorrent possibility of renewed Empire. Too, he knew Falc's regard for Kinneven of Lock. Chasmal would not stoop to making offer for Falc's services. He knew they were not available for payment alone, or without loyalty and esteem. Chasmal could not presently expect high esteem from one with the standards and alertness of an omo; not when a foreigner had to enter in and straighten out the messy affairs of household, family, and inimical rival!

"You will accept my hospitality, Falc, and a companion?"

"I will apologize for having cost my lord three peace-keepers—"

"Three traitors! Would that you c'd bide over and aid us in seeking whether this treachery runs deeper in m'own household! Apology rejected as unwarranted, but you will accept my fervent thanks!"

Falc bowed and ritually stretched forth his weapon hand, palm open. "I shall ride for Lock tomorrow, my lord—"

"Well-provisioned!"

Another bow: "Wi' thanks, and waste no wine on me! If my lord will not take offense, I will partake of his hospitality, but prefer no companion. I have been insulted, and I have slain. Falc must walk the Way of Communion this night."

"That rite of your Order will not occupy you all the night, good Falc!"

"No, but my personal rule is to avoid night-companions after I have spent emotion and life. I might well be too harsh with her, and have no wish to harm one of my lord Holder's valuable ajmini. . . ."

"No five of which are so valuable as Falc of Risskor!"

"Nor ten either, with my lord Holder's indulgence. But I beg my lord not to insist. Once under such circumstances I killed a companion, a mere girl, and without anger or cause. It is embarrassment to me still. I would not place myself in such a position again. Tonight my blood is high and hot, and in such passion the solitary way is best. For me."

"Simayil, p'r'ap," Chasmal began, but aborted the jest at sight of the dark man's face.

"A question, Holder Chasmal. Are the slaves of this household forbidden beer?"

Chasmal's head tilted to one side. "Only in the company of their betters. Otherwise . . . who trusts the water system of Lango?" Chasmal smiled at what the other man presumed to be a common saying in Lango-by-the-Sea, and would remember. "Why d'you ask, excellent Falc?"

"Had the answer been no, my lord's new prefect would have another arrest to make. She might be watched, even so, as she was with me while Alazhar had me awaiting your pleasure. A big woman; her name is Sereah."

"Sereah!"

"I hasten to add that I chose her. Alazhar did not send her."

"Perhaps I were well advised to plan a journey to the annual fair in Darsin. Best I do a good bit of trading. P'r'ap." Chasmal nodded, obviously to himself as he considered, and Falc remained silent. Then: "As you wish it, excellent Falc. With regard to night-companion, I mean. You are like no other man, and while I would gladly give you five of the best-trained, I'll force nothing on you. Except o'course the best mount in my stable, which you will accept else your own suffer a seizure and expire before sun's rise."

Falc bowed low before the Holder's smile, looking as if he too was considering a smile. It did not happen. Chasmal watched that. He felt that this strange, grim, most competent of men was capable of smiling; it was just that Falc refused to do. The man's discipline was as a mountain: beyond any human efforts at breaking or moving. Back before the long-dead First Civilization had reduced the planet's resources to nothing, and men to swords and riding steeds that were the result of mutations from First Civilization weaponry and "technology," such men as Falc of Risskor should have seized all Sij. Perhaps then history, and the whole world, had been different.

Chasmal cast off that thought.

It was stupid to reflect on how life had been then, and what it might be like now were there oil anywhere on Sij, within Sij; or that nitrate of potassium so useful to those of the First Civilization for creating their explosive substances and devices—*or if all of us were not so glued now to a slave-based economy and not so superstitious about anything even smacking of First Civilization ways*, Chasmal mused. Yesterday and would-have-been were not worth tears.

4

And so the omo dined alone and late, waving away her who
brought the repast and the later one sent, with wine (also
cuffed and cross-gagged with a riding crop), by a well-
meaning Chasmal. Falc removed his great crawk-wing cloak
only when she was gone and his door locked. He carried out
that lonely meditation rite which the Order Most Old called
Walking the Way. He ate only the salad and vegetables and
drank some of the beer, which was after all safer than water
and hardly anything approaching serious drinking!

He had wished to be alone in the event of a visit by the
Manifestation, but it—the Messenger—did not come.

Falc slept well, eventually, while somewhere within that
keep Chazar saw to the clearing away of two corpses and
their blood, and while another man suffered alone in the
darkness of the Pit, all deserving, and an ajmil from Silkevare
lost her tongue, deserving or no, and was readied for a
journey to Drearmist of the mountains and the light-mines
whence bloomed that strange glowing lichen that was a leg-
acy of the wars of the First Civilization, and its planetary
despoliation. No one understood it, even while the jar-sealed
lichen lighted most of the world.

It was expensive because the mining of lichen light was a
sentence of death, usually within five years.

Next morning Falc departed overly provisioned and gifted,
having drunk a mug of hot hax, eaten only fowl and without
having trimmed his beard. An early morning shower had
added an empyrean quality to the air; the sky and its light. He
breathed deeply of it. Astride Chasmal's gift of a fine and
well-trained darg, the omo led his own Harr.

The moment he was over the first rise of the Old Road, he
drew the dagger Chasmal had pressed upon him. Its hilt was
studded with gemstones (green, all but the yellow luckstone,
a prismatic, orthorhombic fluosilicate of aluminum). Doubtless it was a fine tool, aside from being handsome and
valuable.

Regarding it, Falc thought, *Nevertheless . . .*

He wrapped it and slid it into the same knapsack from
which he took his own spare Tooth of Ashah; indecently
large, with a guard of dark iron and a hilt of bone-stuffed

black horn. Also in the pouch were the melts of realsilver Chasmal had forced upon him. Re-formed from the debased coins of the First Civilization, these coins were enough to purchase bushel upon bushel of threshed rint or a fine slave, even a well-trained one from such as Kinneven Holding.

What Chasmal thought a Son of Ashah might do with the pot of cvarm, product of the sea off Lango, was beyond Falc's imagining.

Here too was the silly pistol, and the fine aventurine belt-slide. And the message that Chasmal sent to Kinneven. The very, very old nugget of realcoal Falc did sling on a black thong about his neck. It was beautifully faceted and shining, and amused him: the thing might well start a new legend about those whom some others called "Deathknights!"

He would trade the sack of wine for accommodation in Morazain-on-the-Lake, if he decided to spend a night inside.

Hours later, well west of Lango and by now convinced that Chasmal had not surreptitiously provided an escort, Falc twitched a rein to leave the road. Smooth as a night-companion's backside, this darg's behavior. In a grove of sel and canopytrees Falc spoke to Harr while he removed the packs from that broad green-slate back. Next he transferred the old saddle and sacks from the fine new darg to the back of surly Harr, and relocated the packs on the blue-green back of Chasmal's gift. The beast accepted that, without even the dignity to hiss at the insult.

"No pride," Falc muttered to Harr. Man and darg had been together for years, and trusted each other. "Well, and look what we have here," he said, plucking up a dainty little three-petaled flower from amid violet-hued shume in deep shade. "A harr."

Immediately his darg's head came around. Seeing only a flower he did not want, Harr head-nudged his master and turned away. Obviously his master had no need of him, and these butterflies and little moths were both interesting and tasty.

Again Falc swung about himself the voluminous white, hooded robe, although the farmlands between here and Morazain were hardly desert. He had another reason. One of the worst of many difficult aspects of the Order was the required clothing. Unalleviated crawk-hue did draw attention and turn folk away in nervousness. On the other hand, it did not daunt the sun's heat. Indeed, the black clothing attracted the sun unto itself as crellies to the firelight.

Slupp! That from Harr, and two more pretty butterflies, yellow and pink with black, vanished forever. Falc gave the beast's flank a friendly slap. It was the conqueror Sar Sarlis who had carried—or rather ridden, and led—dargoni all over Sij. They served well and bred well, these mutations from the deadly northern area beyond the mountains. They had appeared after the Deathfire war that had been the beginning of the end of the First Civilization. (The middle of the end had come after those folk, mostly yellow-brass of skin and extremely pale blue or even off-white of hair, had tried to live on after they had depleted the sources of energy for all those things they felt necessary. The end of the end was simply the extirpation of that people by the bronze and copper-red races who alone now populated Sij.)

And good, well-meaning Chasmal actually presented me with this foolish 'lectric pistol, Falc mused, turning the thing about in his gauntleted hands and shaking his head.

Naturally one accepted; how could one tell a well-meaning Holder that one thought too much of one's safety to trust such a *thing*, but could use a decent crossbow? Falc of Risskor, however, would no more depend on this sort of First Civilization evil, with its sometime efficiency and range of eight or ten meters, than one would depend on . . . *on another person in a fight*. But Falc aborted that thought, knowing himself for a bigot, even though a competent one who tried to be charitable in opinions.

He tossed the little zinger away.

He started to mount but paused, feeling the tremor of a minor quake. They were a part of life, but this one gave Falc time for uncharacteristic second thoughts. Strange and bulky in many cubic centimeters of long white derlin, he paced over to pick up the weapon—or rather, in his judgment, so-called weapon.

A gift I might make to an enemy, perhap, he mused, as he thrust it into one of two empty stiff pouches on his saddle. "Harr lead walk," he muttered, and was already swinging up when Harr jerked up his head in response.

While Falc drew the robe around him, leaving it gaping

rightward at the waist in front so that he could get at his weapons, Harr turned and paced back to the road. The gift-darg let the lead-rope tauten before he followed, with a hiss of mild complaint. At the road Harr paused and Falc flexed the muscle in his right calf. Harr turned right toward Morazain and Shoe Lake, and thence Secter in Juliara, and eventually Lock.

A wavy shadow moved over the land, and he looked up to watch, briefly, a soaring crawk. Wings aspread, it rode currents of air that men did not even know existed. Falc saw no significance in the overhead passage of the big black bird of prey. He returned his gaze to the way ahead.

"Ashah ride with me," he muttered, and gave Harr's neck a pat.

The omo rode loosely, thinking about Chasmal and Faradox and the oddness of the plot and Alazhar's action, and after a while he picked up the rein. Harr affected not to notice. He walked on, leading.

TWO

The members of a society have a vested interest in its stability, its preservation. A society owes to its members preservation of its stability. That is the meaning of Social Order. Anything else is Social *Dis*order. The previous societies of this world were destroyed by governments; by those very people entrusted with the maintenance and preservation of the social order!

Never again must this beast called government be allowed to grow so powerful. The social order is individuals, who must be cherished —so long as they cherish the social order.

> —the Writings of Sath Firedrake

The sun was a bright flame-yellow coin and Falc wore the derlin, the intelligent traveler's choice. So it was called: der-lin-suma. The phrase had got itself shortened to "derlin," which was meaningless, except that now it meant long voluminous hooded robe or button-cloak, white.

Willingly trailed by the gift-darg, Harr waddled his twisty way along the Old Road. He was pacing due west from Lango on a continent 540 kilometers wide and either 450 or 600 long, depending on whether one measured from the mountain called Granitewall down the western coast to the tongue of land below Mersarl, or from the far northeastern Burning Lands—not that anyone would enter that area of poison death to measure!—down to the east coast's lowest point. That was Risskor, perched on a hurricane-buffeted spit that was like a nipple thrusting into the World Sea.

They had left the area Langomen thought of as their territory. They had passed the rich, more than independent ardom
or barony of Synaven Darg-breaker; he who was as often
called Syneven the Darg, but not within his hearing. Now the
omo and his two dargoni were within Zain.

To their right, on the north across a rising meadow dotted
with the violet blooms of shume, rose and rose the towering
and vasty Bluemoss Wood, which sprawled larger than Lango.
On Harr's southward flank rolled away farmlands in their
tender blue or aquamarine beauty, crowned in great rusty-red
bursts with the ripe heads of rint and barley and decorated as
well by coralgrass. The latter had nothing at all to do with
coral, but in late summer it shot up spears that topped out in
orangey-coralline seedpods. Coralgrass was a friend. Coralgrass
held the land. It also served the purpose of attracting cut-
worms and thus birds away from the food crops.

They evaded a wound in the roadway: a man-deep gash left
by one of the minor quakes that plagued the land. They
passed patches of the beauty of that purple-blooming turnip
some mistook for shume, which grew anywhere and everywhere and was considered by many to be a message and a
lesson to men. They paced past whole fields of it under
cultivation; a plant whose flowers were enjoyable and provided color; whose tubers were eminently edible, raw or
cooked; whose flowers and seeds pressed into an excellent
vegetable oil; whose plants provided fodder.

The fat sun was turning bronze. It was being steadily
overhauled by a mean-looking bank of comminatory cloud,
like a creeping slate-hued fungus shot with deepest blue and
charcoal.

The sun, Falc mused. He knew that the Studiers, back in
the First Civilization, had said that the other light of day, the
tiny one that was often invisible or nearly, was also a sun,
companion to The sun; and called each of them one with the
myriad stars of night. And old stars at that, as Sij they said
was an old world, second from the weary sun that was not
larger but closer—so they said—and still warmed it more than
many would prefer.

"We're going to get wet, Harr."

Harr turned his head a little in acknowledgment of his
name. If he understood, he was surely delighted. He probably

was anyhow, in anticipation. Dargs could smell moisture at impossible distances. Dargs loved rain, or indeed water in any form. And mud.

Falc glanced back at the gift-darg. No one had thought to mention whether it had a name and he had failed to ask. He called it nothing. Falc blinked, glanced up at the encroaching clouds, and again at the rather gloomy deeply blue, purple-and-black barrier of the taboo forest. Many preferred to believe the legend that it *contained* the First Civilization, as a corral contained animals. It was true that many First Civilization remnants existed back in Bluemoss Wood; ruins and worse along with a few intact buildings and artifacts. Another legend held that Bluemoss was haunted. Certainly its dark deeps housed dangerous beasts and reptiles. Visiting there was forbidden, much less hunting or chopping. Old documents claimed that forests would somehow reduce the heat and raise coastlines—by lowering the sea—but no one knew why, or was sure that it was so.

The notion seemed unlikely. Still, many things that men thought they knew were not so, while many rumors and unlikely seeming suppositions proved true; it was just that the reasons had been lost, along with millions of Sijmen and their civilization. In any case, tradition and legend had grown up around Bluemoss and other broad areas of woodland. They were left untouched. At least no one could gainsay their virginal beauty, sunless gloom or no!

Falc thought about that, and about the First Civilization. It was better than thinking about the coming rain. He had given away his wide-brimmed hat two weeks ago.

Once on Sij, up in the northeast where nothing remained, a *different* race had developed; people with unusually pale skin and hair of an extremely light color. Eyes the color of emerald and aventurine and pale new leather, legend had it. Over centuries and centuries and more centuries, that people had spread over and conquered much of the planet. They were arrogant, and strong, and always they came as conquerors bent on rule. For the past century or so, Studiers had sought reasons for such behavior.

A restless folk, some said. They fared south and westward because they were cold, some said; and angry, perhaps, at having such odd hair and weird eyes. Their kind was in the minority by far. Yet they conquered, by arms and tonguetwist and elsewise, most of the other peoples and area of the world, and so came to domination. Of the three continents and few islands, Sijmen now had reason to believe that this continent was all that remained of the world. The conquerors had seen to that, and the War, and the Day of Sun-death that left the planet called Sij worse than restless, complaining of the injuries done it. The planet's quakeful restlessness continued to this day.

Now those people were most often referred to as "the Mechanists." They had progressed into industry, into industrialization, and then . . .

The thing called technology had proven not to be progress. It had nearly conquered them, and nearly conquered the physical Sij itself. Eventually, through dominating along with using and misusing and Using, they became dependent on the rest of the world. And then they had become its prey, and prey of their technology.

Now they were gone. Annihilated. Yes, true, there had been some assimilation, through interbreeding; a mingling of genes. Yet now no one had eyes the color of emerald or aventurine or new-leather tan, or hair of the truly pale blue of the Mechanists. Now those long-faced, straight-nosed people were gone. Gone.

They had not quite taken Sij with them. Sij came back.

The only azure or cerulean hair now came from misdyeing. There were no green eyes aside from that pale blue-gray with a greenish tint. Far more rare were eyes of almost-green. In the language called Sijye the grayish bluish brownish color was *azar;* brue or brown-blue.

Chazar's eyes were truly unique, and Falc's skin like old copper was darker than many people ever saw. Despite the heat, no truly black race had ever developed on Sij. The equator was barren of land.

Sijye was the only tongue on this vast continent and was said to be universal on Sij, if others survived; if other land did. The language had been carried across the world five hundred years ago by the conqueror Sar Sarlis. His empire lasted three hundred years, by which time it had grown huge, impersonal, hereditary of rule and devoted to favoritism;

unwieldy, more and more in need of more and more funding; sybaritic, weak, and plain bad. Intolerable.

Enter Sath Firedrake.

Even now the Master of the Order Most Old assumed, on taking that post, that old sobriquet of Sath the farmer's son: Firedrake. The present Firedrake was quite old, and Falc was sure he suffered in the kidneys and perhaps in his bowels. Now and again Falc wondered who would someday be called Master, and Firedrake.

He was thinking about that when he was interrupted by nature, and Sij:

Ninety-meter treetops on his right whispered and waved restlessly while thunder grumbled across the sky with the sound of a vast empty belly. Harr twitched and hissed, swinging his head to and fro in quest of the source of that noise; of danger. Falc sighed, and rode. He would not hasten. Rain was often preferable to a quake. Patting the darg's neck to instill confidence and calm, he spoke rather than sang the first verse of "Destiny Wears a Black Cloak," in a low, calming voice:

> Troublous time and woe, tyranny of the hoe;
> How these inspire and flame my desire
> To seek the Order Most Old!
> Ashah accept me!
> Ashah ride with me!
> Ashah deliver me!
> Sath guide me!

Falc sighed, and rode. He would not hurry.

"We just plod on, Harr. We've been rained on afore." He patted Harr's neck and muttered a line from Markcun's Soliloquy: "Rain brings unhappiness to some and happiness to many."

And then Falc almost smiled, and began to mutter, and it was not rite or prayer or psalm. Romantic, admiring poems had been written of the Sons of Ashah, and music had been devised for some. Another song had somehow . . . developed, and was known to few if any save the knights of O. M. O. Falc sang that one now; rather he chanted it, for he was no good singer:

Oh how I love the open road!
The sky above sunlit with gold!
Honor lies ahead on this long ribbon of dust—
O let me but ride the open road!

Oh how I hate the falling rain,
For I am not a field of grain!
Weary buttocks tonight and ever more mistrust;
Oh you may have this rearward pain!

Oh how I love my slith'ry steed!
His surly manner I do not need . . .
In him is no care that our cause is just,
But hurries on with jolty speed!

Oh how I love the open trail!
The sun cruelly bakes my hot mail . . .
I love this life as I love swordblade rust—
I also love warts and pelting hail!

Falc sighed and Harr plodded. They would not hurry.

Why bother to hasten and tire the animals when they could not reach Morazain this night anyhow, or even Colax's Wayward Inn? Rain would be falling within three hours, while the inn was six hours distant. Colax had planned and built to accommodate travelers *from* Morazain, not to it. The clever fellow did catch most of both, and had acquired not only a genuinely comely serving-ajmil, but two dargs and a man of weapons as well. Some banker in Morazain must love Colax! So too must he who called himself Arlord and pretended to rule the land called Zain: Morazain, Jayanga, Threeford, and the land round about.

Harr rounded a long curve flanked on the south by a line of spacklebark trees and the bush called flunder, months now from the puffball stage by which it propagated and spread itself. Now they came abreast an open field.

Too open, Falc saw. The farmer had unwisely cut his entire two and more hectares of rint, probably day before yesterday. Expecting no rain, he had ricked part of what had to be his main crop and livelihood. This morning he must have risen to smell a hint of moisture in the air, and hurriedly raked the rest into windrows. They stretched from one end of the field to the other in calf-high cupolas, silvery and bluish with green tinges and glints and of course the speckling of bright red grain-husks. Straight, too, Falc noticed. Good for this farmer! Too bad about the rain.

Did the Arlord of Zain make allowances for crops lessened by rain? Probably not. The farmer was ultimately at fault, with his misjudgment: he should not have done all the cutting at once.

The fellow was in the field now, with what must be his family. He was not so old as forty, a powerful man in the same way that Falc was, without much bulk. Helping him were two others, and a saggy old darg hitched to a wagon in good repair. Its sideboards were up and its wheels were of wood; though metal was available, one must pay the price for reclaiming it and that price was usually beyond the means of a subsistence farmer. This man did have an iron-tined pitchfork, while the one wielded by his presumed son of about eleven or twelve was pure wood.

She who drove the wagon was either a considerably younger wife or the boy's several-years-older sister. Hers was a dull job. She must guide the darg so as to move the wagon slowly: start and stop and start and stop. She and the boy wore sweatbands and he a bright green kerchief or rag over his lower face. Both males were shirtless but wore the long apron-skirts over boots that were best for this job. The skirts were a fulvous hue, tightly woven.

" 'Troublous time and woe, tyranny of the hoe,' " Falc murmured, and added, "They will never make it." He made a little hissing noise.

Instantly Harr stopped. The gift-darg bumbled into his rump, just missing the broad-based round tail, and Harr hissed a lot more loudly than Falc had done. Both stood still. Perhaps Harr wondered why his master had ordered him to halt. Masters were unpredictable, and dargs were not stupid.

"Harr, you're going to get a rest and I am going to go to work."

Falc twitched his left knee. Harr glanced leftward, saw no place to turn, and moved forward. They came abreast of the narrow road that ran yellow-beige back to a farmhouse abut-

ted by a ferg-coop and backed by a barn whose roof could use
some help. So could its owner, right now.

Falc would have taken oath that Harr hesitated beside the
dusty rutty wagon-wheel road on their left, weeds flaunting
their presence in its center; Falc turned his left leg and let
Harr feel just a little heel pressure. Harr turned onto the
rut-road. The trio in the field paused to stare.

"You have another fork?" Falc called.

"In—in the barn," the farmer called.

"Second stall!" the boy yelled excitedly.

"Join you in a drip or three," Falc called, and rode on.

The trio continued to stare. A derlin-clad man riding a
good darg wearing black, and leading one as good or better,
well equipped. His white hood up. This man would fetch the
pitchfork and join them in a few drips of the waterclock?
Strange!

Harr hissed at fergs and sidestepped them. The little creatures were his cousins, off-white or bluish-green with their
scarlet topknots and blue tails. Fergs were welcome mutations, which laid one soft-shelled egg per day. The farmer's
boon, fergs. A few of them hissed back, but most made their
squeaky noises and got out of the darg's way. Harr proceeded
to the barn, wiggle-waddling. The broad wagon entryway
gaped, both doors open. Falc ducked as he rode into the
twilight interior.

The barn smelled of old manure and new hay not yet dry.
Dismounting, Falc snubbed the gift-darg to an upright between the half-doors of two stalls and checked the second
stall for a pitchfork. It was there. He swept off both derlin
and crawk-hued cloak. With a sinfully hurried muttering of
rite words, he removed his mailcoat. It and his sword-belt he
hung on Harr. He kept the dagger. His helmet he fastened to
his belt behind before he resumed the hooded white cloak.
Taking the wooden fork with its once-yellow handle, he bade
Harr follow him out of the barn.

He nearly ran into the farmer. Coming in out of the bright
sunlight, the fellow's pupils were shrunken to mere vertical
slits. Falc watched him struggle to inspect him.

"Name's Falc," he told the nervous, suspicious man. "You
and the rain are in a race and I choose your side. I'll help.
This is Harr. He's very safe, left loose."

"Wh—Harr?"

"Harr, yes."

"Uh—wh-who-o . . . wh—a *Death*knight?"

"Name's Falc. Forget the rest, at least until the rint is in."

"Uh . . . ahm . . . I am Querry . . . uh . . ."

"Falc. Harr, bide around here." And Falc strode out to the field.

To Harr, "bide" meant freeze; the word in conjunction with others meant stay close but to move about was all right. Moving about a *bit*, he had learned; just a bit.

Confused and spluttery, Querry had no recourse but to follow the white-hooded man in the billowing cloak/robe who bore his weak-handled pitchfork, the one he had been going to fix for months. They strode out between two windrows of fragrant rint, all greenish blue and red-flecked. Falc had already seen that Querry had wisely chosen to start bringing in that which was in the lowest area of the field. As they walked, Falc noted their method: the woman guided the wagon up the cleared aisle between two windrows while Querry loaded from one side and his son from the other. The boy, naturally, could not match his father's pace. From time to time Querry must mount the wagon and redistribute the rint to balance the load.

"We could move faster," Falc muttered to the tan-skirted farmer, pausing without stopping, "if I took the boy's side and he was up on the wagon."

"Chalis, this is . . . Sir Falc," Querry told the staring boy. Falc wondered whether his mouth was open behind the scarlet cloth. Likely. "He—he's going to help. If you'll get up on the wagon and keep the load spread even, I won't have to get up and down so much."

Falc was impressed. Rather than tell the boy that this stranger was stronger and longer of arm and would be faster, Querry made it seem that Chalis was doing him a favor; taking some of the strain off his father. That also served to make the boy even more cooperative:

"Be—be better if he—he took my fork then oh are you a are you a Deathknight?"

Falc gave him a pleasant look. "We call it knights of the Order Most Old, which abbreviates as O. M. O.; OMO, you see," he said. "We are omos. My Contractor's business will wait, though, and the rain will not. Right now I'm a farmer."

"Wak!" Chalis said, in the exclamation that seemed universal. "Uh—I mean—here . . . here, ahm, S'r Falc. . . ." He extended the pitchfork gingerly, handle first.

Falc did the same. "Good of you to let me have this one," the omo said.

"It's better. Thisun needs a new handle," Chalis said, indicating the implement he now held. He indicated his good safety-training then, by aiming the fork tines-foremost at a pile of rint on the wagon, and slamming it up and in. Using the hub of the rear wheel, he climbed up.

"A Deathkni—I mean, omo! Wak! Black gloves and all!"

Falc thrust his pitchfork into the end of the windrow to hand. Shoving toward the front of the wagon, he twisted and came up with a load which he slung onto the wagon all in one motion.

"Don't make fun of my gauntlets now," he said, knowing Chalis was not and would not. "The work I do doesn't make my hands good and tough the way yours are." Pacing forward, he scooped up another forkful.

More rint came flying up from the wagon's other side. "You're going to have a sore back, too," Chalis pointed out. "Them's mighty big loads you're scooping up, uh . . . Omo."

"Call me Falc. This—"

"Sir Falc," Querry amended with a grunt, from the other side of the wagon.

"This afternoon is an extra one in my life, though, Chalis. You must have heard that 'no god deducts from a man's allotted span that time he spends personally helping others.' "

Falc heard Querry chuckle. "He's heard it," the man said, and grunted up another forkload.

The wagon creaked forward, and on it went, and on. Long, stemmy rint piled up on the wagon. The graincrop still smelled ripe and moist, but that was because it had so recently been standing. Rain on it lying here in the field would ruin the crop, or at least considerably lessen its value. A really hard rain would pound much red-jacketed seed off and into the ground, beyond gleaning.

Querry judged the wagon to be full, and called to the woman. She rein-jiggled their old darg into a long turn and the wagon creaked back toward the barn. Walking along behind, Falc would have liked mightily to call Harr to him and ride in. That, however, would cost face; too much face. He walked.

"Where have you been, S'r Falc?" That was Chalis, jigging along on Falc's left.

"Lango. Been to Lango?"

"No. That's almost two days away!"

"Tall pink walls like quolina blooms. Guards on top in shiny lacquered armor and helmets. People in bright colors everywhere, but you know that. Too many people. You've been to Morazain?"

"Oh yes."

"Lango has the smell of the sea about it."

"The sea," Chalis breathed, in the same tone he'd have used to talk of gold. "What—what's the sea smell like, S'r Falc?"

"Like nothing else. Wet. Moisty humid, and salty. Sort of like saltwater on the stove, only without the feel and smell of the heat."

"Let him walk quiet, Chal. Let him catch his breath."

"Ohh . . ."

At the barn, the process had to be repeated in reverse. It hardly took as long. The wagon was drawn up beside the big bin with the lattice-work bottom, beneath which was the container to catch the grain itself. With the side of the wagon taken out, amid grunts, the rint could merely be forked over into the bin. It was subsequent loads, Falc thought without cheer, that would be harder. Back to forking rint up and over!

The woman helped. Querry had never introduced her, and she seemed to be ignoring Falc. Querry called her name once: Jinnery. Chalis called her that too, rather than "mother." Querry was probably thirty-five; Jinnery was about twenty-two, or a year or two less or more. Thin, not just slim. Eyes like burnt almonds and hair medium blue, bunned. She probably had a lot of it. She wore not a hint of cosmetic. That added to the fact that she seemed . . . grim. She did not wear her thin-lipped mouth attractively or even very pleasantly, but mostly kept it set. Grinding her teeth down and raising headaches, Falc thought, naturally noticing that her nails were chewed. She didn't look as if she ate much else.

Jinnery.

Wife? Daughter? No one said, and the omo certainly would not ask. Two ideas had occurred to him, and when they finished unloading he stepped back and looked and spoke reflectively, so as not to seem too smart.

"You know . . . if a man were to make a sort of heavy platform, or even a ramp of earth, unloading the later loads wouldn't be so hard."

"Old Catapin doesn't have the strength to pull the loaded wagon up a ramp," Querry said.

"Oh, sorry; I should have thought of that."

For the first time, Jinnery spoke. Her voice was not silver bells or gold; there was more in it of brass. "Catapin is old, and he tires fast," she said. "We do have a second wagon, though."

Falc glanced her way to see that he was being regarded meaningfully, sour-faced. He blinked.

"And you have two dargs, Deathknight."

"Oh." Falc nodded. "Name's Falc. But no. This fellow is a gift from a Holder in Lango, for something I did, and is doubtless pampered.He would need much training. My mount is Harr, and Harr is a war-trained darg."

She came right back: "A war-darg can't work?"

"Harr has his dignity."

"Dignity!" Chalis echoed loudly. "A *darg*?"

Jinnery looked sour. "The dignity of a darg," she said, in a way that invited Falc to take offense. "And so he does not work, and you do. The dignity of a darg. And you, Sir Deathknight?"

"My name is Falc. I am a farmer; anyone can see that. Harr is not. Come. Those clouds have already turned early afternoon to dusk."

It was her turn to walk, Falc saw: Querry mounted the wagon and guided Catapin out the barn's broad rear doorway. Chalis ran and jumped, spinning in mid-air to alight sitting backward on the tail of the wagon. His face showed pride in the minor feat. Abruptly, Jinnery duplicated it. Chalis sat grinning at the omo while Jinnery stared, daring Falc. The wagon rumble-rolled out of the rear of the barn. Falc drew up the hem of his derlin, exposing lots of black boot and leggings. He took four long bounding steps and leaped up between them, past them, into the wagon. He heard Chalis's "Wa-ak!" and instantly felt ashamed; he had done it to show off and very well knew it.

Ashah correct me!

Ashah guide and deliver me from my vanity!

He went up to sit beside Querry.

After a moment Querry said, "You work good."

Falc saw no reason to say anything.

"Raised on a farm, I'll bet."

"No. I've traveled a lot; seen and done a lot, Querry."

Querry swallowed. "You killed?—men?"

"Yes," Falc said, and after a moment decided to say more. "When I am attacked, I have no rules except to prevail. I have been attacked. I have not killed every man who has attacked me or made me draw sword. But they were either wounded or fled, or both."

The darg plodded and the wagon trundled, rocking. "Only when you're attacked," Querry said after a while.

"That's true, Querry. Or when armed men have made me draw sword or just take their cuts or blows. The first thing we do is try to avoid fights. You never heard that, did you?"

"Ahm . . . no, no . . . so many tales about D—omos. Do you know what it is I'm thinking?"

"Oh no, Querry. I just know some of the tales about 'Deathknights,' as others call us, and that gave me an idea why you asked whether I had killed men."

"Hmm. But you stop and help a man get rint in before the rain falls."

"I stop my darg to let women pass, too. Even men. I doubt that the Arlord's men do that. Querry: I am probably speaking from ignorance again, as I was about the ramp. But would it not be easier on Catapin if we drove all the way to the other end and turned, and worked back? He'd have less distance to pull the full load. He'd feel better about it too, seeing himself getting ever closer to the barn. To home."

" 'Course. Stupid of me not to think of that years ago."

Falc shrugged. "A man who lives in the forest can't see it. A man on the road sees only the forest, not trees. So that I make no mis-assumptions, Querry, will you tell me who Jinnery is?"

"Oh. Should of told you already. She's my brother's child—

except that she isn't a child anymore, 'course. He's dead. Killed years ago, in Morazain.''

"Ah. It's a good man who takes in his kin."

The darg plodded and the wagon-wheels creaked.

"It's a more'n good man who stops to help strangers who need it!" Querry twitched the rein. "Nah—keep going there, Catapin. All the way to the end. She needed a place to stay and I needed help. It's an exchange."

"You aren't calling me anything, Querry. Call me Falc."

"Ahm . . . think I'd feel better calling you Sir Falc."

Falc shrugged. "You know I am accustomed to it, but it doesn't fit present circumstances."

Querry glanced at the other man then, and saw that Falc was not smiling. He really did talk that way, then. "My boy'll go skitty if you don't tell him a story or two, Sir Falc. He's a boy. He thinks killing is . . . he'll want to hear some exciting stories. You know."

"I'll not be telling him any you wouldn't care for him to hear, Querry. Well, to work."

They went back to work, in twilight only an hour past midday. When they reached the end of those windrows the wagon was not piled high, but Falc suggested that they unload anyhow. Jinnery seemed inclined to consider that an admission of his weakness; weariness. Falc said nothing to that. The clouds continued to move in and thunder rumbled. Now and again it crashed, distantly. Still, none of them was able to see any rain in the distance.

In the barn, Falc outlined another idea. He was careful with its presentation, as he had been with the others; more careful than he'd have been with a high-placed Holder. Querry was impressed, yet looked less than delighted. He agreed. Falc and Chalis unhitched Catapin and led him out to hitch him to the other wagon. It was smaller and its repair was not as good. It was also serviceable. Realizing the cause of Querry's uncertainty, Falc paced back to him and spoke quietly.

"I will take care of him, friend Querry. Consider: they two should not have to handle the job alone, and you had rather Chalis and I went than that you watched me go out of your sight in company with Jinnery, wouldn't you." It was not a question.

Querry met the other man's dark, dark gaze. "You sure are a strange man, Falc. I think you do read minds."

"No. Probably not so strange a man, either. I just don't fit the concept you have of omos. I will mind the boy, Querry; and the rint."

Querry and Jinnery would unload, then, while Falc and Chalis began filling the other wagon. As he and the boy started back to the field, Falc called:

"Our challenge to you two is that we will be back with this wagon full before you two have that one unloaded."

Chalis grinned. Querry grinned. Falc saw Jinnery accept the challenge. He saw a lot of determination in that grim bony face, and realized that there was more to her than most would surmise.

Thus he persuaded all of them to work the harder, and suddenly the whole job was fun for Chalis. Working with a Deathknight! While they worked, Falc told him an exciting story about a fast ride at night to beat a flooded stream that had to be crossed; he was carrying a message that wanted delivering sooner than soon. He did not ask about Jinnery, and Chalis had no opportunity to ask him about more exciting matters, such as fighting and killing. The other wagon was unloaded by the time they returned, but Chalis's enthusiasm faded only a little. Alone, with a Deathknight! An exciting tale to recount, a story of far places told only to him!

"The trouble with this two-wagon system," Jinnery said as she and Querry prepared to make the trip into the field, "is that it's even more wearing for Catapin."

"Catapin makes no more trips than he would have done," Falc pointed out. "He just makes them closer together. After all, he has a stake in this race with the rain, too. If you lose the crop, he will eat less well but work harder for less happy masters."

"Wak!" Chalis called. "That's right, isn't it!"

Jinnery shot a look at him, and at Falc. Both affected not to notice.

Rain or no, they all had to take a brief rest after that round of hauling and unloading, and Querry doused Catapin with water. The old darg perked up. The gift-darg still waited, hitched in the barn, and was fretful. Querry sloshed water on him, too. It was a kindness Falc noted and appreciated. As he and Chalis prepared to return to the field, Falc specified that they would walk rather than ride the wagon.

"One must be considerate even of dargs," Falc told the boy. "That way they serve better because they are happier. I'm not one of those who believes that dargs do not know what love is."

"Harr serves you better because you treat him better?"

"Yes. And because he knows I merit it and am master. He also—well, I will show you when we have this wagonload ready to return to the barn. Uh!"

The exclamation and their blinking was occasioned by a brilliant streak of lightning, followed several seconds later by a monumental blast from the direction of the wood.

. "A tall, tall tree has just been lessened," Falc muttered, and they began to swing their pitchforks. *Troublous time and woe . . . Ashah ride with us!*

When they had loaded and he had again tugged off his gauntlets to liberate sweaty hands, he laid a gentling hand on Catapin, near his halter. He bade Chalis stand near him. "HA-ARRR!" he shouted, and the war-darg came racing, looking ready to fight. Falc spoke calmly to him, before and while he boosted Chalis up.

"Do nothing, Chalis. Only ride. Harr: come."

They returned to the barn, Falc walking beside Catapin, not quite leading. Harr paced close beside. The gift-darg still waited inside, hitched, and was fretful. They found that the others had not quite finished unloading the second wagon. While Chalis hooted about that, Falc stripped the gift-darg of equipage, leaving only the halter and bridle by which he was hitched. Stepping into the smelly stall where he could not be seen, Falc exercised a bit. He swallowed his groans. He also left his gauntlets off for this load; they were almost squishy-wet inside. A few moments later he accepted the offer of dinner and biding: overnight hospitality. Chalis jigged about and made delighted noises.

They were on the next to last windrow when the first big splashy patters of rain began to fall. They finished loading in the rain. It had become a downpour by the time they were driving the high-piled wagon to the barn. Falc ordered Harr inside to protect his equipage. Harr obeyed with sour reluctance.

"The five ricks will turn most of the water," Querry said,

looking out. "We'll make oil from the rint in that windrow. We have lost nothing."

"Thanks to F—Sir Falc!" Chalis said.

"F—Sir Falc is about twice as weary as you, and trying not to be stiff," Falc said. With water running off his coif, he was stripping Harr. "All three of these fellows will appreciate being outside. Harr will give Catapin no trouble. I think the other darg is too shy to bother either of them."

"Catapin wouldn't give any trouble to a three-legged barga!" Chalis laughed, and his father grinned.

Having said nothing, Jinnery had already raced to the house.

"Querry," the omo said, "I admit that I am too weary to think of unloading that wagon."

"Falc, I admit the same. Think I'll strip and get me a free bath, then see about finding some beer."

Falc nodded, and it was only then that Querry realized he hadn't seen the man smile. "I must pass the bath, but I wouldn't object to helping you with the beer."

Laughing aloud, Querry stripped off long skirt, front-tied crotcher, and boots. Falc saw that he wore heavy cotton stockings, white or once white, and noted that the man was almost ludicrously paler below the waist. So was Chalis, who stripped and ran out to join his father. The omo stood in the barn's rear doorway, watching the three delighted dargs positively wallow in sheets of rain so thick it was visibly gray. Meanwhile he unobtrusively murmured most of Canticle Six of the Way.

2

The rain brought early, extreme darkness. That fact and the presence of a guest prompted Querry to a bit of extravagance, particularly for this time of year. He lit two of the open lamps filled with rintseed oil. It burned with the faint sweet aroma of pressed jarum blooms. Falc was reminded that not all people possessed the seemingly ubiquitous lichen-light from Drearmist.

Oddly, not lichen but algae formed a part of the little house's illumination. Both handsome lamps had been laboriously carved from several-colored stromatolites, fossils formed by algae. The two men munched a sharp, almost snowy cheese, aged in rintseed oil. The room smelled of food, and warmth, and human habitation. Father and son had changed into bright shirts and Chalis's house-pants were a grassy jarum blue with a green stripe down the side. Querry wore green-sashed pants of royal blue with black stripes down the outer seams.

The poor lad had to be told to leave Falc's "warlike things" alone.

"This is barley beer," the man in black observed. His warlike things, sword, helm, and mailcoat, were nearby; but the snug black hood covered his head to mid-brow.

"Ah, good to meet a man who knows the difference. Yes, I trade rint for barley with a neighbor. He's not the cheesemaker I am, so as part of the trade he makes beer for us both. It's many years now we've been trading this way."

Falc nodded his understanding of simple commerce. "It's good for men to trade. How do you feel about the Arlord?" he asked, stretching his legs and affecting not to be so attentively interested in the answer as he was. Carrying messages and advising, passing on information, was the job. So was gathering information, as unobtrusively as possible.

"He don't bother us much. He's all right as lords go, I guess. Want some more, there?"

They ate. More cheese, warmed so that grease rode it, shining, and another kind as well, colored reddish just for the variety and fun of it, with dark barley bread and a sweeter bread made of rint and eggs and fruit from the jonetree out back. Falc complimented the sweet-bread repeatedly; Jinnery's acceptance of the praise was peremptory and short on grace.

"I know you are accustomed to the fine food served in Holders' keeps," she said, in response to the severalth compliment. An apron of multicolored print covered her dress of another multicolored print.

Falc nodded. "That is true. It's also true that I often go without eating at all, for I ride much. What I am *accustomed to*, Jinnery, is whatever I can get! You can believe that any Holder's cook I know of would trade his mother for the recipe for this jonecake."

"Just bread," she said low-voiced, directing her almond-eyed gaze into her beer. Both she and Chalis drank beer with the meal, while the barrels outside collected water. The sounds of the rain continued as background for the meal, and made the small house seem that much cozier.

"Do Holders' cooks trade their *mothers*?"

Querry laughed; Falc shook his head solemnly. "Absolutely not, Chalis. That was what is called a figure of speech. Holders' cooks just aren't usually as good as your cousin Jinnery. Holders, by the way, are often fine men. I would not make Contract with a man I did not respect."

"So it is with Deathknights?" Jinnery said, looking into her brown-and-red mug.

Falc had not fathomed her antipathy, but knew that she persisted in calling him that because he had twice corrected the others and twice corrected her, and had explained to Chalis. He had already pointed out to himself that it meant nothing and did not lessen him, so that it ran off him as water poured off the roof over their heads.

"So it is with us, yes. Ever too proud and never as humble as we wish to be . . . should be."

She raised her head to give him a look, but it was Chalis who spoke:

"Falc—I mean, Sir Falc, do you always keep that little cap on?"

His father gave him a look, but Falc replied equably: "Yes. It's called a coif, Chalis, and all of us of the Order wear one, always."

"Oh. The Order . . . S'r Falc? How did the Order get started?"

"Chalis, we . . . Querry? Jinnery? I'd like to tell him the two-melt story."

Querry looked blank, though Falc noted that Jinnery did not. "Another figure of speech," the omo said. "It means the whole story; the longer version."

"Please do," Querry said. "I've not heard it."

Falc swallowed his surprise. Of course not. Most likely none of these three had any schooling, or could write, or had ever stayed past sunset in Morazain, if until. He nodded, solemnly rose and walked into the other room to break wind, and returned to fill his mug again. *Hospitality from fine people others call simple, O Ashah*, he reminded himself mentally. *One cannot refuse, in honor*. He regarded the wall, looking at the handsome hanging of blue, white, and green braidwork, and decided against commenting on it. If it were Jinnery's work, she would not accept a compliment with grace. If it were the work of Querry's dead wife, he might not care to talk of it.

Turning back to the others, he told Chalis the two-coin story of the Founding:

The death of the First Civilization left a vacuum, into which chaos moved. The great conqueror Sar Sarlis created order from that chaos. Yet what he created became in passing decades more and more despotic, a searing of the souls of men and shriveling of their wills. (Chalis's jarum-blossom eyes were bright and his father nodded at the phrasing, wearing a pleasant expression. He crossed his royal-blued legs.)

This culminated in him who called himself Emperor of All Men: Sai MaSarlis. In those days no free man existed on all the continent and perhaps not in all the world. No one dared disagree with the supreme ruler. Those who even hinted at it were beheaded or ordered to sever the veins in their wrists and thus drain out their own lives. The emperor's many, many officials and even distant representatives had nearly as much power; far too much power. Men, women, even cities were bought and sold. They were even given out to MaSarlis's favorites and the families of his wives and even unto the families of his concubines. Vacuum had led to conquest and conquest had led to tyranny.

Then came Sath Firedrake, third son of a minor farming lordlet of Gunnda, which was to become that strange city ruled by a *group* of men, a "republic."

Sath came, and rose, and people followed him, and more, and Sath rose the more. His acts were just and fair and often heroic. He took as his emblem a simple two-tailed banner of plain yellow, saying that it was not plain at all but the color of the sun, and what could be more brilliant? That was the year and the month of the Shearing of the Tax Collectors.

Emperor MaSarlis sent out men to arrest Sath Firedrake, and they failed. They returned in disgrace and MaSarlis had them publicly slain, in the way of the Empire: their heads were struck with a mighty hammer wielded by a mighty man, so that their skulls were shattered. The emperor sent orders to

Sath to present himself in the capital, alone and without followers above an escort of no more than six men.

Sath Firedrake wisely and rightfully refused, and more people came to follow him as leader. And more came flocking, and he rose the more.

At last Emperor MaSarlis sent forth an army to destroy him, for now the Firedrake had become a threat and a challenge.

Forth marched that army, all tramping men in brightly painted war-masks and their officers in gleaming blue armor under banners of blue marked with the imperial device, and gold and crimson and green and more blue. The sun flashed off helms and upraised spearheads and the bosses of shields. Like a magnificent river they flowed up into Zain to crush one more upstart and challenger, and with them were mighty lords and well-seasoned generals and two sons of the very emperor.

Along the River Nuar, Sath and his followers defeated that imperial army in all its splendor. And more hurried to the plain sun-hued banners of Sath, in number as the chaff that blows like rust in the steady wind of autumn. A son of Emperor MaSarlis died in that battle, and another fled back to the capital with news of the impossible: defeat!

The commander of the imperial army fled to the provincial governor's river-island keep, which rose tall and mighty. All knew that it was surely invincible and well-nigh unassailable. Nor could Sath Firedrake's men gain the isle, for arrows fell upon their boats like hail and sent many good men to lie forever at the bottom of the Nuar.

This is why the waters of the River Nuar run dark, even now.

At last Sath Firedrake divided his force, and sent some of them out onto the river in bobbing boats containing false men, helmeted and war-dressed images stuffed with straw and wet leaves. Above them fluttered two-tailed pennons of sun-yellow. It was they who drew the arrows that day. Sath and the main portion of his force rested, and secretly prepared more boats. They roofed them over and silenced their oars with rags. Well after dark, while those in the well-provisioned keep on the isle were boisterously celebrating another day of lofting arrows at waterbugs (as they in their callous arrogance and contempt called the attackers), Sath prepared his force to move out and invade the island.

Then one of his men, a young and valiant captain named Jalan, noticed something. He called it to Sath's attention: because of the roofing bulwarks over the boats, he pointed out, it would be almost impossible to reverse oars.

"That is a matter less consequential than dust motes or flunderpuffs," Sath Firedrake told him, "for I have no intention of retreating." And he gave the order to embark.

The young man Jalan was sorry that he had spoken, and much chagrined. He was in the forefront of those who charged ashore onto the island, and one of the first into the keep of that great lord, who was brother to Emperor MaSarlis's favorite wife. That Jalan was a brave man, but to this day all boys are urged and reminded to beware Jalan's Utterance, meaning to speak without knowledge and thus to earn embarrassment and loss of face.

By mid-afternoon that great lord of the empire had broken his own war-mask and taken his own life, and soon twin-tailed yellow banners fluttered from his keep. And more still came to join Sath Firedrake.

Now people elsewhere revolted against tyrannical lords and tax-gatherers and assessors—who are always the worse. Then the lords of Juliara and Zain marched against Sath, because the emperor bade them, and Sath did defeat on them. And more still joined him and his cause (which was the cause of Sij!), or proclaimed their allegiance to him, even from afar. In Morazain which was then Jezaina he said that all the land south would *honor* the Emperor MaSarlis, and even send tribute to the capital (which was then where Skeltree lies now, on lower Lake Salarn); but that all men would be *free*. This Sath Firedrake proclaimed in Jezaina where bits of yellow cloth fluttered from every window so that the whole large town was like a field of yellow blossoms: and no imperial soldiery or lord or tax-gatherers would thereafter go to that place.

Thus Jezaina, named after a daughter of Sar Sarlis long before, came to be known as Morazain, which means "field of yellow."

Many prisoners were given the choice of servitude. Many chose it in preference to death or fleeing penniless to the capital—which is not to say that many did not choose death. Even then it is true: thousands of those Sath Firedrake spared, though he was no weak man. It was he who proved that mercy is not weakness. Some of his men and backers became holders of many slaves, which was wealth. Nor would Sath move on then, against the emperor as so many expected, and urged. Nor would he call himself emperor as so many wanted him to do.

He was Sath Firedrake, and in search of a title those men newly free began to call him "the Firedrake," as if it were a title, and so it became one.

Zain flourished, and the land round about Zain, as shume flourishes in an untended field.

A full two years passed before the emperor sallied forth against Sath, and it is said that he led the armies only because his lords and generals would not otherwise march, and by then they were more powerful than he. What a display was there! Carven helmets and plumes nodding all bright-colored above ferocious war-masks, carved and painted; ornate armor all aflash and aglitter, and waving pennons all of a single color: blue, for this was a display of imperial power as well as a conquering force. Battle was joined with a clangor and a shouting of men that rose amid dust into the skies and chased the clouds.

The conquering force did not conquer. The conquering force was conquered.

The Emperor of All Men was defeated, and was slain ignobly and ignominiously by one of his own concubines, who hoped for favor with the conqueror and of course held hopes for her offspring by the emperor; the emperor she slew in hopes of currying favor. With tears on his face Sath Firedrake, all running with sweat and the blood of others and the wound to his sword-arm, saw her deprived of son and life. He wept over the corpse of the emperor, and honored those of his sons who remained living. And the eldest he called by the title Emperor.

By this, many were horrified and angered. They said that the Firedrake should rule. They said it loudly and often. Sath Firedrake, Emperor of All Men by the Choice of All Men!

No, Sath said. No one would rule over the continent. No one could! Furthermore no one should try, ever. The descendants of MaSarlis would be first among the lords of Sij, and no more.

This the young SharSarlis accepted, and agreements were signed and proclaimed far and wide. And that too was on the ninth Sarloj, for it was the Year of Two Calendars.

SharSarlis went so far as to change his name to Shardanis.

Then Sath called Firedrake of Gunnda, Conqueror and Liberator, surprised everyone still further. He doffed his armor and, in sight of many, broke his sword. He removed his yellow sash with the two tails and donned one of dull black, with a ragged edge. In mourning, he said, for all those who had died in his company and in his behalf. He vowed, swearing by his honor and the scar on his sword-arm wrist, never to wear color; only black. He had ever said that it was the god Ashah who guided him, and now he founded the first temple of Ashah and, two years later, that holy order which he called merely "the Sons of Ashah."

There are other orders now, but none is like unto that founded by Sath, for he was both a man of religion and of arms: a monk and a knight. So are we who choose to follow his Way. The Sons of Ashah is the oldest order, and thus is the Order Most Old. It is that, for an Order of Ashanites had existed prevously, but had been disbanded by imperial decree.

"That was two hundred years ago, and nineteen years more," Falc told Jinnery and the others. "Out of chaos came firm government to bring order, and that led to empire. Perhap it was necessary. The First Civilization left only wreckage and useless machines in a world depleted of the fuels to drive them—and worse! For you know of the Burning Lands, and that such creatures as dargs used to be as small as fergs, and other things. Nor is there anything natural about Dreammist, whose jar-sealed lichen glows for many years and is poison besides. It is a Thing that arose from the destruction of the Mechanists of the First Civilization, and in the temples of Ashah Upholder we use no such.

"Out of Empire Sath Firedrake created the autonymous citystates. In them Holders grew up to fill the vacuum left behind by the emperor's dead and enslaved lords and 'lords.' No one rules over all, or can, for the Holders would not stand for it."

Falc sipped barley beer, and shifted his buttocks.

"And thus the world. Gunnda holds to its strange rule still, and it is tolerated because citystates are free each of the others. You have your Arlord and his Militarate of Zain, because ninety years ago a greedy Holder sought to add this land to his. He was destroyed and is one with MaSarlis. I know that his name is not spoken in Zain, and I will not speak it. The emperor does not rule; the emperor now is . . . a symbol. A reminder of the past, a sort of unifying figurehead. A symbol of a continent at peace, united through disunity, if that is what lack of supreme rule means. For unity means rule by one man, and is Not To Be Sought. The Holders rule, and such as your Arlord and a few others on their estate-keeps; ardoms, independent of cities. Because they are well apart in citystates or ardoms such as Lord Daviloran's or Lord Synaven's up the road, they are competitive and mistrustful. We of the Order founded by Sath Firedrake form the unifying bond among all the Holders, all the cities and ardoms. And thus, of Sij. Ashah guide us!"

Falc sipped again with the air of a man who had done with his talking, and Querry spoke almost excitedly.

"Thank you, Sir Falc! Never have I seen it all so clearly, felt so the sweep of history and our heritage. I am glad that my son has heard it—and from one who is in a way a descendant of Sath Firedrake."

"Wak!"

"And now," Jinnery said tiredly, speaking as though she did not want to but could not help it, "Shalderanis is emperor. That . . . boy."

"Yes," Falc said, "now Shalderanis is called emperor. His older brother died and, five years ago his father the emperor died, though he was not old. Emperor Shalderanis is only twenty-six. Some have said that he is arrogant and dreams of the world as it was before Sath Firedrake. But that is silly and I cannot give it credence. No man can take all Sij, now. No emperor may truly rule and thus no empire can exist. *We* see to that, by providing a sort of unity of knowledge, a linkage through communication among the independent Holders."

"What do *you* think of Shalderanis, Sir Falc?"

"I have never met him, Chalis."

"That's not what I mean—oohh . . . but what do you *think*, then?"

"Ashah has said that rumors are weeds that grow without purpose or need, and that he who believes rumors without knowledge is an eater of weeds and thus one with beasts."

"Never met him," Chalis said, while his father closed his eyes, concentrating on remembering the aphorism. "I thought you had been everywhere."

Falc's face easily took on kindly lines. "There are many places I have not been, Chalis. I don't even know the names of some."

"I am going to step outside and increase the rainfall," Querry said, "and take me to my bed. Chalis—"

"Oh! But tomorrow S'r Falc will leave! Let him tell just one story—a story of war and banners and brave weapon-men in battle!"

The eyes of the two men met. Falc blinked in a way that Querry recognized as a nod of acquiescence and reassurance . . . subject to Querry's approval.

"One story," Querry said, and showed his own interest by postponing his necessary trek outdoors.

"A bloody one!" the boy urged.

"No, Chalis; but a brave one that I love. At the battle of the Plain of Tinjurrah, the great Sath Firedrake was set upon by a certain lord's high champion. His name was Bazarga Redstar."

"Bazz-z-zar-r-ga Red-star-r-r," Chalis said, tasting the sound of the words and liking their flavor.

"Yes. A man with unusually long arms and a blood-red war-mask, who used a weapon of his own devising. This he called his 'red claw.' A horrid claw-like weapon mounted on a pole about the length of your father's pitchfork handle. Bazarga used it in the same way another man would wield a sword. Can you visualize that? This long red-painted handle and on its end a hand-sized claw, like this, of red iron. A horrible thing."

"Horrible!" Chalis echoed dutifully, while his bright blue eyes shone.

"With it, Bazarga Redstar maimed and slew many men and good war-dargs. And with it, Bazarga Redstar actually struck Sath Firedrake in the head,'' Falc said ominously, watching Chalis's shock and horror.

"Oh!"

"Yes, for he was still out of reach of Sath's sword. But Sath was of course wearing his helmet, and by chance the claws bit into that black helm and held fast."

"Oh."

"You may assume that Bazarga Redstar was not too ired by this; he had only to drag the great hero headfirst off his darg and slay him by the time he hit the ground."

Chalis was not breathing. Querry was following the story nearly as tensely, and intently. Falc was sure that he had Jinnery's attention as well, though she kept up her hostile pose of disinterest. What soared within her, that she showed him such dislike?

He went on with the story, which was true:

"But! Before the attacker could drag the hero off his mount, Sath Firedrake twisted in the saddle and with his sword swinging *upward*—this way, you see, when a man cannot put as much force behind it—no ordinary man, at any rate. His edge clove right through the bird-claw's staff! Although the claw remained lodged in Sath's helm, Bazarga held now only a shortened wooden stave. It was the jaws of Sath's well-trained darg that put a sanguinary end to Bazarga Redstar's career, for a one-armed warrior is rare. Sath meanwhile completed the Battle of Tinjurrah with that ugly thing standing forth from his helmet like an obscene decoration. Or a trophy, which it was, to the further embarrassment of Bazarga and his lord. Sath Firedrake's force won that day, and the helmet is now in the Firedrake Room of the Mon Ashah-re."

"The High Temple! Oh! How wonderful! I can just see it!" The boy looked ready to wet himself in his delight; his father smiled with pleasure. Abruptly Chalis said, his eyes bright as gemstones, "Will you teach me the use of arms, S'r Falc? Will you?"

"No."

"But . . . why . . ."

"Anyone can use arms, Chalis Querryson. Anyone can maim and kill, and too many do. Bazarga Redstar devised a more evil means of maiming his opponents or bringing them

within reach of his long, long dagger. Anyone can do these
things and too many do. Don't forget what became of Bazarga
Redstar . . . can you imagine what he was later called?''

"Bazarga One-arm!"

"You are right. What the world *needs*, Chalis, is farmers.
For the world must eat. Farmers and Holders and warriors
alike must eat.''

Jinnery spoke. "You are not proud of what you do, Sir
Deathknight?''

"Name's Falc, Jinnery. An omo. Falc. Of Risskor, a far
southern land where farmers are respected and I am not. I
assure you that I respect me and am proud of what I do. No
omo is more dedicated than I, or more competent.'' He
looked away. "Many are more humble, though.''

Querry smiled.

"Competent at killing,'' Jinnery said, pretending it was a
question.

"At many things, Jinnery. Combat is among them.'' He
gazed directly into the repulsion she was at pains to show on
her face.

"Jinn . . .'' Querry began.

"How many men have you killed, Falc?'' Chalis's voice
was bright, unwavering, as he merely expressed curiosity
about that which he thought of as the most exciting and
romantic: killing.

"How many weeds have you pulled and hoed, Chalis?''
Falc returned, in the same equable tone and manner with
which he had answered Jinnery.

Chalis's eyes went huge as he thought he understood: "So
Many!''

"No. I asked you a silly question with no meaning or
purpose.''

Chalis looked at him, blinking, frowning a little. The oil
lamp was low and its light had become a wan yellow.

"Falc means,'' Jinnery said, "that your question was a
rude and silly one with no meaning, Chalis, and asked to no
purpose.''

"Oh I did not mean to be rude! I just—''

"You pull weeds, son,'' Querry said, "and you farm. Sir
Falc . . . does what he does.''

"Which is mostly ride and ride in all weather, carrying

messages and advice," Falc said in a quiet monotone. "Listen, Chalis. Listen. Bad men are as weeds, to choke and spoil the crop of good men. But the sword may cut only one weed at a time, while the hoe cuts many. Praise be to those who wield hoes!"

"Is that from your Order Most Old, Falc?" That from Jinnery.

"It is from an old man I once met down on the Plain of Radd, near Ryar. He was dying, sworded and robbed and left. He would not tell me who had done it or describe the monster to me. Those were his words I repeated. He did not tell me his name and would not have me avenge him. Perhaps it was Ashah Himself, come to teach and test me. Perhaps it is unseemly personal arrogance for me even to consider that. This comes from the Order, from the Firedrake—the Master of the Order—before this one: 'Do not make value judgements,' he taught. 'The darg is a gentle and hard-working creature who serves men and kills only to eat. Is a darg then better than a man?' "

"I believe yes, they are," Jinnery said, in that unfeminine voice of brass, and Falc regarded her mildly. She averted her overcooked almonds of eyes. So much bitterness corked up in that slim and so-young woman with the voice of a pubescent boy!

"What is a—I don't know what a val-you judgment is," Chalis said rather plaintively.

"Today it would have been easy for us to say 'Rain is bad!' That would be a value judgment and it would have been wrong. Truth is that '*Today* rain is bad *for me* because it is going to spoil *part* of *this* crop.' There are those who dislike a particular kind of food or music or people from a certain place, and say 'That is awful; this is rotten; they are bad.' The words 'I think' or 'I believe' and 'to me' are important ones, Chalis . . . and your lids are drooping."

"It is past time, Falc," Querry said. "The trouble is that none of us wants to go to bed and end it. We are not lonely here, but we are alone, and all this is wonderful, like strong wine to us. We will long savor its flavor."

"Your father is both a farmer and a poet, Chalis. An important man indeed!" Falc said. Suddenly he looked at Jinnery, catching her staring all bright-eyed at him.

She said, "I hear paradoxes coming from your mouth, Sir Deathknight."

Falc nodded. "You do! All is paradox, and I can't avoid it, because I am a part of all just as you are. The faith of Markcun Deathslayer teaches that 'Bad' is subject only to a subjective definition, as is Good. Pink, however—the mix of the blood-red of 'Bad' and the white of 'Good'—is the true hue of the universe. In our lives, we can only do what we can to be as pale as the shadeflower in the deepest glen of the forest; and seek ever the pure white of Good as our goal."

"Wait," Querry said, frowning mightily. "Even in that there is a paradox, for what is good?"

Falc shook his head. "That which is not bad." A whimsical smile considered playing tag with his eyes, but gave it up. He gestured helplessly. "I don't have all the answers, friend Querry . . . nor have I managed to turn myself white."

"Beautiful flowers rise from rot," Jinnery said with an air of having stated something of import, though Falc considered the clichéd aphorism apropos of nothing.

Definition was mentioned, and they went off into that while the lamp approached the guttering stage and voices grew gravelly, and then they discovered that Chalis was asleep where he sat. Falc rose.

"Go to bed. I will see to the dargs. I would also much prefer to sleep atop all that fresh-cut rint. Will you grant me that pleasure?"

"You are my guest!" Querry came to his feet. "You will sleep in my house!"

"I am serious, Querry. I had truly rather sleep in the barn. We omos have prayers, and rites before we retire, and I want to be out there. It is nothing against you or your house. Remember that one of us *lives* in a house, and one of us travels. Unless you object to my sleeping on the rint—"

"No no! It is that—"

"Then I will. And may Ashah grant us all a better morrow."

He was partway through the door when Querry said low, "One of us sleeps in a house, you said . . . and you have no woman either, have you Falc?"

"No," Falc said, "and I am not known for smiling."

He went out and closed the door after him, knowing what

Querry had told him without meaning to do: niece or no, Querry had a woman.

The rain had long since become a tired drizzle, leaving behind that familiar clean scent along with the usual paradox: mud. The second moon was up, a pale and haloed little ghost that rode in and out of long gray-blue clouds like tattered banners across the black of the sky.

3

Falc saw to the dargoni, which were coexisting amiably enough. He murmured words of the Way and performed not one but three several rites and exercises as well. Just when he was preparing to lie back on the great pile of still-sweet rint, the pale light came into the barn.

He stood erect at once, head inclined within that ethereal luminosity, as the *Manifestation* coalesced. The Manifestation took as much form as it ever did, until it was a wavery silvery-gray figure, robed and faceless in the last helmet and war-mask Sath Firedrake had ever worn. The Messenger spoke, in a voice that sounded hollow and as if rebounding from old gray stones deep in a well.

"Say to me the Credo of the Order."

"The purpose of the Order Most Old is to preserve the social order," Falc said, from rote but with feeling. "Thus the purpose of the Order Most Old is to hold and cherish knowledge; to hold ever foremost its duty to the social order; to dispense it with love and great care for its value and its danger to the social order; to assist communication among its leaders; and to strive ever to maintain that social order."

That first question always prefaced the communication from the Temple, while the second was never predictable, but taken at random from the Way of the OMO. It was both test and assurance of identification, Falc believed, and assumed it must mean that the Messenger could not see him, but only knew where he was. This time it was the Second Statement the Manifestation wished:

"What man do you serve?"

"A Son of Ashah serves no man. A Son of Ashah does not serve himself," Falc quoted, "or even the Order Most Old, or even the Founder. A Son of Ashah serves the social order.''

Those preliminaries out of the way, the Messenger at once delivered the news in that hollow, echoic voice:

"Five new brothers have been admitted and two applicants have been turned away. Those latter are called Sak of the Berger Steppes area and Sendaven of Darsin. Your brother Ashamal has terminated Contract and will seek another. Your brother Vennashah cannot be contacted. Last contact was somewhere near Silkevare, and we worry. Be alert. The Master and the High Temple abide well. On those occasions when you despair that you are only a chesspiece of the cosmos, consider the despair of the player! May you be granted a morrow no worse than this day.''

"And thou,'' Falc said, an instant before the Messenger vanished, but he thought he was not heard.

Falc of Risskor did not question that the Messenger was the spirit of Sath Firedrake, keeping watch over the Order he had founded and appearing to the sons of Ashah. Always at night, and only when an omo was alone. Falc was sure that the Founder's spirit was with the Master of the Order, and that he donned those relics of the Founder in order to make these periodic appearances to the Sons of Ashah. Since this was invariable, Falc knew that the god was with the Founder and thus with the Master, for how else could he know when the Sons afield were alone and no others would hear the Messenger? Yet he could not see, Falc thought. If any person outside the Order knew of the Messenger by which one-way contact was maintained with those who were afield, none had ever mentioned it. Not to Falc's knowledge.

It happened, and only the Sons of Ashah knew. It happened, and a Son of Ashah did not question the Order Most Old. The Order and its ways were an arcanum that raised cogent questions, which were not to be asked.

Falc was unable not to think about Vennashah, a knight of the Order Most Old now out of contact with the Temple, meaning that the Manifestation could not find him as tonight it had found Falc, in a barn on a nameless farm. Trying not to worry, he composed himself for sleep in the pleasant silence of the barn, redolent of hay and manure. And then he was interrupted again.

Someone was moving toward him, with care for quiet.

Without moving from his supine position, he grasped the hilt of his sheathed sword. He sat up, arm poised to sling the sheath off the blade in a way that would create a noise well away from him and was profoundly disconcerting to any stalker by night. This figure was rather ghostly too, in the darkness, but it was not at all like the Messenger with its strange surrounding glow. Falc made his voice worse than dour, and his question held no sound of query:

"Who is it."

"We are not wholly ignorant of the ways of cities and of Holders, Sir Falc," the voice of Jinnery said, softly. "Querry has sent you companion, in love and friendship."

The omo was astonished. He thought of her antipathy for him, her sharp tongue and looks, the other look he had caught. He thought of how she had listened . . . and then he realized how long ago he had left the house. Long enough for a thoroughly weary Querry to have gone to sleep, while his very young woman waited.

"Querry is kind," Falc said very quietly, not believing her at all. "I would consider him brother, and I would not accept from my brother the companionry of his woman."

He waited, in the silence of the barn aromatic of hay and manure. She said nothing, and he knew he must be even more direct.

"This is no personal rejection of you, Jinnery. Return to your home and your bed."

She stood a while in silence, and Falc sat in silence, and then she turned and left the barn, almost as silently as she had come. He watched the appearance of the sliver of light as she opened the door; saw it close on the interior darkness that shrouded him. Still astonished and rather scandalized, Falc put aside his sword and lay back.

She is years and years younger than he, and than I as well, and she does share his bed, niece or no. And she is no happy woman. Still, I would fault her and not care to be called to attest either to her honor or her discretion.

And he thought, *Ah, Falc! 'Do not make value judgments. The darg is a gentle and hard-working creature who serves men and kills only to eat. Is a darg better then than a man?' Than a lonely woman with the cusp of romance on her?*

Perhap it is her time of year and Querry too weary! Shame, Falc. Tomorrow you are denied a midday meal, for this sad lapse into the Sin of Judgment-alism.

As if it were a psalm, he muttered that threatening, yearning second verse of "Destiny Wears a Black Cloak":

> Pitfalls and treachery and call of lechery!
>   How these conspire to firm my desire
> To seek a different road!
> Ashah accept me!
> Ashah guide me!
> Ashah deliver me!
> Sath inspire me!

And Falc of Risskor went to sleep, mentally muttering the Way of the United Man.

THREE

The head of a Son of Ashah does not succumb
   to passion.
That is to say, he does not lose his control.
That is to say, among other things, that a Son
   of Ashah does not lose his temper.
To act based on lack of control, in passion, in
   anger, is sub-human.
                  —The Way of The Order

Sench got himself out of the Dancer's Luck inn as swiftly as
he was able, trying not to groan or stagger. These confounded
ever-so-manly Missentians just could not be allowed to know
his discomfort. He and the Order just could not lose so much
face. He stepped down into the street with care he tried to
conceal, suddenly feeling like an old man.

He should never should have eaten simiselpis Missentian
style. Even having done, he certainly should have known
better than to compound the error by dumping down three
mugs of ale. It was hardly in accord with the Way or the
ascetic dignity of an omo. Worse, it was far from in accord
with the way Sench's stomach cared to be treated. Even
worse than that would be showing it, in Missentia.

Cloak fluttering black as a rain-laden sky about his heels,
Sench made his way along the street as swiftly as his discomfort allowed. He headed for the alley he had noted earlier. His
stomach roiled and rumbled, thrusting painfully against his
weapons belt. Its sounds were a pleading for relief.

Missentians were not known for high culture, but they did

take pride in their vaunted manliness. Accordingly they were not known for fancy cookery, but for tongue-numbing stomach-burning concoctions the eating of which they fancied proved something about their manhood. Not enough that their simiselpis contained three kinds of pepper, along with onions and those confounded red longbeans; this confounded innkeeper had just had to double the amount of sage as well, in addition to adding radishes which he had first fried.

Sench had been stupid: he had succumbed to the marvelous aroma. Worse, he had not limited himself to smelling, but had eaten. Then, seeking to alleviate the burning of mouth and stomach, he had poured in all that ale. Beans and onions gratefully began to swell. So did the stomach of Sir Sench of Southradd. It no longer pleaded for relief; it demanded it with increasing stertorousness of complaint.

Swinging around the corner into the alley nearly as black as his attire, Sench allowed a groan to escape. Yet he moved along another ten paces before he gave way to the first burst of the wind that demanded release from his body. The sound was not quite so thunderous as he had expected. He kept moving, getting away from the odor. Again, without even a grunt and no effort, he released.

The voice came from behind him, effluvious wake notwithstanding: "Not man enough for our cooking, hmm gas-bag? Here, let me help you loose some of the gas."

Caught by surprise as no omo should be, Sench moved and knew that his meal and his discomfort slowed him. He had an instant of realization that his monumental wind-breaking had covered whatever sound the voice's owner had made in coming up behind him. Hand rushing across his middle to his hilt, Sench spun around just in time to take the follower's swordpoint in his own forearm. It was across his belly, fingers clutching his hilt. Sench groaned and the fingers flexed. Even then his gaze caught the outline of a second man.

The first twisted his blade, yanked it out of the omo's forearm, and drove it in again, under the wrist. It skewered into Sench's guts.

"Here's another, *Deathknight!*" the second man sneered, already driving his long dagger through the omo's cloak and in, between Sench's fifth and sixth ribs.

They stabbed him again, each of them. His face ceased

writing in pain and seemed frozen in tetanic agony as his
legs jellied and he sagged to his knees. By then Sench had
realized that they had been waiting for him or had followed
him from the inn.

*Assassins. They have no other purpose. They are here
solely to kill me.* He was wondering muzzily why when he
collapsed and his legs began twitching.

They took his equipage and his clothing before they left
him, dead and naked in the alley in Missentia.

2

Falc awoke and was up before the sun. A look through the
crack between the barn's vertical planking showed him the
blue dark before dawn, lightly washed in palest rose-orange
over to the west. He did not look at the muddy rintfield, but
Walked the Way. By the time he finished, the sun was a full
disk and all three dargoni were restless. No one had come to
the barn; perhaps they thought he wished to sleep. Surely
such conscientious farm-folk as Querry's family were awake.

He went up to the house to effect his leavetaking and was
fair ordered to sit down for breakfast. He did, his midnight
eyes only brushing Jinnery's gaze in a single moving glance.
They were washing down puffed rint and a little summer
sausage with mugs of hax when they heard the dargs and
voices outside. Jinnery was by the door, and opened it.

"Welll!" a male voice called, all dissembling phoniness in
its assumed joviality and friendliness. "Now here's an attractive greeting to start a man's day off aright! Got something
for us for breakfast, dear?"

Laughter rose, in three male voices. Falc put a hand on
Querry's wrist as the man started up from his stool. Querry
looked at his visitor, who stared his question.

"The Arlord's peacekeepers," Querry muttered, through
tight lips.

"Have they business with you? Do you owe tax or tithe?"

"No."

Querry tugged at his wrist, and Falc rose, sliding his hand
into his gauntlet. Querry rushed to the door then, stepping out

to where the overlord's trio of soldiers still amused themselves by throwing remarks at Jinnery.

"Ah, a man comes. Older, I see. Your daughter, farmer?"

"I am Querry. This is my niece. What can we do for you
today, so as not to hold you from your business?"

Nicely said, Falc thought, easing around the low table.

"Why," one of the men said while another giggled, "you
can paint a pleasant look on your face, farmer, and go finish
your breakfast while we *visit* with your youthful *niece.*"

A small hand touched Falc's cloak and a small voice
quavered, "Falc?"

Falc turned to see the nervous expression on Chalis's face.
"Please stand where you are for a drip or two, Chalis."

Falc swung to pace to the door with a rustle of dark, dark
cloak. He emerged behind Querry and Jinnery, who stood
close. He stepped to their right, beside them. The trio of
mounted men, all in their early twenties, wore flattish but
spike-topped casques with neck-guards of shingled lacquer.
Simple leather hauberks, russet, were decoratively armored
with various square placks of lacquered wood. The lacquer
was yellow into which a bit of red had been mixed, so that
they had somewhat the appearance of gold. All three wore
swords and the two just behind the first held dragonels.

Falc wore a face carved from solid rock and hooded eyes
that stared without any hint of friendliness or humor. "The
Arlord surely does not send forth his brave *peace*-keepers
without letting them first break their fast—and we all eat
together, here."

The trio stared at him. The two rearward glanced at each
other and one suddenly began blinking rapidly. Their leader's
swallow was visible.

"Who . . . are you?"

"I am Falc of Risskor, knight of the Order Most Old. Who
are you?"

"We . . . we are the Arlord's men," the fellow said,
hiding behind the plural "we" and the name and station of
another as such tiny people always did; what else were they
but servants of a Name? "What is your business here, Sir
Deathknight?"

"I told you my name, which is more than you have done,"
Falc said in a quiet and equable tone. "Mine is not 'Deathknight.'

I doubt whether you are empowered to ask my business here, but I will tell you before our breakfast grows cold-er. This is my cousin Querry and his niece my cousin Jinnery. I am visiting them along the way from Lango, through Zain to Secter. I have no business with your lord, though perhaps now I might stop and pay my respects."

"Your cousin!" That from one of the two rearward men.

Falc gazed in blank-faced silence at the fellow, just long enough to make him uncomfortable. Then he said pleasantly, "Even we of the Order have cousins."

The leader said, "Have you, ah, is everything—is everything all right here, Zainman Querry?"

"Yes," Querry said, after a moment of regaining his equilibrium. "We just got in the rint crop before the rain, thanks to Falc."

The three men blinked, one continuously and rapidly, and Falc turned to Querry. "We'd best get that last wagonload unloaded too, cousin, so that we can resume our weapons-practice."

"Well, ah, we'll be on our . . . our way." The leader's gaze flickered to Jinnery, across Querry to Falc. He started to turn his darg, then realized what he'd heard and spoke almost hopefully. Perhaps in the omo's last words he had found his excuse after all: "You have weapons here, Zainman Querry?"

"Since the Zainer sword-hunt of three years back, known to all men on the continent?" Falc said smoothly. "You know better, Arlord's nameless man. I, who am eternally sworn to defend my cousin and his family, of course have weapons. Several."

The man nodded. His face twitched. He nodded again, turned his darg. They left by the road, and one of the trio was scolded—loudly—for having let his mount step off the track into squishy soil "of value to that good farmer and our lord."

"Our *cousin*!" Chalis said, hardly so loudly.

"Hush now, Cousin Chalis. Let them hear nothing. O Ashah, how many such little men have I seen, all big because another employs them! They bask and exult in reflected power. Now listen to him take out his frustration on his own comrade! I doubt that they will return here, Querry, but . . . Jinnery? Their lord may uphold them if they should catch you afield.

'Outrage rules amain and men seek only gain . . . !' Avoid the circumstances."

"You give me orders, *cousin*?"

"Jinnery!" Querry said, which Falc had observed was about all the man said to his sharp-tongued . . . niece. "Falc has just . . ."

She turned with a swish of skirts and went into the house. The two men looked at each other. Suddenly Querry grinned boyishly.

"What fun you Sons of Ashah have!"

"Oh yes," Falc said without expression. "Querry: give me a coin."

"A coin?"

"A coin." Falc nodded. "Any old melt or shaveling will do. And have you writing implements?"

Querry stared, then laughed aloud. "No!"

"Do you fetch the coin," Falc said, quitting the porch and seeing that his cloak's hem stayed clear of the mud. "I have quill and paper in my pack. Does Jinnery read?"

"Why . . . yes," Querry said, obviously wondering how Falc might have guessed that. But the other man was walking to the barn and Querry went inside. He soon had a piece of minglemelt betwixt thumb and forefinger.

"Querry!" Jinnery said. "The man asked for a coin and you don't even know why! I heard him say any coin, even a shave! That's one of the nine true, shaped coins we have!"

Querry gave her a long look in which he let show some pain. Without otherwise replying, he went out onto the porch. Falc wrote, dusted the ink, moved the bit of reed-paper through the air, and handed it to the farmer. At the same time, he took the coin.

"What—what is this? What have we done? Sir Falc? what means this?"

"The nameless men of the Arlord might question your possession of a new darg, Querry, and I have one too many. That is a bill of sale. It does not mention an amount, but does say 'melts of good bronze.' "

While Querry stood with his mouth open, Jinnery spoke from the door. "That coin contains some good silver!"

"Yes," Falc said, "but it seems unwise to let such men as I have seen today know that Querry possesses not only a niece they find attractive but formed minglemelts as well. The darg I leave is unnamed. I suggest that you give him a nice short name that can be uttered or spat in one breath. That way it is easy to train him to come when he is called.''

"Falc—"

'*Wak!*''

Falc waved a gauntlet in a vague upward gesture. "Querry, I cannot be burdened with a darg I do not need and have not trained. Do me this service and keep the beast. I would say that he has never known the whip and will serve you better if he never does. Now I have to be about business that I have interrupted long enough. Farewell and Ashah grant you many good morrows . . . cousin.''

"Falc—"

"*Harr!*''

"Falc, I cannot take such a—"

Harr came waddle-hurrying squishily in rain-soft ground. Falc swung into the saddle he had adjusted in the barn. He extended a bare hand to Querry and his family, palm down in the sign of peace. Then Falc turned Harr and rode along the muddy two-rut to the main road.

"Falc!" Chalis called.

"Falc!" his father called, a bit querulously, in helplessness.

The knight of the Order Most Old rode away. Father and son stood staring, while Jinnery read what Falc had written. The gift-darg of a Holder of Lango was theirs. Its value was at least a score of such coins as Querry had handed the omo. Jinnery looked up. She stared after the man in black.

"A paradox," Querry breathed. "An enigma."

"The greatest man in the world!" Chalis said, far more loudly.

"I do believe," his father mused, "that he was once a farmer and wishes he had never left the farm."

"Not human," Jinnery said, and flounced back into the house. She did bear the bill of sale with care.

The omo rode, and rode, and worked out with sword against shadows while Harr took a bit of midday meal. Falc had forbidden himself food until sunset.

3

At least the four assassins were not cowards. Cowards would have succeeded in killing him.

Falc saw them as he returned through the chokebushes and marlet, down the tree-grown knoll to the road. He had just completed his noonday stop the day after his parting with Querry. He was in Zain still, but this quartet was not of the men of the Arlord.

Though they were not quite uniformed, he recognized their city stripes and House colors: Lango. Faradox. Their purpose and challenge was unmistakable. They sat their mounts across the road between him and Morazain with about a meter separating them, and they gazed at him.

He realized that they had ridden past while he was up among the trees relieving himself. Now they blocked the road before him, forming a short line, and they gazed at him. He saw purpose in their eyes, but nothing of friendliness. Four men, hard-eyed and apparently well mounted. All placket armored. Helmets imitated animal skulls with big ears and long, outward sweeping neck-guards. Their colors were green and yellow, with some strong black piping. That provided Falc with information, like it or not:

They make no attempt to disguise the fact that they're the men of Holder Faradox of Lango—they're flaunting it!

All wore sword and long dagger, with broadened placks of lacquered wood shingling down their left arms, as shields. Two bore those long staffs with hook and spear on the end: dragonels. The man with the long bony face sat his saddle on the far left; the truly ugly one next. Just right of the road's center was he of the everted mouth. Not just the lips; the whole mouth was thrust forward, indicating that the fellow possessed teeth far too huge for his mouth. Since that mouth was compressed, Falc could not swear to the fact. He remarked the fourth man. He seemed to be peering at Falc through a chokebush, blighted black. Big, bushy, unkempt beard that wanted to curl.

Longface, Ugly, Bigteeth and Bushface. Staring at him from either side of their helmets' pendent nasals.

"You seem to be blocking the roadway." Falc's voice was soft and he kept his hands on the reins.

"To us, it seems the other way around, Sir Deathknight."

Falc nodded equably. He guided Harr well to the side, leaving plenty of room. He gestured for them to pass.

They sat their mounts. Two of them looked at Ugly. Their leader, Falc thought.

"Not enough room for us four, Sir Deathknight."

Falc met the gaze of the speaker: Ugly. "Call me by name."

"Falc of Risskor, killer-monk of the Order Most Old."

So. They knew exactly who he was. They were indeed here for the specific purpose of killing him, then. Falc sighed elaborately. *Me, specifically.* Keeping close watch while seeming negligent, he used his left hand to tug open the white robe. He let them see that his right hand remained on the reins.

"You little fellows have friends among the peacemen of another Holder's house?"

"Turn and ride ahead of us, Falc. You are wanted in Lango."

"If someone in Lango wanted me alive, he'd have sent a courier, not four armed men." Quietly he said, "Harr: sit." And as the darg's rearquarters sank and Falc leaned forward to compensate, he went on to his accosters: "I'll not be turning my back on you four. Four! You must have expected several Falcs?"

"You do have a reputation, Deathknight."

"Might I have names by which to know my murderers?"

"You will not need them."

It must be here then, Falc thought. *They have no other purpose. They are here simply to kill me. Four of them. Brave in their numbers, or they would have sent crossbow bolts from ambush—as they should have done. They have all the advantage and full well know it. They will charge and draw whenever Ugly says the word, while I can only wait and hope. A few strokes should do it, with them converging. Then they carry this head back to Faradox to prove their great efficiency.*

So. The only possibility for me here is to hope mightily, but not to wait. Ashah and Sath ride with me.

"Harr," he muttered, and twitched his left foot, moving the heel forward along the creature's side. Harr, crouching on his hind legs and glaring at the quartet, hissed and ran out his tongue. He trembled in his eagerness to be among them smelling blood, and tasting it.

Falc never so much as glanced at the leftward man, Longface on his nervous darg. Falc's right hand remained on the rein; his left on his left thigh. Neither appeared to have any interest in weapon hilt. Now he stared intently *past* the leader, over the man's left shoulder as if looking at something. After a time neither Longface nor Bigteeth could stand it. They glanced at the road behind them and Falc spoke in a low, conversational tone.

"Harr go." He added, "For Ashah, honor, and Sij."

The crouching Harr used his hind legs to thrust his bulk forward at speed. Only when he was on the move did Falc touch him on the neck with his left hand while his right swept to his sword's hilt. The derlin's flutter was bothersome, but that couldn't be helped. Shouts rose from the four. Two drew while the others wielded their dragonels, preparing to take the entirely unexpected charge of their quarry. Bushface raised his back-hooked spear while Longface started his across his mount's neck to intercept the charge. Harr plunged directly at him, hissing and glaring.

Falc's shrill whistle discomfited every darg while telling Harr it was each for himself in a concentration on warfare. He had already been guided toward Longface, to put Ugly on their immediate right. The leftward darg stared at that glaring inimical face of his own species rushing toward him. He heard Falc's ridiculous shouting and yowling. Its sole purpose was to disconcert.

Harr ceased hissing and opened his mouth, wide.

He was less than a meter from Longface's darg when that beast broke, as Falc had hoped. He had not expected the trick of looking past them to work. The lack of real experience and attendant incompetence of Langomen continued to amaze. His left hand brought the knife from behind his right shoulder and snapped it at the leader.

Ashah chose that moment to remind Falc that no man was perfect. The blade banged off the ugly man's helm. Still, Ugly was badly disconcerted, ducking, with his sword-stroke spoiled. That persuaded Falc to change his plan at the last possible moment.

He had charged Longface in the hope that the darg would break and Harr would tear open a mount's neck or human leg as they passed, while Falc slashed the eye of the leader's darg; anything to reduce the odds in such an uneven rencontre. Now since Ugly responded with near panic to the thrown knife, Falc instead jerked up his sword. Ugly's darg did not bite at him. The hard jolt on the left brought a loud grunt from the omo at the scraping pain to his leg even as he smashed his sword directly into the leader's midsection. The armor turned the blade but the strength of the blow, combined with Ugly's imbalance, conspired to spill the fellow off the far side of his mount.

Falc caught his balance and yanked his right heel into Harr's side.

Twisting with that serpentish sinuousness so dangerous to a darg's rider in crisis, Harr flung himself rightward in a swerve past the rump of Ugly's mount. Harr even snapped at it, to no effect other than discommoding his own rider. That was all right; Harr was doing his job. Falc had not had time to see whether Harr's mouth was bloodied and so did not know how many foes remained dangerous. He did slap the rump of Ugly's mount with the flat of his sword, hard. The darg bolted. That was Falc's purpose. Now the Langoman leader must remain afoot.

Somewhere a waterclock might have dripped twice since Falc began his charge.

He gave no time to subtlety now, or to consideration of niceties. Bigteeth, trying to haul his mount around to meet an attack that was suddenly at his right rear, heard a roaring bellow and received a sword blow in the back that struck with all the force of a thrown log. Armor straps snapped. Bigteeth arched violently backward and his sword jumped from his hand as if catapulted.

Falc had a moment in which to wish he had attacked differently. Now he had two men with long-hafted dragonels to deal with. He did not fancy himself a match for Sath, to slice through such poles against their natural yield under such an impact.

The accoster farthest to the right had wisely ridden forward to turn. Now he came back at the charge, dragonel long and ready and deadly. Obviously he was a good dargman, confident to ride and guide a trained steed without using the reins. Harr came full around past Bigteeth's darg and for an instant Falc and the bushy-bearded man were looking into each other's eyes. Both were moving precipitately forward to collision and there was no pause for that exchange of glares. Both Bushface's hands were on his dragonel's long, round haft for a right-to-left slash. They rushed together. . . .

Again Falc applied pressure with his right heel, and Harr swerved.

The surprised Langoman saw his enemy swing broadside to him, forming an easier target. He slashed at it while Falc cut horizontally across himself with every bit of his strength. It was not the desperation stroke it appeared. Blade met rushing wooden pole and the outcome surprised him. Because both men were smiting at each other with muscle behind the strokes, their weapons came together with terrific force. Falc's blade did indeed slice through the dragonel haft, partway; the staff broke and snapped its head straight along its original course. Falc saw dancing lights and reeled as the haftless spear-hook combination slammed into his helmet and fell down his back. It caught in the white robe and dangled for a moment before it fell.

The jerk of Falc's left foot was an accident; an involuntary reflex.

Harr responded with speed. So did his master, though he was only partly aware of what he was doing. He was unable to reverse his arm to launch a truly damaging cut at Bushface, who struck the omo's arm with his big wooden stick while he drew his sword. Falc kicked out with his left foot. Toe slammed into knee at the same time as Harr chomped.

Bushface and his mount screamed simultaneously. Falc groaned. He would have a fine big bruise, for the jagged end of the other man's haft did its best to pierce his mailcoat at the left armpit. Bushface's mount plunged away in pain. Harr clung, so that Falc had to hang onto the horn of his saddle to avoid being wrenched off Harr's back.

Then Bushface's bitten darg was bolting, while his rider fell. Falc had no time to watch. He had other business. Kneeing Harr, he looked to his right.

Ugly was on his feet, with his mount twenty meters away. The leader of the hired murderers held his right arm up, hand

back over his shoulder. He was moving, and Falc recognized
the stance and intent. Hurriedly he braced both feet and
leaned back and back. That way the flat, leaf-shaped knife the
Langoman threw—Falc's knife—whizzed over his chest with
seven or eight centimeters to spare. Immediately straightening, Falc again whistled the shrill note and bawled out other
things, although Harr was already charging the Langoman
leader.

Behind him lay Longface on his back, rolling to and fro
and clutching his leg. Harr's teeth had bitten it more than half
through and destroyed his kneecap in the process.

Falc showed teeth. "*Good* Harrrr!" And he snapped his
left heel inward, hard.

That did not sit well with the beast, despite the welcome
"Good" sound that he knew; Harr wanted to charge in and
eat Ugly up. The trouble with that was that the Langoman
was fully ready. Harr was more likely to lose eye or snout
than to taste new blood.

Falc kicked again, while bawling the darg's name and
dragging the rein leftward. Harr responded with an angry hiss
and what Falc knew was a deliberately violent slew to the
left. Sinuous as a snake, Harr was, and Falc was a long time
aware of the precarious delicacy of his own spine. For a
moment he had a vision of Sir Chondaven of Ryar, lying
forever on his broken back in the High Temple. . . .

Falc kept his seat and his spine. Ugly's swordcut at the
darg's face had already begun. Falc leaned out, cutting upward to intersect the blade, using his own sword to save Harr
while Harr veered left. Harr was angry. He would vent his
war-lust on this other enemy then, the one on the ground!

Blades rang together with a loud clang and screech of metal
sliding on metal. Falc felt the shock run up his arm, but hung
onto his hilt. Meanwhile his right foot shot out. Iron-tipped
wooden stirrup drove into Ugly's face with a disgusting sound.
Blood rilled. Suddenly much uglier, the Langoman was catapulted backward, bubbling vocally. He hit the ground with a
rattle and clatter of placks like nuts dumped out onto a drying
frame.

Harr was already bent on his new target. His master did not
deter him. Poor Longface was after all in real agony with his
knees, which would never let him walk normally again or ride

without pain. Having already destroyed his career as a man of weapons, Harr now destroyed him utterly, by trampling the long-faced man with some care.

Falc reined, muttering calming words for both Harr's benefit and his own. He had time now to see what he and the war-darg had wrought.

All attackers were down, while the sword of their intended quarry was unblooded. Harr had fully accounted for Longface. There lay the leader, his face a hideous mess and his body still; the kick had blasted him into unconsciousness. Near him lay Bigteeth, horridly still but breathing; his back was broken and no part of him would move except relaxed sphincters. Falc would grant him the death the Sons of Ashah prayed for … . in a while.

And there went Bushface's mount, bolting . . . dragging his master by one spur-equipped boot caught in the stirrup. It was one of several reasons why Falc was no friend of spurs, although darg-back combat without them was nearly impossible.

He gave chase on a darg that was far from winded and still excited. He overtook the other beast after nearly a kilometer's gallop, and Harr wanted very much to bite and chew. Falc prevented that. Since he who had come to murder was being dragged on the left, the omo forced a reluctant Harr to come up on the other side. Almost from the moment he leaned out and caught the fleeing animal's halter, it began slowing.

"Come," Falc said, with a tug. "Come," he said again, and tugged, and a third time.

With his other hand he slowed Harr and guided him into a long turn. They returned to the scene of combat with the would-be assassin still dragging. No matter; he was not conscious and had not long to live anyhow. Falc had already decided what he was going to do. The treacherous Faradox must have a message, with proof. Falc pulled off the derlin and alit, limping a little.

Three dargoni suffered themselves to be approached, soothed, tethered. The omo wrapped various weapons in a Langoman cloak and tied the package on the back of one of those quieted animals, retaining Bushface's unused sword, which was all freshly sharpened and shining. Harr and another darg bore four overmatched hired assassins up into the woods. Again Falc exerted himself without strain. Bushface's sword flashed six times, chopping. A few moments later four corpses rolled down into the ravine Falc had recently used for the purpose of relieving himself.

One man and two dargs, one bearing two fat knapsacks and Bushface's smeared, dripping sword, returned to the other three dargoni. Falc collected reins and prepared to assume the role of drover. Ugly's darg watched, bearing the two swollen knapsacks that were not all that heavy.

"Go home," Falc bade it. "Home! Go home, darg! Wahaaah! When you reach Lango, the men at the gate will recognize Faradox's colors and see that you are returned to him. Go! Every master of murderers has a right to learn how they fare, be they competent or no. Go and bear him my message. WAHAAAHH!"

He sprang at the darg, waving the derlin. The creature hissed, wheeled, and hurried back the way it had come. It bore Falc's message to Holder Faradox of Lango, in two saddleborne knapsacks.

His three new animals Falc deprived not of their valuable heads but of nearly all evidence of Lango and Faradox. Knapsacks swelled. Then he and Harr set about conveying the spoils of successful combat to Morazain-by-the-Lake. Falc did not have to clean his sword; he had not blooded it. It was bent a bit.

4

The hill just east of Morazain was called Naragane, so that the temple of Ashah there was Ashah-Naraganit-re. It stood with seeming serenity unmarred by haughtiness atop the tall steep knoll colored deep blue with only the hint of a greenish cast, and made glossy by longbean. A carefully arranged and attended patch of shume formed a purple A for Ashah. The access road was terraced and both narrow and circuitous by design. Having passed up Colax's inn without even pausing for water, Falc kept his animals to a sedate pace as he mounted the hill. He knew the monks maintained an effective and totally unobtrusive watch system. He made no effort to penetrate it, to seek the watchers with his dark gaze. They proved their presence without his ever seeing a sentry: the pryor met him in the courtyard.

He was tall and broad, young in his hooded robe of very plain, dark green mossweave and cinctured with plain bell-rope, and he limped.

From within, Falc heard the low chanting of the monks repeating the Litany of Purpose: *"The heart of a Son of Ashah does not bleed. Instead, the mind and body of a son of Ashah are dedicated to justice.*

"The head of a Son of Ashah does not succumb to passion. Instead . . ."

The pryor said, "Hail, brother."

"Be with Ashah, brother," Falc said, and dismounted onto cobbles between tall, tall mossed walls grown with ivy. Characteristically he went directly to business: "I have use for two of these captured animals. This darg is the best of the three. Its packs contain various weapons, helmets, and pieces of armor. Do have the colors changed on all of them, and accept them in Ashah's name."

"Their owners, Sir Falc?"

Falc directed a pleasant look at the priest, quite young and crippled in the calf in his first year as a knight of the Order seven years ago. "Their *riders* were waiting for me on the road. They were sent to slay me. They failed. Their heads are on their way back to their master."

(". . . of Ashah sees each individual as an individual, and knows that only through individuals is there that which is called society, and social order. Ashah accept me! Ashah guide me . . .")

The pryor nodded solemnly before smiling. "With our thanks, Sir Falc. There must have been four. Most impressive, brother!"

"My sword is not blooded. My darg and I are a team."

"So I have heard, Sir Falc."

(". . . does not do murder. Ashah deliver us! A Son of Ashah does not do theft. Ashah inspire us! Neither does the Son of Ashah refrain from killing. Ashah guide . . .")

"And how did you arrive at the number four, brother?"

"Because you arrived leading three dargoni, whose bridles I can see were made or at least decorated in a certain city well east of here, overlooking the sea. You said the assassins' heads are on their way back there. Therefore one assumes that they are borne by a fourth darg, which was presumably ridden, before the encounter.''

"Ah," Falc said, laying a gauntleted hand on the broad shoulder, "you have the eye of an eagle, Sir Coineval."

"It is 'Pryor,' Sir Falc; just Pryor Ashahnaraganit."

(*"To be a Son of Ashah is not just to have faith and duty . . . or to be faith-wedded and duty-bound, but to be dominated by one's duty and faith, which are one, in every aspect of one's living of one's life. Ashah deliver us . . . Ashah inspire us . . . Sath ride with us . . ."*)

"Not to me, brother," Falc said, staring into the young man's eyes. "To me you are ever Sir Coineval, knight of the Order Most Old, and I shall not swerve from that."

Coineval compressed his lips against their tremor. "With thanks, brother omo," he said throatily. "Do stay and refresh yourself. Doubtless your darg could use the rest."

Falc shook his head, once. "No, brother omo. I have business down in Morazain. Oh; have you heard aught of Brother Vennashah?"

"None."

"Should a monk happen to be journeying toward the High Temple, the Firedrake should be advised that in Lango I foiled an apparent plot of Holder Faradox against Holder Chasmal, and that four men in the colors of Faradox of Lango sought my life, not capture, a day east of here. Just for the sake of the information, Sir Coineval. We don't know enough to say more."

"I understand. I am sorry you will not tarry here, Sir Falc. Rest aids the soul and betters a man in the service of Ashah. There will be adequate place, as a brother will be journeying within a few drips. Besides, several here would love to work out with you in the morning!"

Falc was no longer comfortable with this man who had been knight of the Order and could no longer be because he had been wounded, and yet who still possessed the eye and the instinct—and the firmly muscle-padded shoulder. Too, Falc did dislike taking leave more than once. He turned, mounted, pulled Harr around, and with his two dargoni rode down the hill from Ashah-Naraganit-re.

(*". . . Sath ride with me . . ."*)

A moist-eyed Coineval watched him all the way down to the main road.

5

Once Harr had paced through the Princehead Gateway into Morazain whose men preferred women well laden with fat, his master turned to call to the arrogant men in the round-house above and beside the gate of red and orange.

"Remember my name! Keep me waiting this long next time I come to your gate," he said, emphasizing "your" with sarcasm, "and there will be trouble."

The omo turned his back on a shocked expression along with a glower, retort and ready crossbow, and rode directly to the temple of Avmer Tyrvena. He did pause to allow the passage of a beige-robed monk or priest of This, and bowed low. Showing surprise, the priest signed him and went on in silence. It was about then that Falc remembered, and sighed.

"That is to say, among other things, that a Son of Ashah does not lose his temper." Well, one tries, O Ashah, one tries! The opposite of "sub-human," after all, was not "superhuman!"

Falc rode on to the Tyrvena-re.

"A gift of my Order to the temple of Her whose name men do not pronounce, my sister," he told the tiny woman with the strangely unlined face; what he could see of it above the yellow cloth covering her mouth and nose.

"It is most kind, my brother of Ashah, but what use have we of a darg?"

"His equipage should remain with you, my sister of the Tyrvena. He is trained, though, and at market will bring whatever your temple needs most."

The blue-black eyes crinkled and he knew she smiled behind the yellow concealment, this tiny not-old woman wearing an ungirt brown garment like a tent. "And who makes us this gift, brother?"

"The Order Most Old, my sister."

"No," she said quietly, with a half-shake of her head. "It is Falc of Risskor who makes it."

"You know me then, sister."

"I know your behavior, Sir Falc, and this is part of it. I know the name of that son of Ashah who is not seen to smile. I shall not ask which two men were so foolish as to challenge you and so unintentionally make you this gift which you now press upon us." She extended a voluminous brown sleeve at the end of which no hand showed. "Risskor lost much, when it drove away Falc into the Order Most Old."

Falc's face tightened and his body showed sudden stiffness. He turned away to mount and ride from her without another word. Now he led only Longface's darg, slung with a saddle-bag of battle-won provisions and another containing four daggers. All other arms he had left with Ugly's mount up on Naragane.

The pryoress of Morazainit-Tyrvena-re watched him until he turned a corner and was gone, and then she wiped her eyes and took up the darg's bridle in her small brown-gloved hand. She murmured words she knew, though they were not of Avmer Tyrvena:

" 'The heart of a Son of Ashah does not bleed' . . . but Sir Falc's does."

6

"For the Arlord of Morazain, Threeford and all their environs," the man in black wrote, "from Falc of Risskor, K.O.M.O., against the next seven years' taxes of his Cousin Querry of eastern Zain, and in hopes that knights of the O.M.O. will not be kept waiting before the closed eastgate of Morazain."

The garrison commander's aide spoke without having read the note. "You are most kind, Sir Falc." He accepted the message and the reins of the darg formerly ridden by a nameless long-faced man of Lango; the skittish and therefore the least of the three captured dargoni. The linked knapsacks were slung over Falc's left arm. "The Arlord will be appreciative."

A certain gatekeeper will not, Falc reflected with serenity.

He would have liked to give the man one of the daggers, as glue, but it was too obviously of Secteri manufacture. He had no wish to create enmities or suspicion based on false premises.Well, one could not give presents to everyone, though as Sath Firedrake had said: "Little gifts and kindnesses are the glue to bind men to men."

"The Order Most Old has no enemies," Falc said with studied sententiousness and a certain sanctimoniousness that he felt this man would appreciate, "and many friends. I am Falc of Risskor."

"I am Bellenevin, Sir Knight of the Order."

"Well met, Sir Bellenevin."

"Well met, Sir Falc."

Falc rode away from the garrison, to the inn bearing the sign of the White Horn.

FOUR

To seek the happiness of every individual is
stupid; an unworthy and unattainable goal. Each
individual must seek its own happiness. Some
few are even happiest when they are unhappy;
that is, under stress or in some want.
——Writings of the Masters

Just as Falc set foot on the single front step he heard angry
voices from inside the White Horn and recognized the sound
of an overturning chair. He thrust open the door and took one
pace inside. Freeing his arms of cloak, he stood staring. Two
men were on their feet in bristly, combative stances, glaring
at each other across the small semicircular table. Since they
were broadside to him, each man's peripheral vision noted the
omo's entry. Both glanced his way, at a face somber as his
garb. They blinked. One licked his lips. They glanced at each
other. The one with the belly opened his fist and took his
hand off and away from his dagger's handle. The other
pretended that he'd been intending to pour from the yellow
pottery bottle he held, rather than use it as a weapon, which
had been his obvious intent.

Both sat down. Both affected not to have noticed the
black-clad man.

Falc glanced around. Other patrons were openly gazing at
him. Two looked distinctly unfriendly, resentful. A couple of
others, one of each sex, were obviously fascinated. The inn

was like unto nearly every inn Falc had visited and guested in, except that the walls of the White Horn had recently been repainted. He found them restful, long vertical triangles of medium blue and pale yellow, alternating up and down. The suspended lichen-light globes looked new, too. *Recent repairs after a quake*, he mused. He had noted the lowered level of the lake as he rode in.

He paced through the room toward the empty table he had spotted, not quite in the corner against the rear wall.

"A decidedly timely entry, Sir Omo," a voice said as he passed.

It was obvious fawning, and Falc did not glance that way The innkeeper, a slender man save for his pot, arrived at the table at about the same time as the omo.

"I am Corunden, Sir Knight of the Order," he said, "and I am grateful that you arrived in time to save my furniture and floor!"

Falc gave him a kindly look. "A happenstance, host. I but stood prepared to defend this life and honor. No, no wine, thank you."

"They were arguing about the severity of a recent quake, Sir Omo," Corunden said, with a smile moving the veinous purplescence of his cheeks. "One allows that it was not much of a shock. Well, I've endured worse, though thisun certainly cost me! But—your honor? Surely that was not at stake in such an argument!"

Falc's brows lifted. "Had such trouble taken place while I was here, that would have embarrassed the Order and thus diminished me."

The innkeeper blinked several times. "Uh . . . yes. Will you have food?"

"Please," Falc said, and sat.

Within an hour he had both eaten and ascertained that Holder Arisan and his Housechief were still not getting on. Corunden was happy to send his son of twelve or so to the Household of Arisan with the omo's message to Housechief Baysh:

RISSKOR WOULD HAVE CONVERSE WITH YOU. HE STOPS AT THE WHITE HORN.

He went for a walk, then. Naturally he was noticed as he paced along the streets, but he assumed as usual that no one one knew what he was doing: being about his business. He was observing Morazain, noting sights and faces, tones and words, the condition of buildings and of people. It was the business of an omo, and yet so few took pause to consider that information had to be learned before it could be passed. Among other things, he saw unrepaired damage of the sijquake that had so recently rocked Morazain-by-the-Lake. He decided that he'd have taken the side of the arguer who said it had been severe—although like Corunden, Falc of Risskor had seen and experienced worse.

When he re-entered the White Horn, Baysh was waiting.

He was a shortish, bony man with a great deal of nose and mouth and large round eyes that emphasized the vertical lines of his pupils. A dark gray hat with a broad brim lay on the edge of the table, and under his big gray cloak Baysh wore a tunic purple as the bruises of love. Falc ignored the tunic and studied the face while he went to Baysh's table, which was the same one the omo had occupied earlier. *Not happy*, Falc had decided, by the time he reached the corner and his fellow native of Risskor was rising to greet him. Falc thrust back his cloak, clapped the other man's shoulder, and sat. They ordered beer and said nothing of importance until Corunden had brought the mugs and departed.

Omo and Housechief exchanged news while they sipped. Falc noted that Baysh continued his habit of using his thumb to turn his ring of office, consistently if not constantly. The conversation meandered onto the subject of Emperor Shalderanis, and the situation of Sij and its citystates.

"I doubt whether he is any happy man," Baysh said, turning his ring.

Falc shrugged. "Oh I don't know. That youngster lives the life of the wealthiest Holder, and does nothing!"

Baysh grinned. He was one of the very few who knew that Falc of Risskor did indeed smile, though only with the eyes. Abruptly the grin faded. "Falc . . . I heard that 'a Deathknight' was attacked, in Secter."

Falc recognized that as a question, but had nothing to offer. He said so. Then: "I hope it is not so. Baysh . . . as I said, I've just come from Lango." Quietly he told the other Rissman of the need of Holder Chasmal. "An agent of his will stop here for two days, as of either tomorrow or the next day. Should you have occasion or desire to speak with him . . ."

"Hmmm," Baysh of Risskor said, pretending to consider though Falc had already seen his interest. "I am well established here . . ." He broke off to wait for comment. None came.

Falc merely hinted at a shrug, the faintest rise of one shoulder. "I know of his need, and that he would value a good Housechief, not to mention a superb one." He paused, and understood the meaning when the other Rissman sighed and looked down. "You and he would get along, Baysh That's all I have to say. You know we monkish murdering monsters are not seeking to start trouble between excellent Housechiefs and their estimable masters."

Baysh rapped the table and sat back. He spoke to the tabletop, in a quiet voice: "Well you know that my lord Arisan is about as estimable as a rutting barga, old know-all."

The faint rise of one of Falc's shoulders only hinted at a shrug. He said nothing. With a rather jerky nod Baysh leaned forward to touch the other man's black-clad arm.

"Wi' thanks, Falc."

"Just being about my business, Baysh."

"This fellow serves good beer and I like the décor," Baysh said, wearing a face of exaggerated innocence. "I may happen by here again, soon."

Falc nodded.

"What do you need, Falc?"

Falc gestured with his head. "That hat."

Baysh rose. "Good night, Sir Omo. Ashah ride with you."

Falc showed no surprise. It was not an unknown phrase, after all, and surely there were some outside the Order who had heard some and perhaps all of "Destiny Wears a Black Cloak." He watched Baysh out before he picked up the hat and rose to go to the private sleeping room Corunden had been fortunate enough to have available.

With the door locked, Falc began the ritual disrobing.

The Messenger did not manifest itself.

2

In the morning Falc presented the innkeeper with a sack of wine and a pair of captured daggers in payment of his bill. Purple-cheeked Corunden held both palms out, but all six fingers and both thumbs were turned down, in rejection.

"I have already been paid by your keeping order, Sir Omo."

Falc continued to hold out the knives. " 'Success has a handmaiden, and her name is Luck.' And I have many weapons, good Corunden."

"And I have sufficient knives, Sir Falc. Such a gift far exceeds your bill."

"Good!" Falc said, and placed the unmatched pair of daggers on the counter, almost soundlessly. "Remember Falc of Risskor next time!"

"Such a gift will cover several next times," Corunden said, regarding the knives without touching them.

"Fine. Pack me a knapsack, then, and let us stop this unseemly haggling. Oh—don't bother putting in wine!"

With a ridiculously full knapsack slung on Harr's back, Falc rode out of Morazain. He did not head westward, but through the Princehead Gateway and back the way he had come.

On a high place overlooking the road he had used yesterday, he kept watch on that dust-colored ribbon. Long ago he had learned that form of patience that came from doing something, almost anything, while he waited and observed. Today he quietly sharpened all his blades as he muttered psalms and homilies of the Way. The sun dragged its feet across the sky. Today's meditation was on the first statement of the Credo: "To be a Son of Ashah is not just to have faith and duty, or to be faith-wedded or duty-bound, but to be dominated by one's duty and faith, which are one, in every aspect of one's life."

Falc kept ordering himself to dispel the unworthy and contentious thought: "Not, O Ashah, easy!" The meditation taught to the Sons of Ashah proved that the individual contained within itself the power to change itself, but . . . not, O Ashah, easily.

At a bit past noon he tugged off his gauntlets, opened the

knapsack, and ate sparingly of the several days' provisions Corunden had packed. A large butterfly chanced too close and Harr snacked. The sun edged across the sky. Clouds intervened and birds complained. The sun reappeared and birds rejoiced noisily. Harr found a lovely ant-infested stump and enjoyed a late lunch. His master watched the passage below of the man he assumed to have been sent by Chasmal, in hopes of doing business with Baysh.

Without conscious thought, Falc mentally registered the dusty orange cloak and the silly feathered hat.

He maintained his watch. He saw no band of swordsmen, no one he deemed suspicious, and none on the darg he had sent back toward Lango. The sun lowered and began to take on the color of the cloak of the presumed Langoman.

When the road was clear, he rode down. This time he was admitted to Morazain without delay. Falc passed through the red and orange gateway without comment or a glance at the roundhouse. He paced Harr carefully to the White Horn. He stopped twice for others, despite being waved on. A man scowled. Falc affected not to notice. A darg hissed and Harr affected not to notice.

Corunden showed his surprise when the man in black re-entered his inn, but Falc made no explanation. He had already see the orange cloak, draped over a chair. The man at the table there, seated so as to be able to see the door, was unfamiliar to him, and looking at him. Falc approached and the fellow rose. He did not wear Chasmal's colors, or Lango's colors, or any colors at all that Falc recognized.

"I am Falc of Risskor. You are from Holder Chasmal?"

"Yes. I—"

The accent of those two words told Falc that the fellow was Langoman, but that did not make him Chasmal's. Falc insisted on a test: "Who is his Housechief?"

"You know he has none, and was you helped put the Eye on his son's finger. Will you sit down, Sir Falc? My lord Chasmal has naught but good—better than good!—to say of you. I am Arle."

Falc was convinced. Moving a chair so that his back was not to the door, he sat and drew off his gauntlets. Quietly he told the bulky man about the killers sent by Faradox.

"My lord Holder will soon know about this, Sir Falc. You were unscathed?"

"Yes, and my darg, and the one Holder Chasmal gave me. I hope that he employs better weapon-men."

"That is worth mentioning to him too," Arle said. "I can tell you that he employs no murderers! About this man I am to watch for, B—?" He broke off when Falc touched a finger to his lips.

Falc said, "*That man* knows. That man decides for that man. You were bidden to wait for two days?"

Arle sighed and showed him a small smile. "I am to wait for three."

"I doubt whether that will be necessary," Falc said, and went out to wander about a bit before dinner. He did not eat with Arle or anyone else, and retired early. He set his mind to the statement "Consider that when you lie sleeping, you dream that you are awake, and know it not. How then do you know that you are not dreaming even now?"

As usual, attempting to ponder that put him to sleep.

He was up and out early next morning, with a fat sack newly packed by Corunden. Once again the man in black did not resume his journey west. He dismounted to lead Harr up that same hill and kept that same vigil from concealment high above the road. Meanwhile he mouthed and muttered psalms of the Way and reviewed the Words of the Firedrake. Today he pondered the sub-meanings of the statement that "A single grain of sand can close the eye of the mightiest of men." Now and again, making sure he was invisible from the road well below, he exercised. Surging cumuli seemed to harry the sun across the sky, as smaller birds sometimes harried the crawk.

The surprise came along about noon: the fast-moving darg was the gift-animal of Chasmal of Lango, and its rider was Jinnery. Her medium blue hair strung down and blew back wispily from her disheveled bun. She was alone and lightly cumbered.

That was interesting, even fascinating. Falc remembered the determintion he had noted in that bony face she wore in such a grim expression, and knew that he had been right: there was indeed more to her than most might think.

Whatever the reason, she must be following me.

With derlin on and hood up, he trailed her into Morazain. He watched her go to the White Horn and enter. He was watching when she left. He saw two men take note of her, two poorly dressed louts suddenly interested in a young woman alone and well-mounted. When they exchanged nods and began following her, Falc of Risskor was watching. He followed them through Morazain and out the Gate of Gift Pearls, to the west.

The two men tracked her all afternoon, and Falc tracked them, maintaining the derlin and hood. She was hurrying. Misusing Chasmal's fine pampered darg, he mused. The sun dragged across the sky with its almost effulgent crown of cumulus, and Falc followed, keeping his distance. To his knowledge Querry's niece was so ignorant as never even to glance back. Staying well behind, her pursuers had eyes only for her and naturally no fear for their backs. Nor did Falc give them cause. Once he put back his hood and wore Baysh's broad-brimmed hat for a time, so that at this distance he could be taken for a different man.

He thought it was unnecessary; he never saw them so much as turn. Why should they, two armed men? She, however, had much to fear and should have thought of it. Could she suppose that she was too unattractive to draw attention—on that obviously excellent darg?

Single-mindedly intent on following me, Falc thought. *Why?*

Toward sunset he paused atop a long, long slope that ran down ahead of him. After a straight stretch, trees rose and the road curved almost sharply. If the two followers continued, he thought, he would cut across to come between her and them, beyond the curve. Dark, dark staring eyes saw her pull off the road just at the trees; watched her followers hurriedly turn off also, this side of her. Furtively, just as they had trailed her.

They are cutting across, Falc thought. *They plan to take her, in the woods.*

He threw back the white hood. He was opening the derlin as he signaled to Harr and braced himself. The darg objected but raced down the hill at a slither-gallop anyhow, because that was what his master demanded.

When Harr reached the trees, drooling, Jinnery's darg stood

waiting and the bony-faced woman was just emerging from behind some bushes at the trees' edge. Falc and a disappointed Harr did not have to do or say anything; at sight of him the two men gave up thievery; for the present, at least. They cut wide around him and fled back toward Morazain.

Omo and darg had a brief disagreement as to whether to give chase or remain here. Falc won. A staring Jinnery was hurrying toward him, wisps of hair blowing loose from her moribund bun. Still mounted, he was about to tell her what had happened and what had almost befallen her when she produced a dagger, or rather a farmer's knife. She lunged into a charge, blade upraised. Falc made a clicking noise to Harr and threw up one arm. Harr lurched forward, trailing drool. The knife raked Falc's gauntlet. Harr hissed and tugged at the rein, wanting to turn and bite.

"Harr BIDE!"

Still mounted, Falc released the rein. His gloved hand snapped around her wrist, the one above the nail-bitten hand sprouting the broad blade. She made nasty noises, then pained ones as he lifted her by that wrist, one-handed, until only her toes touched the ground. He ordered her to drop the knife. Since her choices did not exist, she did, oddly not weeping but looking angry. Not, he thought, ferocious.

No girl, indeed, he mused. *A woman indeed!*

Though dangling in air by one wrist and surely at some pain to her shoulder, she batted at him with her other hand. The action hurt her. He saw that in the writhing of her face.

"I've just saved your life, twice," he told her. "First from those two men who trailed you all the way from Morazain while you never had sense enough to glance back!—and secondly from this darg, who wanted very much to turn and eat your hand off. Harr's had sharp metal in his teeth before, sandwiched in fingers."

With a sudden flex of his arm he swung it, and opened his hand to sling her from him. He was dismounted and standing over her before she had ceased rolling and fighting to regain something approaching equilibrium. He spoke quietly.

"You do not want to kill me, Jinnery. You never did."

She sat up without looking up. She covered her knees with her skirt of bright print. Without looking at him she began telling her story to the ground between her outstretched legs.

She stammered only a little, but as she went on in that dull voice of brass, Falc's heartbeat speeded and he began to breathe more and more heavily.

Hours after he had left the farmhouse three days ago, four men had come riding, asking about him. Four men in matching colors. No, not the Arlord's hirelings come back; other men. Unfortunately, Chalis was happy to tell them excitedly and proudly that Sir Falc had been there, and indeed had helped get in the hay, for he was their cousin.

"I saw one of them strike him down, then, with a long pole-sword thing, and I saw the blood and Querry went running and they just stood waiting and then they killed him, too. I saw it. My legs were quivering and my head went all silly and I thought I was going to fall down. I told myself that if I fainted I was as good as raped and murdered, too, and I just ran, and there was this darg, and I got on and kicked and kicked it and we galloped across the fields. When I looked back they had . . . had set f-fi-ire to the barn and the house." She paused to fight the quaver out of her voice. "I took next to nothing and didn't even think of getting to the road. Not for a long, long time. Then, in the woods, I hid and cried all day, trying to think of what to do. Then I decided to try to catch up to you, but I was afraid to ride at night."

Suddenly she looked úp at a man whose face had gone shades paler. "Did you know that darg was trained to race, to *jump*?"

"No," Falc said.

He stood staring down at nothing; at the ground between Jinnery's ankles. Her head tilted a little as she became aware of his pallor and saw the working of his mouth, of his temples. The knuckles of his gauntlets shone with the clenching of his fists.

At last, at long last he asked her about the quartet of murderers. Her description told him what he had already decided, in horror and anguish: they were the four men sent by Faradox of Lango. *To murder me, not that innocent boy and his good father; too good.*

With confirmation, Falc was even sadder. Conscience-stricken. He already knew, and did not need her reminder:

"They were after you. You are the cause of those deaths."

Staring down and then at the trees, Falc nodded.

"Yes."

Never mind that he had stopped in a spontaneous act of kindness, to help strangers in trouble; any explanation or remonstrance against his guilt would be unworthy. Because of him, Querry and Chalis were murdered and the farm burned, destroyed. Jinnery had nothing and no one.

She is my responsibility.

"All I knew to do was follow you. I have no one, nothing. I am noth—you are responsible. All I knew to do was follow you."

After a time Falc brought his eyes into focus and looked down. He found that he had to refocus still again. She was staring up at him. Old, faded blue-gray cloak thrown back. Smudged, rumply white blouse, long skirt of medium blue dotted with little flowers in yellow and green with a touch of pink. Clothing and skin-over-bone legs were floured with road dust. She did not even flinch when he drew his sword, but only kept glaring large-eyed up at him from that gaunt face. Even the pupils of those burnt-almond eyes were enlarged almost to roundness. Yet she merely sat, at the feet of a large black-clad man who had just bared the long blade she knew had been smeared with blood rather more than once.

Falc strode past her with a sound of creaking leather and soft boots whispering through grass and long cloak whispering in air. The innocent sapling was perhaps as thick as his arm; he chopped through it with one vicious, grunting stroke and the fledgling tree sagged and toppled against a larger companion. The sapling shifted slowly, and fell by degrees. Whirling, Falc chopped twice into a huge tree before he wheeled and hurled the sword to drive into the ground.

Jinnery was twisted half around, watching. She looked from man to weapon. It stood, quivering.

From ten paces away, he said, "How can I let you accompany me? I can't be on my guard all the time. You tried to kill me."

"No I didn't. I wanted to prove a point . . . no, I *had* to. And you *are* on your guard all the time! I know you Deathkni—omos can't be killed that way, so easily. I don't want to kill you, *Cousin* Falc. I need your protection, *Cousin* Falc, as you have proven and besides you are responsible to begin with. How can you refuse me?"

She watched leathern mailcoat gleam in various places, the points of stress and reflection shifting as his chest filled and slowly subsided in a great sigh. Her thin lips were a straight, grim line; her jaw squared with the clamping of her teeth. He could not refuse her, and they both knew it. Unattractive or not, she was on a more than attractive darg. Such a young woman alone on such a fine animal would not long be allowed to survive; indeed, she almost had not made it much past Morazain.

Falc sighed again. This was not going to be pleasant for him.

3

It was not pleasant for him.

"Back on the dargs," he had said after a long silence, and turned away as she got to her feet. "We'll go a bit farther and stop for the night within the woods."

"After I've been racing all over the world following you?" Her unfortunate voice had become even less pleasant. "We're stopped; what's wrong with this place? I'm *weary*!"

"We will stop at sunset," he said, mounting.

"It's almost sunset now!"

"Almost. We still have light. Best to use it." He turned away and made a little noise. Harr began to move.

"Well, wait a minute, damn you! I'm not experienced at swinging onto a darg in a skirt!"

"I can't spare you my leggings." He didn't look her way, and despite what she had said she was in the gift darg's saddle and alongside him within a half-minute.

"You really are a conceited dictator, aren't you!"

" 'Conceited' is a child's word," Falc said pleasantly, looking straight ahead. *Though it does go with your boy's voice.*

"Arrh! Damn! Arrogant, then! Arrogant! You're an arrogant . . . *Deathknight*!"

"Yes," Falc said, and they rode.

They rode in silence.

A little over an hour later he had nudged Harr and realized that he was about to turn left into her darg; he had quite forgotten her silent, skinny presence there beside him. He pointed beyond her.

"We'll go into the trees past that big rock beside the little derrberry grove," he said. "There's a little clearing back there, and a stream. We can eat derrberries and—"

She interrupted. "They're not ripe, this time of year."

"Oh," he said, although he could see by the low hang of the spindly branches that the berries were ripe.

"I can't say that I care to go back in there and camp with you, out of sight in the woods," she said with an attempt at haughty asperity. "Why c—"

"Oh," Falc said.

He had paced Harr forward, across in front of her, and up the little incline toward the almost snowy boulder rearing up amid the bushes at the woods' edge. He heard her mutter. He could not make out what she said, and supposed that was fortunate. She was coming. He did not glance back. He noted that the derrberries were ripe. He lifted his helmet off with care, so as not to disturb his skullcap.

A few seconds after he had passed the bushes, he heard her mutter sourly and knew she had seen the color of the berries: that deep, deep purple that might as well have been black. They passed in among the trees, and around the truly gigantic one, and there was the brook, narrow and shallow, but alive. The small grassy clearing was dotted with the pink of quolina. Falc swung down, removed saddle-sacks, and unsaddled Harr.

"I never saw berries ripe this time of year before," she said in sour admission of error, working at her mount's saddle straps.

"You've lived in Morazain and on a farm," he said. "One."

"Oh you really are a superior son of a barga, aren't you!"

"Yes."

She made an exasperated "oo-*oh!*" sound.

After a while he realized that he must leave off being unfair and unpleasant to her. She was, after all, bereaved. "Derrberries that get as much shade as sunlight ripen faster than those in open fields," he told her.

Rather than saying "Oh," or "Thanks," she chose: "Why didn't you tell me that before?"

That was the sort of question Falc did not trouble to

answer. He heard her grunt and glanced her way. Deceptively strong for someone so thin, she had just peeled the saddle off Chasmal's gift and was swinging it as she turned. She staggered a little, forced to replace one foot as she sought a place for the saddle. She glanced at him.

"On the ground anywhere," Falc said. It was something one appreciated about dargs; the saddle came off dry and could be put anywhere. Dargs didn't sweat. They just drooled. He gestured at his own saddle. "You might want it well away from mine."

Her question was her usual challenge: "Why?"

"Because I'll sleep with my head on my saddle and you certainly don't want to have to sleep close to a murderous Deathknight!"

She carried her saddle well away, walking spraddle-legged under its weight, and nearly fell with it when she dumped it to the grass.

"You have water?"

She turned. "I have a little left." She glanced at the stream. "It doesn't matter now, does it."

He nodded. "That's good water. Comes off the mountain. You have something to put derrberries in when you pick them?"

"Yes! My mouth!"

Falc sighed. "Take this pan and pick for us both, Jinnery."

"And what will you be doing?"

He could have told her. Her stance and tone and face were all so unpleasant, so challenging, though, that he decided against it. He stood gazing at her.

"Pick your own," she said, and strode away, dusty skirt swishing. She ignored the proffered frypan.

Falc had murmured a hurried version of the Credo and a few other rite-things while he removed gauntlets and cloak, loosed his mailcoat, and sat on the ground to open the knapsacks. He shook his head, gazing down at one of the two daggers he had given Corunden. The fellow had packed all this food and returned part of the "price" Falc had decided on!

When she returned, lips and hands empurpled, he was sitting on the ground holding a piece of ferg breast, cooked but unheated. He was chewing. She stopped, stared, blinked, stared. Falc said nothing.

"What's that?"

"Ferg," he said, and took another bite. "Breast."

She looked at her hands. He watched her grow just a bit smaller and assumed that she was realizing what she had done to herself. "It . . . didn't occur to me that you had food."

Falc saw no reason to say anything.

"Do you think you have enough for two? One and a half, really; I don't eat much. It's just that it's been a long time. Querry says I just pick at food. . . ."

"Pick your own," Falc said, chewing.

She stiffened, showing that she recognized her own words. If she felt guilt, she recovered swiftly:

"You are an *exassperating* man!"

Falc saw no reason to say anything. He did make certain that his equable expression did not change.

She walked past him, upstream a little, and without turning he heard the little splashes as she stepped into the water and washed her hands and face. He heard her drink from cupped hands. After a time she returned, barefoot, to stand over him.

"I suppose the message is that I pick and share berries and you share what you already had."

"That's a nice offer," Falc said. "I'd love some berries. And of course I'll share. Fair is fair."

She picked up the frypan and went to pick some more berries. He saw that her straggling hair had become more forlorn now with some of the straggles wet. She had made no attempt either to repair her bun or to take it apart and let her hair hang free.

Falc glanced at the dargs. They had drunk a little, and had found something to eat. Dargs always did. All he had to see to was that they didn't go too far upstream when they decided it was time to wallow and muck up the water. He thought they'd choose the pool a few feet away. That way clean water would remain, upstream behind him.

He stood and, in the ritual way, disencumbered himself of his weapons belt. He had just dipped out a drink and was returning to the scene of his repast when she returned with newly purple hands. The frypan held a pile of derrberries. Falc gestured.

"Sit or squat," he said. "Thanks."

She sat, arranging her skirt. "What may I have?"

"Anything you want. I don't even know what the sack contains. My host at the White Horn packed it."

She ate bread, more berries, and a ferg leg. She picked little bits off the bread and tucked them into her thin-lipped mouth to chew ruminatively. The habit was unpleasant to Falc and he ceased watching.

After a while she had said, "Shall we gather wood?"

"The food doesn't need a fire and neither do we. It isn't chilly and this isn't wild animal country."

"Oh."

The dargs had decided it was time to get wet, and then thoroughly wet. They had chosen the nearby pool. Even happily and noisily wallowing in shallow water, the greenish blue and blue-green creatures were somehow more graceful than on land. Or less ungainly, at any rate; grace might not be a word applicable to dargs.

Now Falc and Jinnery sat in silence, watching the beasts flop and slop about in their beloved water.

She sighed. "This is twice I've been orphaned, in a way. I was staying with Uncle Querry when my father was killed, in Morazain. Now . . ."

"I'm sorry, Jinnery."

"Are you?" Her tone was satiric. Ah, how sharp that tongue was!

Falc nodded, looking at the grass. "Yes," he said low-voiced.

That was so obviously real that it shut her up in something approaching shame. Neither of them spoke for a time. Then Falc did:

"Have you wept, Jinnery?"

Her sigh was almost silent. "A little."

He nodded. He saw no reason to say anything more.

After a minute or so she said, "Why?"

He looked up. For once her tone sounded not challenging, but curious. Nevertheless he was not about to tell her: because she was even more defensive than when they had met, more challenging and unpleasant so that he preferred not to talk at all, and that the probable reason was that she was holding in the grief, even justified self-pity, which needed to be let out in tears or yelling or both.

"You probably need to weep a lot," he said. "It helps. It's just something that has to be done."

She cocked her head. "Have you wept?"

"Whether I've wept or not doesn't have anything to do with anything."

"Meaning that you'd never admit it if you had."

Falc saw no reason to say anything to that.

The dargs splashed and Harr snapped at the other darg. It squealed. Falc said, "Harr," sternly, and looked at Jinnery. The hatchet-carved boniness of her face seemed to have softened, and he realized that it was because the sky was nearly dark.

"Have you given that darg a name?"

She shook her head. "Chalis wanted to call him Falc." Seeing what that did to his face, she chuckled. "I won't."

He fell into a trap: "Thanks."

She snapped it shut: "He's too nice a beast."

Falc ran a few lines of the Calm Psalm through his head. With his face arranged in quite pleasant lines, he said, "This is most unpleasant for me, Jinnery. I am more than reluctant to have you with me. It is possible that you could be less deliberately unpleasant."

Jinnery stared, blinked, and at last began to weep. *There*, Falc thought, and rose and went into the woods to relieve himself. He was careful to stay away longer than necessary. Complete darkness closed while he said prayers and hoped the Messenger would appear. It did not. Falc looked up and could just make out Orlam. It showed as about half a moon, with Jera's shadow on it.

He took care to make noise in returning to the clearing and could just make Jinnery out, standing well away. He thought he saw the knife in her hand.

"Falc," he said, and saw her hand go behind her back.

"Good. Tha-thanks for . . . for privacy, I guess."

"Um. Remind me tomorrow to show you how to hold that knife."

He saw the swift flurry of movement and knew she was embarrassedly stowing away the dagger.

"I do recommend a short name for your darg," he said.

Fully clothed, retaining his mailcoat, he stretched out on

his back and arranged the saddle so that it was partially under his head. The dargs were silent; Falc and Jinnery were silent.

"How old are you, Jinnery?"

"Twenty," she said sharply, and he was sure her expression was as sharp when he heard her head turn to look at him or in his direction. Very little moonlight filtered down into the small streamside clearing. Whether his reaction indicated that she "should be" older or younger, he assumed that she was ready to be defensive. Probably offensively so.

"In a way you look younger," he said, to the sky. "In a way, older. The eyes. And perhaps the set of your mouth."

"Twice orphaned, Sir Falc of Risskor. Should I be a sweet li'l girl with laughing eyes and upturned mouth?"

Falc saw no reason to say anything.

"And besides, Ashah saw fit not to give me lips or breasts."

To the sky he said, "I ride to Secter, and then to Lock, where I am Contracted to a Holder."

"I ride with you, Cousin Falc," she said, and he heard her movements as she turned and curled to sleep.

He remembered his thoughts about her that night in the barn, and considered it again, reminding himself. *She is years and years younger than Querry was, and than I am too, and niece or no, she shared his bed. And she was no happy woman, even three days ago when she had family and home. And she probably just told me what it is that soars in her to make her so bitter. Thou art not known for being fair, Ashah my god. We men invented that.*

He lay long awake, staring up at nothing save a dark blue sky cut into interesting segments by the black shapes of tree branches.

"Chalis, Chalis," he muttered into the night. "And Querry, good man and good father! I would take vow this moment and ride back to Lango for Faradox's head! Yet I do not know whether I may do, for I am not my own ruler. Falc does not decide, for Falc."

Sadly, Falc stared up into the night, seeing nothing.

FIVE

One need not love his neighbor and thus all men. That would be ridiculous and lead to great frustrations and crippling guilt, as well as encourage a society based on the impossible—egalitarianism—and pauper the people to make them "equal" while less free. No. We say that you must instead deal fairly with each individual as an individual, whether he or she is loved (or even lovable) or not.

—Sath Firedrake

In a dark area of Ryar where he really had no business at this time of night, Sir Relashah came upon three footpads in the act of attacking a man, who was down on the pave. Relashah called out, drawing as he broke into a run. In the pale light of the moon called Jera, one look at the charging man in black persuaded the trio to flee.

Relashah of Kem saw that they were still running as he reached their victim, and sheathed his blade. His cloak made him resemble a great bat alighting as he went to one knee beside the poor fellow. He put a gauntleted hand gently on the fallen man, who, twisting with inordinate swiftness for a wounded victim, stabbed straight up into Relashah's throat.

Making gargling sounds in his own blood, Relashah caught that murderous wrist and used it to yank the blade out of his neck. It fountained. He forced the treacherous barga's hand down, and down, and forced the dagger into his killer's chest. Or tried to; it skidded off well-lacquered armor under the man's tunic, and the fellow chuckled.

"No such luck, Deathknight swine!"

Sir Relashah sagged, spewing blood as he died.

The supposed footpads came hurrying back to speed him along with vicious kicks. Drenched with Relashah's blood, their supposed victim hustled to his feet to help.

"Fell right into it, didn't you, *Deathknight* swine! Uh! Feel that one?"

"These swinish *Deathknights* can't resist aggrandizing theirselfs by helping poo-oor people in trouble! Here's one in the—uh!—nuts!"

"That's enough; look, he's running out of blood. This ain't a *Death*knight, it's a *Dead*knight!"

They laughed. Swifty they stripped off the dead omo's equipage and clothing, which they stuffed into a waiting pair of rough-cloth bags.

"Look how pale the pig is under his blacks!"

"Huh, look at the size of these stones! No wonder he's a monk!"

The victim laughed as he peeled off Relashah's coif. "And look at this! Ever see anything so ridiculous?"

They left him there, dead and naked in an alley in Ryar.

2

Falc tried to forbear telling his companion that with her hair down this way, long and mildly wavy past her shoulders, the lines of her face were softened to her considerable benefit. She had risen the instant he had, and waded upstream to wash body and hair and clothing. She rode with wet hair and wet clothing, a condition soon remedied by the sun. At last he succumbed to that impulse to say something nice, and was immediately sorry.

"You mean with my hair hanging I've suddenly become almost attractive?" Her voice was scornful. "Well, try to contain yourself, *Cousin* Falc!"

Falc rode for the next three hours in silence. He hoped sincerely that she hated silence. Not singing, or at least executing his version of singing, was not easy. He would give her no chance to make fun of his voice or ability to carry a tune. He already knew about those lacks.

The sun moved slowly across the sky, and the road stretched on. They met no one save a pair of laden wagons with two outriders. When Falc reined aside, Jinnery did. Two drivers and two outriders nodded a greeting; one outrider lifted a hand. Falc did both.

"How far is Secter?" Jinnery asked, after three hours of silence.

"Not far."

"Will we reach it today or tomorrow?"

"Yes."

After waiting long enough to be sure that he meant to say no more, she said, "Which?"

As before, Falc continued to gaze straight ahead while he answered. "Which what?"

"Will we reach Secter today or to— Will we reach Secter today, or will we reach Secter tomorrow?"

"Tomorrow."

"Thank you."

An hour passed in silent plodding. They met a trio of riders who gave them nods and strange looks. A Deathknight with a woman!

"Oh," Jinnery said a while later, "I am to remind you to show me how to hold a knife."

"Yes, I had forgotten," Falc said. "It is important. We'll do that when we stop for the night."

"You think I hold a knife by the wrong end, perhaps?"

He compressed his lips and said nothing for the better part of an hour. Then:

"The very worst way to attack or defend with a dagger is to brandish it; that is, to hold it high for an overhand swing. It leaves you open all the way up and down and the length of the swing makes it easy to dodge or defend against. Hold the knife down, near your side and at the waist, and keep it moving. I will show you."

"I see. You must know all about knife-fighting, hmm?"

"Yes."

Falc said nothing more. He tried to meditate on the statement: "Treat the day as if it were the morrow, for soon it will be." *Not soon enough this time, O Ashah*, he thought.

Later, seeing a farm wagon about to emerge from a side road ahead, Falc decided to trot for a while so as not to have to trail the wagon and breathe its dust. That was wise; as they approached, they saw that the wagon was laden with *shab*: manure. They trotted until Falc decided to slow.

"Falc?"

Since he said nothing, she said "Falc?" in that questioning way again.

He glanced at her for the first time since he had complimented her. "You are here and I am here. You know I heard you."

"So sorry. I was going to ask why we have so little new steel. All of us, I mean. Everyone."

"Society, you mean." Falc's face tightened. "We have none. We are Sij, now, and Sij is confined by its resources. Steel requires iron. The only iron left by the First Civilization is available only as something called oxides."

"What are oxides?"

"I can't tell you."

"Can't, or won't?"

"I don't know what an oxide is."

"The Sons of Ashah don't know everything?"

"The Sons of Ashah do not know everything," he said, and heard her sigh.

"Oh, I am glad of that! And fuel . . . what about this thing called coal? That black thing you wear around your neck; is that coal?"

"Yes. Coal is too deep inside Sij for us to get at. So I am told. These are the things called 'technoscience,' Jinnery. I know nothing of it, and do not care to."

"Would it burn as fuel, that bit of coal about your neck?"

"I suppose."

"You're not afraid that this hot sun might set it ablaze?"

"I know that it requires more heat than that," Falc said, with some pride.

"Hmm! Have you no handy saying for all this?"

"I can tell you words. These are the words I know, and I am not sure of their meaning, or whether anyone is: 'The only available oil, sulphur, copper, coal, iron are buried so deeply within Sij as to be irretrievable . . . not only irretrievable, but inconceivable.' "

"That . . . I don't know what that means."

Falc shrugged one shoulder. "Neither do I. It means that

any return to what Sij was before is impossible or at least extremely improbable because the First Civilization, the techno-society, used all non-renewable resources, and *used them up*. This is written, and I will tell you before you ask that I am not sure what it means."

She rode in silence, chewing on all those words, before she said, "Well, at least now I know more than I ever did in my life."

Falc saw no reason to comment. *Ashah guide and deliver me!*

When they camped, he spent some time demonstrating to her the use of a knife as weapon. She assured him that she did not intend to use this knowledge. He assured her that he never had or did, either. He reminded her that such knowledge might possibly have served her in good stead had he not rescued her from the two bent on taking her darg and "whatever else they intended to take."

"Would you call those two men bad?" she asked, surprising him with the sudden switch of topic.

"They were intent on a bad act."

She surprised him further by showing him why she had asked; she introduced a subject they had touched on that night in her home.

"If pink is the color of the universe and the red of blood is the color of bad, why then should men—should *we* strive to be better than the universe?"

Ah, a surprised Falc mused, *she both remembers and thinks!* "The universe is composed of all," he told her, not quite from rote. "The bad and the good. No one has stated that everything should be attainable. We can only try."

"What's 'attainable'?"

"Means you can get it, reach it."

"And do you seek that perfect and ungettable-unreachable goal, Falc of Risskor?"

"I seek unity. The natural enemy of humanity is chaos. Perhaps it is our natural state; I don't have that answer either. Surely the highest goal, though, is unity."

"Unity."

That hung there in silence for a while, and she said, "Perhaps that is what I came seeking, that night in the barn."

He saw no reason to respond to that, but did anyhow: "That is not what is meant by unity."

She did not, Ashah be thanked, ask.

3

Under a graying sky along about noon next day she announced that she had chosen a name for her darg. Falc looked over at her, her face shadowed dark under the hat Baysh had given him. She had restored her hair's bun last night, probably because he had said she looked softer with it down and loose. Now she told him the name she had chosen for her mount. He assumed that this too was spite, since he had praised the excellence of the creature and advised a short word as name. She would call him Shabtain.

"Dungheap!" he echoed.

"I certainly wouldn't name him after a *flower*," she said with scornful emphasis, gazing straight ahead.

Let her misname and mistrain the animal, then. I shall soon be rid of her, and thanks be to Ashah!

A surprisingly chill wind gusted at them for an hour or so, and gave way to a slashing rain. Alone, Falc may or may not have sought shelter. Not today, not with Jinnery like an anvil attached to his leg. He had ridden in rain many times, and was accustomed to it. Unworthy or not, he hoped that she was not and that she hated it.

His helmet turned water. His cloak did, for a while. Hers was sodden much sooner. She did learn one trick: now and again she tilted her head to the side to let water pour off the big gray hat's broad brim rather than run off in front or back, onto her. She said not a word, but rode as he did. They even passed an open barn, very close to the road. No one would have denied them temporary shelter. Falc passed it without a glance.

The rain lasted about an hour. After that, the sun returned with a vengeance, as if seeking to suck up every drop of water at once. Both travelers shucked their cloaks. They steamed. Both knew that the omo suffered the more, in his blacks. He said nothing and showed nothing.

•   •   •

Just over an hour from Secter, they met two other pilgrims, not farmers or men of weapons either. Male Sectrans, both gave respectful nods to the omo and looked questioningly at his companion. Falc greeted them both. His asking what news in Secter was only politeness, in passing. Both smiled; one said "All's well," and they rode on.

Far behind them, Falc and Jinnery saw the approach of another rider from Secter. Tall and broad, he paced his mount as they did. He wore a hooded derlin as Falc did. Falc noted his boots and saddle and bags before faces were recognizable, but said nothing to his companion. She seemed nervous; Falc was not. Then the pilgrims came together, and the other man hoisted an arm.

"Hail, brother, in Ashah's name!"

"Hail, brother," Falc echoed, "in the name of Ashah. How do ye, Ashamal?"

"I am well," the other omo said, and put back his white hood for the first time. "You ha' taken on a bodyguard, Brother Falc?"

"Ah yes, she protects me well. She is Jinnery, Sir Ashamal of Mersarl."

Seeing that no explanation was forthcoming, Ashamal nodded to Jinnery, who nodded back without a word. He said, "Would you excuse us to exchange a few words?"

Without a word she twitched her heels and Shabtain paced forward, past Ashamal along the road to Secter. She paused in the shade beneath a hugely spreading barrtree. Ashamal of the thin, hooked nose and intense, royal blue eyes had already reined close to his fellow omo. He spoke in a quiet voice.

"Falc: d'you know 'bout Sench?"

"Contracted to Havenden of Kem."

"Falc, Brother Sench was slain just outside Darsin, 'nd left naked."

"Naked! How slain?"

"Set 'pon. Stabbed repeatedly. Dishonored and stripped. That is abs'lutely all we know of it. No one knows anything, 'cluding the High Temple."

Falc nodded, grim of face. He saw no reason to waste words on comment, since Ashamal had said this was all anyone knew.

"You knew nothin' of this, Falc?"

Falc shook his head.

"I'm on my way to offer Contract to Havenden. You have not been . . . Visited?"

"I have not seen the Messenger for several nights, Brother Ashamal. I have that woman with me. It's not my wish. She lived on a farm other side Morazain, and her protector was murdered because of me. They also burned her home and barn. She has . . . attached herself to me."

He told Ashamal about Faradox and Chasmal then, and the rest of it.

"So. You avenged her uncle and cousin 'thout even knowin' it."

"No. The four were hirelings. Revenge is located atop Faradox's neck."

"Um." Ashamal glanced Jinnery's way. She had dismounted and was moving about, exercising her legs. "She's grateful to you, 't any rate."

"I have not told her."

Ashamal jerked his head back to stare. "What? Why?"

Falc shrugged. "I'm not interested in currying her favor and I do not need her gratitude."

"Beware vaunting pri-eede, Ole Brother Stoneface," Ashamal said, and smiled.

Falc did not. "You beware pride, Brother. I'll keep mine. Ashamal: Holder Chasmal of Lango is a good man. I recommend that you go to him and offer Contract."

Ashamal cocked his head. "You think that I deserve a good man, Falc? Thank you."

"Tell Holder Chasmal I suggested that you approach him, and he will know that you are a good man, too."

Ashamal blinked, nodded, glanced away. Oh, this ever serious outcast of Risskor and his sky-high self-esteem! Aloud Ashamal added, "Deserved."

"What?"

"Only a mutter, Falc. I will think on it. P'rhap I should vis't Lango, hmm? What will you do, Ole Brother Stoneface?"

"I would ask you to do me service, Ole Brother Dragonel-nose."

Ashamal smiled. "Ask, Falc."

"I would ask you to escort Jinnery to Lock, Ashamal. Explain to Holder Kinneven that I have delivered his mes-

sages to Holder Chasmal, who is now beholden to both
Kinneven and Falc. Advise Kinneven that he was most certainly right about Faradox, who now has reason to hate Falc
unto vengeance. And tell him that I have had to go to confer
with the Master of the Order.''

"Had to?''

Falc nodded. "I must. Will you do this, Ashamal?''

"You've never asked any sort of favor of me, Falc. Is't
ridiculous that I feel honored? Yes, I will do it. And as for
you, Brother: Enjoy your clean head!''

"Shh—we will not tell her until morning,'' Falc said.
"Will you ride back to Secter with us?''

Ashamal shrugged. His whimsical little smile said "Oh
well.''

The three of them rode into Secter of the richly patterned
carpets and women in baggy pants rather than the dresses Falc
considered proper. There they took a room in a second-class
inn. Falc left them to deliver his brief oral message to a
Holder, turned down the man's invitation to night there, and
returned to the inn to dine with his companions. It was Falc
who laid down the few melts the innkeeper wanted for the
meal and a good-sized room. No one thought anything of that
sensible three-way sharing of a nightchamber, unless they
were surprised that the men had taken up with such a homely
woman. Surely a pair of Deathknights could do better.

They would have been far more surprised to learn that the
three slept apart and shared only the room, not bodies.

In the morning, after they had breakfasted and were mounting, Falc advised Jinnery of his plans.

"I must go to the Mon Ashah-re,'' he told her simply: the
High Temple of Ashah. "There you may not and can not go,
Jinnery.''

"What!"

He but gazed at her; not only did Falc of Risskor avoid
saying the unnecessary or the obvious, he tried not to lie, and
so would not mouth the standard "I'm sorry.''

She made more noises, not at all happy about this sudden
development. Sir Ashamal was rather surprised that Falc
allowed this skinny girl to insult him. Surprised too at her
desire to continue with stern Ole Brother Stoneface and at the

same time wary of her mount Shabtain, Ashamal held the
creature while Falc rode away.

Once he was outside the city he set Harr to the gallop, and
held that pace for an hour. It felt very good to be back in his
natural state: alone.

4

Despite the quake that enforced several minutes of great
care, she overtook him just under five hours later.

"You're right," she said, patting her mount's thick neck
and shaking back her tangled hair. "He *is* a racing darg!"

Falc made no comment on the fact that she was wearing the
ballooningly full leggings of a Secteri woman, a garment he
deemed unfit for any woman. "Jinnery: I am going to the
High Temple of Ashah. The home of the Master of the Order;
the very home and keep of the Order! There no woman may
go. You can *not* accompany me!"

"Look at me, Ole Stoneface. Look upon Young Stoneface."

He looked into those nigh-black eyes. In the brightness of
the sun her pupils were mere vertical lines. He saw the
purposeful look in her eyes, and in the set of her mouth and
strong straight-boned jaw.

"I am looking, Jinnery. You may not and can not accompany me."

"Very well then, Cousin Falc. I will follow, for you can
not leave me!"

He showed a face of affliction and turned his anguished
eyes upward. Ashah gave no sign and Falc saw not the
faintest hint of a cloud from which might come a lightning
bolt to remove this sapling-thin woman's anvilish weight
from around his neck. Again Falc tried.

"I have been riding for years, girl. I can live in the saddle,
eat in the saddle. I can sleep in the saddle. You can try to
follow, but you cannot keep the pace I and Harr can set."

"That may be." She smiled and stroked her mount's neck.
"But I'll bet Shabtain can!"

He could only stare. So this was the meaning of the phrase
"helpless rage!"

"And," she added after a perfectly timed pause, "I'm no girl."

He drew in a deep breath, let it out slowly through his nose. He was stuck with her, and he knew it. "If you must follow me, at least resume your womanly skirt and rid yourself and my sight of those sections."

"Sections?"

"That's what those most unfeminine leg-balloons of Secter are called."

She glanced down at her grass-blue sections. "Oh. But see, since I'm to follow, they'll not be in your sight, Cousin Omo."

Ah, Ashah, the mockery of her voice, the smug satisfaction in her face of planes and angles! Feeling most unwontedly helpless and wondering what inner force or newly manifested weakness was preventing him from slapping her off her mount, Falc stared.

Suddenly both her face and her voice became less harsh. "Falc . . . consider. You ride and you wear leggings. I have ridden without complaint, and yet I could not keep my skirt between my bare legs and saddle or darg-hide, and my legs have been chafed constantly. Besides . . . every time you decided that we would speed up, my skirt blew and I had to use one hand to hold it down. I considered trying to tie or sew it together between my thighs, but without a pin or needle or thread I couldn't think of a way to do it."

"Jinnery—"

"Just a moment, now; there is more. You are a monk, a Son of Ashah, and you have no business seeing a woman's legs. Now you cannot: they are covered. Further, the covering is loose and does not even outline the female legs you have no business seeing. Sir Knight of the Order: do you hear logic? Your argument is not an argument, it's a reaction. It is not logical. Do you hear the voice of your illogical prejudice, Sir Falc, or do you hear me?"

And that was that. Falc of Riskor, O.M.O., must accept her aquamarine balloon-pants and her sour companionship, such as it was. And yet he would not. She had said that she would follow. Very well, then.

Without taking his gaze off her, without a word or a movement that she could see, he signaled Harr. The darg turned and set off along the road. Smiling, her eyebrows up in a serene expression, Jinnery waited several seconds before she set off after him.

She trailed him all afternoon. She trailed him until dusk, and after. He made no camp but rode on. When the sky was a deep slate hue, he swung down and walked for a while, knowing that Harr would not stop or meander. As they approached Hazne's Wood, Falc pretended to be inspecting his saddle so that he could snatch a backward glance. She was there, walking beside her hideously misnamed darg, sections flaring. Falc brought Harr to pause and swung into the saddle. He rode in among the trees without looking back. Within the forest the road was no narrower and Harr needed no guidance.

In that greater darkness Falc hauled a saddlebag around before him without turning, found a piece of fruit just on the point of slimy death, and ate it. He was kind enough to Harr to dismount for the fording of Stinking Creek. He spoke soft kindnesses to Harr as they crossed, without looking back.

Jera rose, and Orlam, and presumably The Loner, too, were up there in the sky of night. Falc did not look up and did not look back. It wouldn't have mattered; within the forest, night was a thing of black onyx.

Having started the day with an hour's gallop, Harr was ready for rest and deserved it. He grew draggy and then definitely surly. When Falc hauled out another moribund fruit and proffered it, the beast seemed as interested in taking off his hand as in eating the gift. His yellow eyes glared. Falc wiped his pulp-slimy hands on the darg's hide. A bat swooped and Falc ducked at the sound while glimpsing only a movement in the air.

He listened hopefully, but heard no sound from behind to indicate that Jinnery and the bat had encountered each other.

Harr turned uncooperative; three times his master drowsed off in the saddle and each time the darg awakened him by stopping. This was not training; this was the opposite of his training. Falc had slept many times in the saddle while his superbly well-trained war-darg bore him on his way. Now Falc slapped his neck and Harr hissed genuine malice. His master knew better than to repeat the act, for the darg would only force him to discipline it more sternly, and that would not be fair.

When Harr blundered in among the trees and bushes and nearly caught his rider by going under a low branch, Falc knew it was deliberate. He hauled the hissing creature back onto the road and forced him to pace angrily along for a few minutes more—hissing—before urging him into the trees. That was important to both of them; this way it was Falc's decision, not Harr's.

While he unequipped the darg and relieved himself, Falc did not know whether to think about Jinnery or to try not to. He did neither, and the choice was not his. Within bare minutes man and darg were asleep under the trees.

When he awoke, Harr was breakfasting on this and that and Jinnery was on the road a few feet away, waiting beside her darg. Wearing the big gray hat and her green-blue sections.

Falc rose, muttered rite-words while he exercised briefly, and murmured to Harr all the while he harnessed the beast. Then he led him out onto the road, passing Jinnery without seeming to see her, and began walking on his way. An hour or so later he stopped to enter the woods and relieve himself as he should have done upon awakening. Furtively, from cover of woods, he ascertained that she was still there. He emerged to mount, but paused while the brown-and-gold butterfly flitted too close. He heard the slurp and saw it vanish, and urged Harr into a trot.

Falc's stomach rumbled.

5

Two hours out of the woods, he had donned derlin and raised the hood when he heard the approach of a single darg from behind, at the canter. He did what he'd have done had he been alone and overtaken by another rider in more hurry: he minded his business. He rode on without looking back.

That did not mean he didn't stiffen when he heard the other darg slow. Then he heard a male voice, speaking low. Falc missed the words.

"No," the rather loud voice of a pubescent boy replied, "I'm with him!"

This time Falc heard the man's words: "Oh? So far behind? Who's he?"

"Sir Falc of Risskor," she said in that unfortunate voice, still too loud, "Knight of the Order Most Old!"

The man speeded to come up alongside Falc, who glanced over at someone's courier. Young and brawny and cocky, he was liveried under his derlin in a painfully bright green and reddish brown, with yellow trim.

"Hot sun today."

Falc nodded. "Yes."

"I'd think a noble Son of Ashah'd let the girl wear the hood and derlin," the fellow said, and was away at the gallop, as if hurled from an invisible catapult.

Falc sighed. "I was too young and too snotty once, too," he muttered, and Harr's neck rumpled as he glanced around. Falc's stomach rumbled as he gave the darg a pat. "Want to trot?"

Harr didn't know questions, but heard a word he knew. Harr trotted.

6

Sunset was a half hour away when Falc terminated a half-hour's gallop and nudged Harr into a turn. Broadside, he watched Jinnery's racing darg terminate its gallop. She brought him to a stop twenty or so meters away. Wild of hair and flushed of face, she returned Falc's gaze.

"Isn't galloping glorious?"

He shook his head, but not in negation. She was still with him; she looked hale; she acted hearty and even friendly. She was no more fathomable than the deepest well, he thought, who had never paused to consider that he was quite unfathomable to all, including himself. He sighed.

He thought, *How many sighs has this impossible woman brought from me?* And he said, "What soars in you, woman?"

She had adopted his set face and equable tone. "Hunger, mostly."

Falc's big chest heaved in a sigh.

SIX

We believe that individuals should receive fairness, which means that which they merit and deserve, which means justice.
Justice cannot be "gentle," as it cannot be "stern."
Justice is justice; that which is merited for that individual:
reparation, not retribution.

—the third Master

The man was big, and all in black. His much smaller companion, in long white derlin with its hood up, might have been a tall boy or an unusually thin man. No; she was a woman, and they were companions without being friends. They had ridden for three hours through ever-rising, increasingly rugged country that led them to the Mountain of God. When they reached the tumbled rocks and rocky debris at the foot of the mountain's long sloping east face, the woman could only stare up and up that towering mass of stone. She saw mostly gray porphyry shading to the black of jet with shades of russet and dirty gold. Here and there she spotted a sort of scraggly imitation of a tree. Each stood from the mountain at an odd angle that fascinated her.

The man in black was moving, though, and she must follow. They and their mounts climbed up toward those scoriac crags.

The High Temple of Ashah and His Order, Falc had told Jinnery, was tucked away well up within the mountain, and invisible. Access was by one pass only; a narrow slice between high granitic walls. First they must climb to the pass. He had seen to it that the derlin concealed those Secteri balloon-pants which he considered awful.

They were challenged twice before they reached it, and they were watched all the way through its half-kilometer length. Jinnery found it hard to obey Falc's injunction not to look up. A giant had surely chopped into the mountain with his prodigious sword, and she rode now in the bottom of the deep wound. It seemed the narrower for its depth. Bits of something shiny and tiny twinkled at her from the walls. Worthless, Falc said. She knew the sentinel guardians he had mentioned were up there on the wound's lips: trainees, semi-retired omos, and a few zealot monks who possessed keen eyes and high skill with the bow. She was grateful that he had warned her in advance, and warned her also to keep her mouth shut while he identified her as his cousin, a fugitive from evil.

Even so, one mailcoated guardian of the Order was sour about it, because of her.

Flanked by two older men who were obviously in better than good condition and in possession of bows and hip-slung quivers bristling with arrows, he maintained his suspicious eyes. When he asked a question, Falc called him by name, and repeated what he had already told them. Falc used precisely the same words. The sentinel continued to scowl. Falc gave him his dour look.

"You know me, Brother Provalk. I am come home to the Temple. It is irregular that I bring someone with me, and I will answer to the Master for it. You will stand aside." Falc made one of his soundless and invisible signals to Harr, who began pacing forward.

That guardian and his two men looked even more stern and disapproving. They also stepped aside. Jinnery was aware of their glowering eyes while she passed, and after. She sat stiffly, staring at Falc's back as she rode close behind him. Her skin prickled and her armpits were wet. The assured *presence* of this dark man with his twice-dark eyes that evaded no gaze! Was there anyone who dared face him? Could there be anyone to whom he could possibly defer?

Next they had come to a wall, and a gate. Again Falc identified himself, and this time the guard smiled.

"Welcome home, Falc!" he called, and signaled.

Jinnery heard the clink and rattle of chains. The prodigiously thick gate swung in. She saw more armed men and she blinked at sight of another blank wall only a few meters away. Falc turned rightward to pace along between those walls of thickly massed stone until they came to another gate. It opened before they had to stop. They passed through.

The vision within was a revelation that assaulted Jinnery's senses, but in a purely positive way. Here lay what she had least expected to see, despite what Falc had told her. She could only stare.

Mon-Ashah-re, Falc had told her yesterday as he began to prepare her for their arrival, was self-sufficient. She had begun to have doubts about that, as they proceeded up into solid rock. Now she saw the gardens, the beautiful and well-tended shrubs, the trees, and she knew that he had not exaggerated. Years upon years ago wagonload after wagonload of soil must have been fetched up here at the cost of much labor. Such shrubs and trees and gardens could hardly grow in the bare rock all about them!

The Temple itself was still invisible within a fortress that seemed to grow from the rock itself. Carefully tilted back from them, it consisted of stones piled upon stones in a strangely smooth yet multi-hued way so that it resembled less a wall than a rearing mosaic hill of rock. They passed through another gateway and dismounted. Two men, a quite young and a quite old, came to take their dargs. Falc greeted the older by name; that man was pleased to introduce him to the younger, an apprentice omo.

As soon as he spoke, with rich respect and deference, Falc told the omo-to-be where he was from: Darsin. The youth showed his wonder at the big dark man's perception and knowledge; Falc was right. What Jinnery noticed most was how very impressed the youth obviously was to meet Sir Falc of Risskor; "the legendary Sir Falc," as he put it.

That impressed Jinnery. It also increased her surprise at the respectful attitude Falc adopted toward the next man they confronted. Falc! Falc as she had never seen him or dreamed he could be: deferential, respectful!

This aged, wispy-haired fellow in the black-trimmed robe

of dark brown did not repeat the put-upon act of Provalk, but was most stern indeed.

"This was not well done, Son of Ashah. Special quarters will have to be arranged for this woman."

Falc's head was unusually low and he spoke very quietly. "I felt myself without choice, High Brother. She is as I said my cousin, and I dared leave her nowhere. I apologize to you for the trouble I am causing, and will apologize and defer to any you indicate."

"I have heard you. Woman, you will receive quarters, where you will *remain*. You will not speak to those who escort you, or who provide you with food and water."

On the point of saying "Yes sir," Jinnery decided to begin her silence now. She only bowed as she had seen Falc do.

She straightened in time to see new astonishment: the man addressed as "High Brother" was in the act of clapping Falc fondly on the shoulder.

"I'm glad to see you, Falc! The Master will be stern about your cousin but glad to receive your report. Do you bring aught else? No new wounds, I hope?"

"None, High Brother. I bring nothing but myself, but have given to more than one temple in Morazain. Some weaponish hirelings afforded me spoils. And I have seen Ashamal, who is probably in Lango by now. I recommended that he seek Contract with a Holder there—you know Chasmal."

"Of course. Later you must tell me what need he will have of our brother Ashamal. For now, Falc, we will see to your cousin's comfort; you must go at once to the Master. He has known you were coming since minutes after you started up the mountain, of course."

Falc nodded, started away with him, and paused. He glanced back at Jinnery. All but swallowed in his derlin, she looked small and quite lost and pitiful in this holy place of men. He who was home could do nothing. He nodded to her, and walked away with the High Brother.

2

Falc entered the big barren room with its high, vaulted ceiling on encircling columns, smooth cylinders of pearly marble

streaked with red and gray. He walked silently to the line of
cream tiles set across the otherwise unrelieved black of the
floor. There he paused to kneel and unfasten his weapons belt
and helmet. Leaving them there on the floor, he rose. The
click of footsteps in such a chamber might have been dramatic, but as ever Falc wore his dull, soft-soled boots. There
was nothing dramatic about his entry, for he was most sub-
dued and deferential in pacing to where the Master of the
Order stood just outside one of several shafts of light admitted
by small, high-set windows.

The Firedrake was a big man, a barrel-chested truly *big*
man, who had attained his age without attaining girth. For
that was the rule, and it applied to all from the newest recruit
to the Master himself: the Sons of Ashah did not grow fat.
The Firedrake had been an omo, as all Masters had been. He
had ridden all over the continent and knew its cities and its
rivers and mountains and most of all, its roads and weather.
His attire was severe. His snug black coif concealed all of his
head save his face, and covered his neck as well. From there
only his hands, large and visibly very old, and the toes of his
black felt shoes appeared from a snugly girt robe of heavy,
dull black. He had never been handsome and never worn
facial hair. His face was as severe as the minatory sternness
of his attire, all vertical lines like crevasses save for the
straight horizontal slice of his mouth. Two lines slashed down
his forehead to the inner edges of his eyebrows, which were
not quite white.

All of this emphasized the youthful alertness of his eyes.
No lichen-light glowed in the High Temple of Ashah, but
even lit only by thin shafts of sunlight and a single oil lamp,
the eyes of the Firedrake were blue as jarum-blossoms and
very, very bright.

He stood with one hand upon the smallish round table of
hard old wood. Despite its age it was well polished and
showed few marks. The great slice made when the fifth
Master had lost his temper was still there, in its ugliness so
full of meaning. He had succumbed to rage that day, and
resigned the next, to disappear forever. Some said that in his
shame he had thrown himself down the sheer precipice of the
mountain's south flank. Some said that Sath Firedrake had
come for him, and dragged him away as unworthy. Others

said he wandered the world still, and must do so forever. Falc
thought that he must have gone away and died, that Master of
a century ago.

"Welcome, Knight of the Order Most Old."

"No knight, my Master, but an unworthy son of Ashah
begs the blessing of the Firedrake."

"You have it, in Ashah's name and in Sath Firedrake's
name, O Son of Ashah."

"You will call me Sir Knight, sirrah, for I am blessed by
God and Firedrake!"

The Master of the Order Most Old bowed to complete that
ritual of mutual abasement, and straightened to gesture. "Sit,
Falc. What has befallen you, and what soars within you that
you bring a woman to the very Temple?"

No chairs were provided at that table; only two plain stools
of wood, and neither was different from the other as neither
was reserved for the Firedrake. It was the Knight O.M.O.
returning to Mon-Ashah-re who must first choose a stool and
sit.

Falc did, and held his tongue until the Firedrake seated
himself, not quite opposite his omo. "It begins in Lango-by-
the-Sea, Master. I have much to tell."

"I have ears, and time."

Falc told his story.

The Master raised a hand for pause. "You delivered
Kinneven's message by mouth? What was it?"

A knight of the Order Most Old told his message to no one
save its intended recipient, and all knew it. Only omos knew
that an omo told anything and all to the Firedrake.

"Holder Kinneven's words were these, Master: 'Here is
something no one knows about the purple shume. Not only
does it stand tall and its main stem grow ever thicker, but it
puts forth aerial roots.' "

The Firedrake's lips moved as he gazed at the vaulted
ceiling of this chamber, repeating words he would not forget.
Down came his head and those bright and alert eyes of
intelligence gazed into Falc's. "It has meaning to you, Falc?"

"No, Master. Since the shume does not stand tall, I knew
it was a code between Kinneven and Chasmal, who seemed to
understand."

"You can think of nothing he said; no action he took or

order he gave that might have stemmed from the message?"

"No, Master, and I have thought on it."

"I am sure you have. An enigma. Oh, but these proud Holders will have their secrets, even from the trusted bearers of their messages! Tell on, Sir Knight."

Falc told on, until the next interruption:

"You slew them all four, Falc, and they sent to murder you? And you and your darg took no wound?"

"I took a bruise that lasted for days, Master."

"A *bruise*! That is not a wound! A *bruise*! Brother Chernis *bruised* his knee just today when he slipped on a step!"

Falc bowed his head. He had tried to diminish his feat, to pretend modesty by mentioning that he had been hit, but the Firedrake would have none of that. Falc should have known.

"Forgive me, Master. I took no wound. Nor did my darg."

Instantly the Firedrake reversed himself: "Ah, Falc! What a fighter you are! You have an extra weapon few men have, or use: your brain! You are a fighter beyond even that one called Sir Sijamal!"

Falc bowed his head low. "It is not possible, Master," he said, for the omo Sijamal of Missentia had become this man now across the table from him.

"You think I'd say it if I did not believe it, churl? You think Sijamal was less the vaulting egoist than you?"

Falc's head remained down. "I have no ego, Master. I am part of the Order, and that only."

The Master shook his head. "Oh, Falc, Falc! What lies— and yet I think you believe that you are truly a most humble man! No no, let no more lies and flattery fall from those lips, Sir Knight! What next then, after you did death on four men and sent their heads back to their master?" Abruptly he added, "After an afternoon in a hayfield and a night in a loft, indeed!"

"My Master: I must return to Lango."

The Firedrake seemed not to hear that, but only gazed expectantly at him. Falc dutifully continued the narrative, this time without interruption until he reached the point a few days ago at which Jinnery had overtaken him.

"Incredible! How do you suppose she slipped Ashamal's charge?"

Falc shook his head. "He could not hold her mount forever. Once he had released it and was less attentive, she left him at the gallop. She had only to follow the road, at the gallop. My Harr is the best of war-trained dargs, but he is no racer.''

"Have you made her the owner of that animal?"

"Yes, Master."

"Too bad. It is a superb one, isn't it."

"It is, my Master, and I am sorry."

"Sorry, sorry. Always ready to be sorry, to bow to the Firedrake, so-o respectful Falc of Risskor."

Falc lifted his head with anguish in his eyes. "Two men I love and respect above all others, Master, and between them there is no comparison. You know this. You are the first."

The Firedrake sighed. "And Falc is the other. You are more abjectly respectful of me than any, Falc. Perhap overly so. Do not confuse me with your father."

Falc's face stiffened and he looked away. "Never!"

After a few moments of taut silence the Firedrake said, "So. She overtook you, and you brought her to our keep, to the very home of Ashah."

"Not . . . exactly so, Master," Falc said, and told of his "accepting her offer" to follow him.

"Falc the cruel, yes. We all know about that, do we not?"

"I have never denied it, Master. Nor ever will I deny that I do all I can, short of running, to avoid armed encounters . . . and glory in it when I am forced to fight and kill."

It was the Firedrake's turn to look down. "I know, Falc of Risskor. An honorable man, a truthful one, and a cruel one . . . and a killer."

Yes. This time Falc sat very straight, with his head high.

"So. And after all that she had endured, she said only that she was hungry?"

Falc looked away. "Master, I . . . weakened. I . . . melted. It was then I vowed, though not aloud, to see to her, to look after her, to bring her here with me. And to take her hence to Holder Kinneven. It is unworthy, but so I have vowed."

"You have a carnal interest in her, Falc?"

Falc made sure that his gaze met that of a wise old man's startlingly youthful eyes, and held. "None."

"Shall I believe that, Falc?—of Falc?"

"My Master knows it is important to me that he does."

"Hmm. And so you came here. You have just departed Lango and Morazain, on your Contracted liege's business, and you flaunt that business by interrupting it to come here. And yes, I heard you tell me that you wish to *return* to Lango. Why?"

Falc blinked. It was as if this man he respected above all others had heard nothing he said. Why must he be ever such a stern father? *He is my only master; from him I take what none others would dare, and live.* Falc took a breath. Above all men, Falc of Risskor would not make an angry retort to the Master of the Order Most Old; to the successor of Sath and Ashah's representative on Sij.

"To kill Faradox, Master."

"*Kill!* A Holder!"

"It is a matter of honor, my Master."

The Firedrake's big fist of veins and wrinkles and pale bony knuckles struck the table between them. "*Personal* honor! A Knight of the Order Most Old has neither personal honor nor personal business, Falc. This you accepted in your vows to God and Founder . . . *Son of Ashah.*"

"My Master, this man has done insult to the Order and its honor by sending men to *murder*—"

"—to murder *you*! You, *Falc of Risskor*—a man, not the Order!" Up came the fist, and a finger snapped out of it to point at Falc like a skewer ready to impale him. "You confuse pride and anger with honor. You say 'my master' to me when only you and your pride are your master! You assume that an affront to you is an affront to the Order and Ashah. I am surprised at you, Falc."

Falc too was surprised, although he doubted that his Master really was.

Stiffly, formally, he said, "Master, I request permission to return to Lango, and—"

"Denied. Expressly denied. Return to Lango except on the order and business of your Contract liege or the Order, Sir Falc, and you are only Falc, for you will have made yourself no knight of the Order!"

Feeling his anger, Falc sought to deflect it or contain it. That hurt; it burned his very guts, but he had done it before. He had no choice. He could not disobey for he could not leave the Order, which was his shelter and his life, his very life. He accepted with a bowing of his head. This was the Master of the Order, and Falc was of the Order. Falc did not decide for Falc.

The Firedrake pushed it; forced him. "Speak, Falc."

"Falc does not decide for Falc. I submit, Master."

"You will recite the Litany of Purpose fivescore times in penance, Son of Ashah, and meditate on the sin of pride and honor that is not part of the unity of the Order."

"This son of Ashah submits and agrees without question, my Master."

" 'My *Master*,' " the Firedrake muttered with sarcasm, and gave his omo a look.

Abruptly the Firedrake stood and paced, with the faintest rustle of his robe but without the hint of creaking joints or a grunt on rising from the bare wooden stool.

"The Order thanks you for your news, Sir Brother, and we give you ours: a quake so rocked the southern coastal area that the city of Tem was almost totally destroyed, with many lives lost."

Falc compressed his lips and stared at the floor. He saw no need to say anything.

"Falc, our brother Sench has been slain."

"Sench!"

The Firedrake stood with his back turned, speaking to a bright spot on the floor where the sun streamed in through a high-set port. "It would appear that he was set upon and murdered. Too, Sir Senithal was attacked in Jayanga and we have no idea why. Sir Vennashah has been missing for nearly three weeks. A naked corpse was found down in Silkevare, and burned as is customary there with alley-dead. No one remembers seeing the Scar of Sath, but the corpse did seem to possess the Curse of Sath. And Falc: Sir Relashah was slain only a week ago, in Missentia. Missentia! Home of the second temple and our twice-friend Kaladen the religious! Relashah was stripped of everything he wore; everything. He had been both stabbed and kicked, repeatedly."

"Ashah sustain us!" Falc had pounced to his feet. "Master! These men were . . ." He broke off, working to compose himself. Sench! Senithal! Vennashah presumably dead; Relashah, old Relashah the Gasser dead in an alley! "Master!

Could . . . could someone be . . . attacking omos, *because they are omos?*''

The Firedrake turned to gaze at him. "Naturally such a thought occurs, Falc. However it is difficult to give it serious consideration, certainly without further evidence. Why? And who? Think of the incredible magnitude! A cabal that unites Holders and *citystates*?! The number of people of disparate places necessary to such a . . . such a plot! What could unite them? Who would dream of such a course of action, much less dare—and to what end? What possible motive could there be for attacking the Order? We have represented a form of peace and order, through communication and respect for the Order—us—for over two centuries.''

The two men stood gazing their incomprehension at each other. Falc wondered, but he kept it to himself. He would try to learn.

"Welcome back, over-proud Son of Ashah. Go and cleanse yourself.''

Falc bowed low. He returned to collect his weapons and helmet before leaving the presence of the Firedrake.

3

In the Inner Temple, Falc muttered the rite-words while he stripped at the edge of the Pool of Complete Cleansing. His scarred, powerfully built body was not all he revealed in that cool, ever dark place where none might go save omos and resident monks. Here, where none but those of the Order might see, a Son of Ashah stripped completely. That meant removal even of the coif or skullcap to reveal the Curse of Sath. While he bathed all would disappear at the hands of a silent acolyte, who would leave a robe for Falc to wear while his blacks were thoroughly cleaned.

He felt the chill when he bared his utterly bald head. Sath Firedrake had gone prematurely bald, and despite his later asceticism he was sensitive about it. That "curse" had been incorporated into the Order to be shared by all the figurative descendants of Sath. Since it was considered a secret and a Mystery of the Order Most Old, an omo removed his skullcap noplace but here.

Falc reflected in outrage and some horror on Sench and Relashah, stripped utterly . . . and Vennashah too? He hoped his brothers had been dead before they were subjected to such humiliation and disgrace.

He tested his wind by muttering his penance while he swam in the pool in that complete cleansing he and his fellow Sons of Ashah received only here. It felt sinfully wonderful. His penance-litany he dedicated to the dead of Tem, victim of the angry planet, and to the survivors, who might by now be envying those who had died. His breath held well. He did, as Ashamal had wished him, enjoy his clean head.

He did not enjoy visiting poor Chondaven, but was glad he had done it. *O Ashah! Give me death that is my lot, but I beg you not to cripple me!*

He had to force himself to concentrate on the balance of his penance. He had memorized the Litany long ago. Repeating it required no conscious thought. His mind kept wanting to slide off into consideration of the murders and disappearances that might well also be deaths. His mind wanted to betray him by pondering his words—could someone be attacking the Sons of Ashah, murdering omos, *because they were omos?*—and those words of the Firedrake: What possible motive could there be for attacking the Order?

4

It was worse in the morning. Falc emerged from an hour's visit and meditation in the adytum of the god to learn that Vennashah was not just missing but assuredly dead too, murdered and stripped like the other two. It was, Falc mused, as if some ritual were being practiced on the Sons of Ashah. That led to two interesting thoughts which he deemed worthy of the Firedrake's consideration. Still loosely robed while his uniform was allowed to dry in the air, he requested another audience. The Master was not immediately available. Falc waited two hours, his mind busy without thinking once of Jinnery.

Then an aide to the High Brother came, with the summons from the Firedrake. That second entry into the great chamber and the recounting of those ideas led to further embarrassment: Naturally both had occurred to the Master. He was kind about it, though, and for once Falc left his presence without feeling like a chastised child.

He had agreed not to return to Lango save on orders. Therefore he would go on "home" to Lock, to place Jinnery within Kinneven's protection. Completely uniformed in his blacks once again and having persuaded the High Brother to "loan" him another derlin, he sent for Jinnery and their dargs. She was led to him, long white traveling robe covering her full sections. She looked either unhappy or angry or both. Falc affected not to notice. He knew she had been cloistered absolutely in a small room and was sure that it had not been to her liking. He would not give her opportunity to complain by asking how she was!

Besides, he was sure she would tell him.

SEVEN

Enforced sharing is both evil and a redundancy. Sharing is a voluntary act. Involuntary sharing is theft, whether it is accomplished by individuals or a group or large group called government; the State or citystate.

By the same token, no one shall be deprived of sharing all that she or he wishes!

—Sath Firedrake

He was right; Jinnery complained freely once they had traversed the pass and were making their way back down the mountainside. Falc saw no reason to try to explain or even respond, and did not. He did notice with pleasure that she had arrived at an important decision, in her solitude: she was calling her darg only "Tain," now. "Knoll or small mount/mound" was a silly name for a darg, but of course so was Harr. It was at least one swiftly pronounced syllable! Falc noticed, and perhaps he smiled inwardly. He made no comment.

After they had made fireless camp and eaten, she remarked that he had said nothing about what she called "her treatment" in the High Temple.

Seated comfortably on the ground across the little clearing from her, Falc saw no reason to say anything.

"Falc!"

He looked questioningly at her.

"Have you nothing to say?"

"You have been a guest in—"

"Guest!"

Falc went silent.

"Well? Is that all you're going to say?"

"I began, but you interrupted. Now I am waiting to be sure you are finished talking."

"Damn you for the most exasperating man on Sij! I am *through*, then."

"You have been fed, and been an overnight guest in the High Temple of Ashah. It's possible that no other woman has been so honored. It is a place of monks and their rites, of the Mysteries of Ashah. Naturally you could not wander about within a temple of men. Shall I say that I am sorry no one entertained you?"

She said nothing. Her angularly bony jaw was taut. Perhaps she was grinding her teeth. She stared a few inches above his head at the tree against which he had placed his back.

"I thought I might at least see something; see the Master, perhaps."

"You saw much. You saw the Mon-Ashah-re. You saw some of its people and its defenses. As for the Master . . . he looks like a man."

"You saw him?"

"Yes. I made my report. We shared knowledge. I stated my desire to return to Lango and punish Faradox. It was denied and I was given penance for the request. I was also chastised for bringing a woman into the Temple."

"Really!"

Falc only nodded.

"And your . . . your uniform was cleaned."

"Yes."

"Did you do that? Is that some ritual, too?"

"No. Yes."

"What? Which?"

"No I did not clean my clothing. An acolyte did. And yes, a ritual is involved."

Her tone continued querulous. "Yet no one offered to clean *my* clothing!"

Falc sighed and crossed his outstretched legs the other way. "Only men inhabit the High Temple. You expected a man—a monk—to clean your clothing, woman?"

"No, I just . . . oh thunder and blazes! I just didn't see or hear anything! I didn't know where you were and I had no one to talk to and nothing to do."

"You could brag the rest of your life about being the only woman to have guested in the Mon-Ashah-re, Jinnery. All there stay busy, and when they are no longer busy they pray or chant, and then they sleep that they may busy themselves on the morrow. No one was available to come and listen to you complain."

"Complain!"

"You said that you had no one to talk to, Jinnery. With you, 'talk' and 'complain' are the same."

She made her exasperated noise: "Oh-oooh!"

Certainly Falc made no reply to that.

After a time she snapped, "Complaints are not all you have heard from me!"

"No; sometimes it is an accusation disguised as a statement. Sometimes it is a cutting remark designed to hurt. For some reason you think it necessary to be unpleasant."

Her voice was very small when she said, "oh."

She said nothing after that, but sat thinking, as he did.

Next day he was aware that she was trying not to be unpleasant. That was less a positive act than the lack of a negative, but he wondered if she knew how to be pleasant. Having had that thought, he strove to be pleasant, and discovered that with her he was not sure how. He tried.

They rode, they talked little, they tried. That afternoon they heard the rumble and felt the tremor and swiftly dismounted. For a full minute they lay still and listened to the low rumble of the world, and to their heartbeats. Another minor quake had rippled through Sij, and was gone. Somewhere rocks probably fell. Somewhere trees may have toppled, and even buildings. Falc mouthed a prayer for the Temple. People alive and at work or play or asleep one instant might be dead the next, and even buried within the planet, by the planet. The level of a lake might have risen or fallen, and new scars might mark the seamed ground. Not here. For a full minute they clutched the tremorous ground, but nothing came of it.

They rose, they mounted, they rode on, thinking of insulted, ever-restless Sij. The sun at last quit a hazy sky and they camped under a rednut tree. He enforced some knife practice on her while he exercised. A writh's wail sounded and forced them both to pause and listen, but it was far away. What voices those creatures had!

Afterward they ate from knapsacks, along with rednuts. They made no fire.

"Falc," she said, just as it grew dark, "do you like women?"

"I'm not sure what you mean or want, but I don't dislike women."

"Not disliking isn't the same as liking."

"You didn't ask whether I liked men. The answer is the same. I don't like or dislike anything as a class. Not all dargs are likable, or all swords or food either. In general, I don't dislike men and I don't dislike women. In particular, I like some and don't like others."

He was uncertain as to what had prompted the question, but Falc was uncomfortable. He remembered her coming to the barn that night, and he was nervous, for it was night now and they were alone together and he could not send her back to the house. After quite a time of silence, she surprised him.

"In . . . in general and in particular," she said in a measured way, apparently having a difficult time making the statement rather than considering each word, "I don't like the embrace of men."

"Umm."

"Isn't that of any interest to you? I mean, it's hardly natural, is it?"

He kept his yawn quiet, so that she wouldn't think it was a deliberate comment. He could no longer see her face at all clearly, and was happy that they were both almost invisible to each other. Their facial expressions were, anyhow.

He asked the darkness: "Do you mean the sexual embrace?"

Her voice was tiny: "yes."

"Always, do you mean?"

"yes."

"Hmm. Excuse me, but . . . what about œstrus? Twice a year, when all women. . . ?"

"I feel it," the darkness said in her voice, still only just audible. "But even then the urge is not great. Not the way it's . . . supposed to be."

"The way it is with other women, you mean—or seems to be."

"Yes."

"It is . . . unusual," he allowed. It was easier to talk of such matters in the dark, and he knew it was for her, too. He surprised her by saying more. "Yet you came to me that night, in the barn."

"You didn't believe me, did you. I really was sent. I didn't think you would welcome me . . . that way, but he *sent* me."

"Querry."

"Yes."

"You're right. Even though you had been hateful to me, sneering and scornful, I didn't believe you when you said he had sent you."

"Do you now?"

He took care to pause before he answered, so that she would perceive it as a considered reply and be more satisfied with it. "Yes."

"Good."

"Querry sent you to me in friendship and some feeling of guilt. You slept with him?"

"Yes. *Slept* with him. And . . . let him use me, when the need came upon him. I didn't really respond or care for it, but didn't let him know that I really wasn't interested. I mean it really wasn't fun and I'm really not interested. Really. I know that makes me strange," she went on in a sudden blurt, "but it's the way I am."

"It's not an entirely new concept to me," he said into the darkness.

"You . . . don't think it's freakish . . . Falc?"

"It's the way some people are," he said. "Women and some men, too."

"Really?"

"Yes."

"I mean you're not just making it up to try to make me feel better?"

"Jinnery: have you ever told me anything just to try to make me feel better?"

"Umm . . . no."

"Neither have I."

She was emboldened to amplify on her admission, or declaration: "What I mean is that I am not a sexual creature, and would prefer to do without the sexual embrace."

"Uh . . . I have not been considering it, Jinnery."

"That is not what I meant! I was *not* intimating—" She broke off.

He said, "Sorry, Jinn," which surprised her. "I did want you to know that." Then: "Some women are able to live so."

Her voice returned partially to the scathing tone he knew better than this soft-voiced admitting: "Are they? In a world where strength counts and men rule and women serve them? How?"

"By being strong. Being unpleasant as a ward against being embraced is not always necessary. Some run away and hide," he said, thinking of the Sisters of Tyrvena. "Women can—you can substitute strength for resentment."

Minutes passed, and he was sliding down into sleep when the darkness spoke again, in her voice:

"That's your history, isn't it. The essence and philosophy of Falc of Risskor."

Falc did not reply.

2

Next day they were more comfortable with each other, and they talked. They talked of the weather, the countryside, the places and things they passed, and of the old Empire.

Falc had just realized that he had ceased being offended by her sections—most because he hardly noticed them anymore, when she much surprised him with an admission and a question he certainly did not expect:

"Falc . . . uh, f-freak or not, it keeps getting harder for me to see the purpose of life. Does the Order have an answer for that, too? Just out of curiosity, you understand!"

Falc ignored that disclaimer and spoke solemnly: "Years ago I had cause to ask the same question," he told her. "Fortunately, I was speaking to the Master."

"The present one?"

"Yes. I am not so old as to have outlived a Firedrake, Jinnery."

"I thought that perhaps to be Master a man had to be old to begin with. Besides, everyone's old when you're twenty and twice an orphan. And the Master—did he have a satisfactory answer?"

"That depends on what you consider satisfactory! It's enough for me. Rather than reply at once, he asked me a question in return. He said: 'Men create suffering and women suffer. Should we then consider this their purpose?' "

She looked at him with her brows up. "The *Firedrake*! I am amazed that a *man* would say that! It's truth, of course, and part of what's been bothering me! And did you have an answer to that?"

"He didn't expect one; I knew that. I waited, and he gave me what might be a parable. ' "No," ' a retired warrior and conqueror and liberator once replied to the same question, long ago. ' "Let us not then question the purpose of life, but Life itself. Has yours purpose?" ' The seeker to whom Sath Firedrake said those words went away, saying that he had not been helped and might as well have stayed at home."

She stared away into the distance. "His mind was closed," she murmured at last in a faraway voice, pursing and working her thin-lipped mouth as if physically chewing the concept.

Falc was pleased by her perception. "And his heart," he said.

"Careful. I hear paradoxes coming from your mouth, Sir Fa—Sir Deathknight."

Falc nodded. He remembered that she had said just that to him, before. He made the same reply as he had in the farmhouse that night in Zain: "You do! All is paradox, Jinnery. Isn't a religious man and a monk who is also an extremely competent warrior—and killer—a paradox? A woman who does not care for men and thus presumably does not want children? Are we not a paradox, just the two of us in company?"

"Perhap I'd best *meditate* on that for the next few kilometers," she said with a mild satiric emphasis.

He did, whether she did so or not. Now and again he glanced at her, still surprised. Rather abruptly he realized that they were riding along under an amber sky. The day had passed faster than others had done since her joining him.

"I've been trying not to complain," she said soon after that, at sunset, "but I'm tired of our junky cold meals."

He thought about that. He had noticed the first, and he agreed with her in the second. "So am I. Let's go into that little wood and see if another sort of dinner presents itself."

They rode in among the trees. He found a ricker's trail and new droppings, and said so.

She smiled. "Shall I collect some dry wood?"

Falc nodded. He set off stealthily, and was able to kill a chubby gray-blue ricker. He carried it rather proudly back to her, along with some old dry wood. He was pleased to discover that she had been collecting herbs and tubers—and kindling. She cooked as if she enjoyed it, with nothing to prove. The crackle and the aroma were beyond welcome, and their mouths watered. That anticipation helped turn this little hot meal into a feast.

When they had eaten he got her to practice some more with the knife. He told her that she showed promise. He saw her practically glow at being complimented and remembered how badly she had responded that night in her home. *How she has changed*, he thought, but forewent mentioning it to her.

What she could not do was cut at him. Yet after watching him exercise and practice, she agreed to use a stick as substitute for a knife. She attacked him three times. He blocked each "cut." Once he remarked also that he had just cut off her arm. The other two times he disarmed her *relatively* painlessly; the second time her fingertips tingled. When he stopped it, she was panting and noticed that he was not.

"Falc . . . what you said this afternoon—is that what you are, Sir Falc, Cousin Falc, Sir Deathknight, Son of Ashah, Omo?"

"I am all that," he said, with a satirical note.

"No, I mean what you said: an extremely competent warrior and killer?"

"Yes. I am that."

"Is that why that youngster was so respectful at the High Temple?—and others?"

"That's part of it. I am . . . they also know me as a dedicated servant of Ashah and the Order, and of my Contractor."

"Kinneven, Holder of Lock."

As she had grown to expect with regard to unnecessary comments and questions, he saw no reason to reply.

"A servant, to Holder Kinneven of Lock."

"Yes."

"The ever-confident man who can face down anyone, best anyone if he won't face down; the arrogant Falc who chooses when to answer and when not to answer . . . a *servant*? Another paradox."

"So it is."

"I—what?" She broke off, because as she had started to speak he raised a hand, palm out and all three fingers up. She recognized his staying motion.

"I have just decided to tell you. I didn't before, because I don't need your gratitude and had no care what you thought."

"Does that mean you care what I think, now?"

"Don't push, cousin," he said, and at that instant Jinnery saw what few others had seen: that this man did smile, but only with his eyes. "The four men who—who destroyed your fam . . . your life . . . they are dead."

She swallowed. A long breath left her and she sort of sagged back against the tree he had twice chopped in the drama of his practice. She looked down and ran both hands along her section-clad thighs.

He waited.

After a minute or so she asked, "You?"

"Yes."

"All four? You alone, Falc?"

"Yes. They waylaid me. Got ahead of me, somehow; some mighty fast riding while Harr and I only ambled. They were stretched across the road, waiting to kill me. That was their purpose. They wanted *me*. Perhap if Chalis hadn't said I was his—your cousin. . . ." He broke off to gesture helplessly.

"At any rate. Their mistake was in facing me. They could have slain me from ambush, or perhap succeeded if they had merely charged. Instead they wanted drama. They had to prolong it, to gloat, and at last I charged them."

"What!"

When he said nothing but only stood looking down, she said, "Falc? Four men—very well-armed men, and murderers—

lay in wait for you, and gloated, and *you* charged *them*. I'm
sorry I made it sound like a question; it's so hard to *believe*!''

He looked embarrassed, or something like. ''No matter
how good a man is, four have an advantage over one. Taking
the attack to them gives me a brief advantage: surprise. I've
done it before. It serves to cut the odds by one, at once.''

He described the murderous quartet. She nodded.

''Yes,'' she said softly. ''They are the ones.''

Then she surprised him anew: she turned away. Falc sighed
and told her no more. He should have heeded his original
decision, he thought, and kept to himself the fact that he had
avenged Querry and Chalis, although without knowing it.

Later, after they had weathered a minor quake and a scary
windstorm that snapped and hurled branches as if they were
twigs, they sat watching the fire without feeding it. The fire
drew crellies. They danced about it, flirting with the brightness; flirting with death. Some found it. Falc asked if she
would care to have him train her darg to come to call.
Deliberately he referred to it as ''Shabtain.''

Yes, Jinnery would. And perhaps . . . perhaps they should
use just his *nickname*, ''Tain.''

''Good idea,'' Falc said, solemnly and with no sign of
comment or amusement. ''And let's both be sure to call him
that, a lot. He must be made to understand that it's his
name.''

''I think he already does, Falc.''

He nodded. Yes. They were not stupid, these ugly creatures of mutation. And, he at last knew, neither was Jinnery.

3

The rain was hard and violent that night. They survived
it. Next day Falc of Risskor made a woman a valuable gift:
the jewel-handled dagger from Holder Chasmal of Lango.

''You know how to use a knife. You can be safe with it or
dangerous with it. You deserve a good one.''

She stammered surprised thanks and flushed at accepting it.
Moments later she turned her head away and kept it so, and
he pretended not to notice that she was quietly weeping and

striving to keep him from knowing it. Falc saw no reason to say anything and saw definite reason to say nothing. He was content to ride in silence for a while, trying to look dour while feeling very warm and pleased that he had given her the knife—and further, that she was touched.

When she again turned her profile to him, riding beside him, he pointed and suggested that they go into that meadow to begin the training of Shabtain-no-more.

"Falc," she said slowly, in that quiet voice that made him give her his full attention, "later. I want to hear about it. I want you to tell me about it. About those four men."

"Uh . . ."

She turned her head with a jerk to show him a fierce-eyed glare from pupils expanded to roundness. "Tell me, Falc! All of it! I want details—everything you can remember!"

"Uh . . . Jinn . . ."

"What? What, Falc?"

"I'm . . . I'm not sure I can do that. For one thing, I don't always remember anything like every detail, once my my blood's aboil and my sword is out. For another—"

"Is that what happens? The blood boils?"

"Something like. I hear it roaring; I hear my heart pounding in my ears and yet I feel chill—cool, I suppose; just doing the job as fast as I possibly can because if I don't one of them might do it better."

She stared, and her hand left her thigh to start toward him, quavering. Almost she touched the black-clad arm of the man riding beside her; almost. Then she drew back her hand. She had heard him. Did he know what he had just told her? Had he intended to tell her so much about himself? Her teeth dented her lower lip, deeply. Tain plodded on beside Harr, and she continued to stare at the side of the face of this too often dour, too often silent and more than competent man of weapons. He was gazing straight ahead, and she was sure it was because he did not wish to look at her. It was hard to know whether a man's jaw was tight, when he wore a beard!

Suddenly her hand leaped across that space between them. Thumb and all three fingers clamped his arm, clamped and squeezed.

"Falc! I need to know, cousin. I *need* to hear it! *I need to see those men die*!"

He turned to look at her then, and down at her fingers on him, the knuckles all pale with her clutching, and back into her face. Torture showed in those deep midnight pools that were his eyes, and she saw that he hated this. This man among men—this almost superhuman man really did not like talking at all, really, much less telling of his—his feats. And she wanted details.

She ignored the anguish in his eyes, the tortured set of his face. Jinnery only stared, waiting.

Slowly, Falc nodded. Her hand dropped away. He turned his head to stare ahead again, and he began talking. Very quietly he talked for the next several kilometers, and he answered every question as well as he possibly could. He even told her of the beheadings, and his sending the heads off in the direction of their unworthy master in Lango.

At last she said, "Thank you, Cousin Falc. Thank you for killing them, and thank you for telling me." She heaved a huge sigh. "I know you didn't want to, Son of Ashah. Thank you for letting me force you."

Falc did not reply. Falc said nothing for the next several kilometers.

4

"A darg is not stupid," he said, when they dismounted under a big lone lajenta tree in the sprawling meadow and he glanced about, as he always did. Ever cautious, ever suspicious. Never, never had Jinnery felt so secure, or Esphodine either. She saw that he saw nothing, no possible menace.

"They enjoy serving," he said, "and they like to please. It isn't difficult. It's done with kindness."

She put her head on one side. "Kindness. Dargs."

"Yes."

"A strange concept, kindness to dargs or to enemies."

"I have been known to be kind to enemies. It is easier with dargoni, and feels much better. Come."

The dark man began walking through the tall blue grass into the field. He heard the rustle of ballooning aquamarine leggings whispering together, and knew she was coming.

The dargs watched while their masters walked away; twenty

paces, then a few more. Falc stopped. He glanced about. He squatted, white cloth folding about him like a tent, and she watched him overturn a palm-sized stone.

"Ahh." He straightened. She saw him transfer something from one gauntleted fist to the other as he turned. He bellowed the word: "HARR!"

Harr rushed to them at the waddle-trot, an ungainly hulk in greenish slate-blue whose each step was a lunge through tall grass the color of manganese. Falc spoke nice words, just words—many of them "Harr" and "good boy," she noticed—and opened his fist to the beast. For an instant Jinnery saw the pallid, fat worm in the gloved palm; then she saw Harr's tongue, and the grubworm was gone. Falc patted his darg's nose. Suddenly impossibly dark blue eyes were looking at her.

"Call Tain. Just the name."

"Tain!" she called, and saw the creature's golden-eyed gaze shift to her. He looked alert and attentive. He also did not move. "TAINN!"

"Take this," Falc said, extending his fist.

"Wha—oh. Another of those worms?"

He nodded, gazing at her, and his arm remained extended. Not wishing to take it, she did. He saw a tremor run through her as he deposited the squirmy grubworm in her palm.

"Some farmgirl," he said, but his voice was not unkind and she swallowed the rejoinder that tried to leap to her lips.

"Wait here," he said, and strode back to her darg.

She watched the flutter of the white derlin and thought how pretty it was, how graceful on such a big man; such a big dark man. White and black. It was what he believed in, she thought in a burst of realization.

He began talking very quietly as he approached Tain on silent feet, with much use of the creature's name. Then he was beside Tain, patting its thick neck. His hand slid into its halter, between cheek-strap and head.

"Call him, Jinnery!"

"TAINNN!"

Falc felt the darg quiver, but it did not move. At once he began walking back to Jinnery, hustling the creature. Harr watched.

"See how he comes when you call? Goo-ood Tain. Open

your hand and extend it to him. Hold it flat. No, Harr; Harr bide!''

Tain flicked the grub from her hand and Jinnery immediately wiped it on her derlin, several times. Harr's hiss sounded like a sigh.

Falc returned to the stone. He used his dagger to dig in the softer dirt under it and straightened with both fists closed. "Now back to the tree, Jinn.''

Once again they walked away from the dargs, and turned to look at them. Once again Falc called Harr, who came at the galumph. This time he received only rubs, pats, and words.

"You never know do you, big boy?'' Falc said, and to Jinnery: "That's important, too, Jinn. You won't be able to give him something every time, and he needs to know that early.''

She nodded. "Now?''

When he nodded, she called Tain again. The darg definitely came to attention and definitely stared at her from bright yellow eyes. Then a flit of purple and yellow with tan caught his attention, and his tongue shot out to take the butterfly out of the air. Tain missed and looked shocked. Drool dripped.

Falc extended a fisted hand to Jinnery.

She showed him a distasteful look. "Ugh.''

"We are training a darg,'' he reminded her, with an exaggerated air of patience. "*Your* darg.''

"*You* have a glove and don't have to feel the icky wormies squirming in your hand,'' she pointed out, with an exaggerated air of . . . something.

Solemnly he removed his glove. He handed it to her. With exaggerated unconcern, he transferred the grub into his bare hand. Once her hand was lost in his big gauntlet and she extended it, he placed the wriggly white creature in the palm. It looked twice as white there, against the black. He turned with a rustle of his derlin and strode toward her darg.

Tain was still looking around for more butterflies when Falc approached. Again he took the creature's halter. Again Jinnery called. Again the omo hustled the darg to her, and Tain took his reward from her hand while receiving lots of undeserved praise. Harr watched, drooling while he let his tongue loll, definitely trying to look as pitiful as possible.

With a sigh and a shake of his head, Falc helped him find some large ants.

On the second try next day Tain came hurrying to her when she called, and was rewarded, praised, and petted. Within another day he was following her around unbidden and they began the harder task of training him to stay, on command.

EIGHT

The gods create life, whilst mortals take it as if
they had the right.
　　　　　　　　　　　　　　—Sar Sarlis

The dead have advantage over the living and
this is why: the dead need never fear dying.
　　　　　　　　　　　　　　—the fifth Master

For once, Falc was caught by surprise.

It very nearly cost him his life.

He and Jinnery had stopped a few meters off the road for
rest and more defense tutoring and practice for her, with
knives. He was showing her the silly 'lectric pistol and
lecturing caustically on the thing when the three men came
along. That was what saved Falc's life, that and Jinnery.

They were three riders, male, wearing no city's or individual's colors. One was obviously sick or hurt. He reeled in his
saddle, head down and back bowed, hands clutching the
pommel. The round-faced one with the bushy beard seemed
preoccupied with him, but noticed the two beside the road
and called out in a nervous voice.

"Know anything about what do when a man's had a—a
stroke's what I think it's called. . . ?"

"Get him over here in the shade, to begin with," Jinnery said.

The men turned their dargoni off the road to ride across the
grass toward her. She and Falc had dismounted under two

155

patriarchal finleaf trees so huge that they practically formed a grove of themselves. A few seconds ago Jinnery had not only put the throwing knife into one of them, but into the area just above the light patch in the bark that was her target.

Falc remembered later that he had glanced over at his mailcoat, slung over a branch just low enough for him to hang it there. Because they were working with knives and Jinnery's throws sometimes went wild and worse, they had tethered Harr and Tain well away.

Just as the trio of travelers entered the coolth of the shade of those towering trees, the sick man swayed and began to tilt. Clearly he was about to fall off his mount. Falc forgot the little pistol still in his hand as he pounced to break the fellow's fall. That was when metal rasped its way out of its sheath: one of the other two drew and struck so fast that Falc had no time to do anything save try to hurl himself backward—not far enough—and to grunt, as the sword chopped into his left arm and he felt the blow to that side.

"—*that*, Deathknight!" he heard his attacker's raspy voice snarl.

Even as he felt the horribly forceful blow that staggered him, the "Deathknight" was jerking up his good arm to squeeze the trigger of Chasmal's gift pistol. He heard a faint crackling sound, smelled the acrid odor as of fried air, and watched his attacker stiffen in his saddle. The man shivered. Then he fell. Even while Falc realized that the blood was rushing from his head to the detriment of his vision and thinking, he knew a sensation of wonder mingled with elation.

The damned technoweapon had worked! He had just shot a man with the device he had always thought of as described in one complete phrase: silly little pistol.

But there were three of them, and Falc was wounded. The man supposedly in need of help experienced a miraculous recovery. All in an instant he became very much alive and very healthy. Short and burly, he kicked a russet-clad leg at the man in black at the same time as he straightened in his saddle, to draw sword.

The pistol was in Falc's fist. It had worked. It had served him. Too, he had been wounded in his sword arm and knew he was bleeding. The blood was rushing straight down from his head and out of him, leaving him increasingly light of

head. The zinger was in his hand and it had proved not silly;
it had served him. He twitched that hand over and triggered
the weapon.

He heard nothing and smelled nothing. Neither did the
short burly man who was not ill; obviously he also felt
nothing. His sword scraped out and started coming around at
a dizzy and increasingly weak Falc of Risskor.

Something made a *whish* sound past the omo's cheek, from
behind.

The guardless hilt of a throwing knife—his—appeared in
the man's thigh. He let out a yell as he jerked violently and
actually dropped his sword.

Incompetent ass, Falc thought, whose life had just been
saved by a woman. The un-sick man's legs had jerked invol-
untarily and his darg responded to the inadvertent signal with
dargish reflexes and competence. It lurched ahead at speed,
and kept going. Sudden acceleration combined with laxness
of hands and body caused its wounded rider to be thrust
violently and jerkily backward. He toppled back over his
mount's croup and fell off. The darg kept going. Falc moved
swiftly, despite his pain and the effort that exacerbated it. As
he rather stupidly bent for the fellow's sword, he heard the
stomp of darg feet and something made a *whish* sound above
his head. He knew that this time it was no knife intended for
another; he had just accidentally and most fortuitously ducked
under a vicious sword-slash at the back of his neck.

Oh. Oh yes, he thought muzzily, or almost-thought. *There
are three.*

One leg stiffened while one bent to throw himself aside. He
grunted again at the pain that tore into his arm and up his side
like a bolt of lightning. He sagged to his knees while some
invisible beast gnawed at his whole left side and murky water
flowed through his brain. He was aware of a growing light-
ness in his head, and a faint humming that existed only inside
his skull. He hated it. He felt ridiculous, and shamed. Caught!
Hurt!

And with Jinnery to see!

Even then he was dropping the pistol and, awkwardly
cranking his right elbow high and out to the side, drawing his
dagger. The fallen man was moaning, awkwardly scrabbling
to retrieve his sword even though one leg clad in russet and a

spreading blotch of darker red was useless to him, its thigh muscle pierced through and pinned almost to the bone. The ground rumbled and no one could afford to pay attention. The omo's lurching slash at the downed man's wrist missed as Falc lost his balance. He succeeded only in cutting the man's weapon-hand open and felt stupid, incompetent and ridiculous. He heard the fellow cry out but that small exertion sent more pain sizzling into Falc, and he fell.

What a mess, he thought, while the pain lessened with the muddy water enveloping his brain, turning the hum to a buzzing sound. *The only competent fighter among us is Jinnery!*

He didn't even know that the third man was wrestling his semicompetent darg around again, intent on his omo quarry, stupidly and incompetently forgetting or ignoring the skinny woman in the silly blue-green balloon-leggings, who blind-sided him and stabbed him just below the ribs with a jeweled dagger, and that the fellow cried out and rode away wounded and reeling in his saddle, wearing that handsome sticker of Chasmal of Lango in his side. Many meters away, it worked its way out and fell to the ground. Falc knew nothing. Falc was down, lying sprawled as if dead.

2

"Falc! Oh Falc, you're *hurt*!"

"Uh," he said, and saw no reason for further comment on the obvious. "The—the dismounted one . . ."

"Two fled, both wounded. The one on the ground I—I just saw to. But Falc, you—"

"Saw to?"

She answered in a rush of words: "If you must know I picked up his sword and chopped his neck." She shuddered. "This is not my blood."

Falc tried to look at whatever she was showing him, but couldn't see very well. He knew what she was trying to show him: blood. She had gotten caught in the red fountain when she chopped through the jugular of the man with the wounded thigh and hand. It was unfortunate that she had put him beyond telling them anything, but Falc refrained from castigating her. It looked very much, he thought muzzily, as if he had been the target not of thieves or highwaymen but of assassins. Again.

Because I am Falc or because I am an omo?

"But about you, Falc—"

"My left arm. It is leaking quite a bit."

"Oh!"

"Little matter; my right's the better one anyhow. I'n do 'thout the left awhile. No wait—woman, I am an omo! You can't—"

Yes she could. Ignoring the Order and its rules, Jinnery sliced open his left sleeve to find a deep chop-wound that was beyond "leaking quite a bit"; it had bled a lot and was still flowing. She told him so, and that the same swordcut had hit him in the side, too. That slash had made a shallow gash and might have hit a rib.

"I can hold it. I—I'll just mount . . ."

"Can't even bring yourself to say 'Help me onto Harr,' can you?" Then she tried to mitigate that sneering although entirely true observation by saying, "You do have an arm like a big gnarly branch! And if you had any meat on your body this cut in the side *couldn't* have hit the rib!"

"Got to—got to get on . . . Harr . . ."

Her breath came out hard, with a gusty sound. "You are not going to like this or find it easy, Sir Falc of Risskor, but . . . you needed my help just then, and still do."

"N-n . . ."

"Your job is to be quiet and be still. My job is to patch you a bit. Here, this will work," she said, and he heard ripping cloth. He lay supine, staring upward, and suddenly the sky looked like trouble.

"Sky's gone . . . all . . . hazy . . . darkening . . ."

"Oh, Falc! No," she said in a pained voice, working, hurting him though he would never show it. "No, cousin; you've lost so much blood that it's affecting your—you can't see straight."

Damn, Falc thought, *I am hurt!* But Jinnery was talking on, far more rapidly than usual.

"You could spend the rest of the day trying to get up and get to Harr, too. No; you'd not last that long; you're 'leaking' too much. I have an idea that just getting him loose is beyond you right now, much less mounting.''

She grunted with effort, talking to be talking, babbling because she had fought, and had even killed a man, and Falc was hurt and if she didn't talk she was sure she'd get the shakes and she needed to do something other than look at all this blood. She kept talking, in a rush that left her brain no time to find proper words. It and she were functioning on pure adrenaline, anyhow.

''That's a—whatever you call it, when you tie something around a wound above the around your arm above the wound to stop the blood from just pumping right into it and out; I saw a phik—physikan do that once in Lango and I've got a bandage on it, too. Now listen, Falc. You be *still*. Just rest a minute while I go fetch the dargs over here. Then we'll see how many people it takes to get you on Harr.'' She rose with a rustle of her sections and stood looking down at him. ''We really should stay here for a while in the shade and let you rest and better still sleep, but those two might come back and maybe with friends too and besides staying here isn't doing anything really good for your arm. Remember the house you said you saw, way over there? I hope you were right. We'll head that way, and just stay off the road. Be still and quiet now. I'll be right back.''

Sure does talk a lot, Falc thought.

He passed out or at least drifted off for a minute or three, to regain some semblance of his senses when she was again standing over him. So was Harr. Harr was nuzzling his master.

''The dead one's darg stayed instead of following the others isn't that ridiculous I think he's interested in Tain anyhow we have the beast. Oh, my blood did *not* boil I just just had to uh I barely knew what I was doing. Now we have to get you on Harr.''

''I'n do it,'' Falc said, and started to rise, and accidentally put weight on his left arm. Lightning jolted through the rush of darkness in his brain and he fell back.

''This sure would be a good chance for me to get you to admit a few things, wouldn't it! Well, I won't. Shall we leave the—Falc? Can you hear me?''

"Yes." He waited a moment before making a sentence's worth of effort: "Can you get the dead one on his darg?"

"Oh Falc! You mean you want to take him along?"

"Yes."

"Ugh."

"I under . . . stand. Perhap . . . tie a rope around his . . . ankles and . . . to saddle?"

"Oh, oh, that's worse! The trouble is he's so messy and besides a dead man weighs a lot more than a live one!"

How do you know that, Falc of Risskor thought, but said only, "Yes."

"Well . . . I'll *try.*"

"Wait. I'll get . . . I'll—" Falc broke off and released a long sigh. "Help me up and I can help."

She heard his words all right, heard what the massively independent Falc of Risskor said: the admission. Yet contrary to what she'd have thought, she wasn't quite able to smile. "We can get you on your feet easily enough but that won't make you able to help."

"Yes." Falc gave her instructions.

She was right; geting him onto his feet was not all that difficult. His left arm was obviously totally useless to him, but he had his legs and his other arm, and skinny or not Jinnery was a farmer and stronger than she looked. Then he proved to be right, too: with Harr crowding the dead man's mount while Falc leaned against the dutiful and seemingly placid darg, he and Jinnery got the short thick man across the saddle. She had not exaggerated: he was a mess, with his head dangling sidewise on half a neck covered with blood. Acting on Falc's instructions, she was even able to use the man's own rope to tie both his ankles, pass the line under the darg, and secure it to both his dangling wrists.

"Pull," Falc enjoined.

She grunted to let him know she was, and tied the rope.

"Should I use cord from your pack to tie to the darg's halter, to lead him?"

"He stayed," Falc said. "He will follow. Let's . . . mount."

You mean let's get you somehow into the saddle, she corrected mentally, but uncharacteristically kept the thought to herself. She no longer felt the need to push it.

It took a while. Once Falc's wounded arm got some-

how between his body and Harr and took pressure, and Falc
blacked out. Jinnery held him up until he came back and they
began again. Harr helped by standing still as rock. Somehow
the three of them got his master into the saddle. Wincing and
trying not to show it, he laid his useless arm across his left
thigh and accepted Harr's reins from Jinnery. She patted his
thigh without thinking, and swung to her mount. Falc saw
that one of her sections' legs was torn and missing some
fabric.

The dargs bore them slowly, plodding away from the trees
into a grassy field dotted with bushes. The dead man's darg
followed. Pausing only long enough for her to retrieve her
dagger, they rode across a broad field and descended a short
şloping hill to cross a tree-edged gulley, where for the first
time Falc let her hear him groan. Somehow he managed to
stay in the saddle while they ascended the other side. His
head was aswim and after a while he dared not look down.
Through more grassland, and around a bushy outgrowth left
alone so long it had achieved great height and spread wide
with aerial rooting. As they rounded it they saw that Falc had
seen aright: here was a farmhouse with two outbuildings.
They heard hammering, inside the smaller building.

Fergs hissed and hurried, getting out of their way. The
shed door opened and a man appeared. He wore farmer's
skirts and a great big old wide-brimmed hat, and he bore a
hammer at the end of one burly arm. His brows were dark
and what they could see of his hair was too, while his
unkempt beard and mustache were gray and white with a few
strands of slate blue. His big-nosed face was adorned with
something one seldom saw, despite the glass industry and old
knowledge: he wore spectacles.

They did not have to say a word. He saw it all in a glance.

"Must have been more than just that one, Sir Knight of the
Order, since you're hurt. Let's get you off that darg and into
the house. I've got some good powder, and sure do know
how to make a poultice."

"So do I," Jinnery couldn't help saying.

Falc tried to refuse the bed, but Parshann told them it
had been his son's until the boy had growed up and took off
for city life. It was unoccupied and had been for two years.

Parshann lived alone, unless one counted no fewer than six lean and sinuous cacks, all meandering in and out of the house at will and draping themselves colorfully anywhere they pleased.

Parshann joined Falc in his insistence: Jinnery must not help get the omo's clothing off, and furthermore must leave the room. Parshann closed the door and Jinnery fumed. A cack brushed her balloon-legginged ankle. She glanced down and said nice words. Red and gold and white with a bluish tail, the cack paused and looked back. Jinnery squatted and the cack quite forgot where it had been going. Soon Jinnery was sitting on the floor holding and stroking the animal while she wept and wept.

Parshann and Falc were meanwhile relieving the omo of his upper garments. The farmer saw the dark man's pain and only nodded, saying nothing; to mention such a man's stoic bravery would be to insult him.

He removed the tourniquet and rubbed the arm, muttering an apology. It leaked a little more, and then the flow slacked. Parshann eased off the bandage.

"She done a good job, Sir Knight of the Order."

"Name's Falc."

"No! I've heared of you, Sir Falc! I'm Parshann, 'n' you'd never believe I was born just within Risskor, would you! Never mind, never mind. I'm older'n you and remember it but just sort of hazy. You've sure atoned for all of it an' more, bein' not only an omo but the best, for a lot of years. 'Nough about that, Sir Falc. Let's see . . . huh! This rib's cracked, sure. Feel that?"

"Uh."

"Sorry. Cracked all right. Hurts worser'n a big cut, don't it! Well, we'll powder the arm and get a poultice on it. A little powder on your side'll do. Then we'd best see how tight we can get some cloth and maybe rope around you. That'll keep that rib from biting you ever' time you move. I've heared you've took as many as four sworders at a time, Sir Falc. How many'd it take to do this?"

"Three."

"Um. Sometimes a man gets took by surprise, don't he. That hurt?"

"Not for long."

"Good attitude. Now we'll just . . . there. Ever hear of Sir Parneris?"

"Of course. He—ah! Kin to you, friend Parshann?"

"My brother. You know all about 'im, then. Joined the Order long 'fore you did b'cause we're both a deal older'n you. Died three years ago. Is it true it was just natural causes?"

"It's—uh! Sorry—true, Parshann. Our brother Parneris was visiting the High Temple, and one morning he just didn't wake up. Heart, likely. It happens."

"Um. Now if you can just bend this way a little—good! Now what I need you to do, Sir Falc, is just lay back and be real still while I go put together a poultice. That's something I learned real good, when Helky was alive."

"Your wife?"

"Nahh. Widow of a neighbor who died. Pretty homely, but she was a good worker, cooked good, and knew how to give a man a good screw even when she wasn't in heat."

"Ah." Falc saw no reason to say anything more.

"She died last year, damn it—no, it was year b'fore last. Real shame, her leavin' me that way. About the same as Parneris, I guess; just keeled over one day. Couldn't breathe and her arm had gone dead, and then she did. Damn. You get to like a woman, you know? I'd lived alone ten years before that. But her man died and there was Helky, needin', and I didn't even know I was. But I must've was; I sure got accustomed to company. A man gets accustomed to company, don't he."

This time Falc elected not to reply. He couldn't say no to this man, and didn't want to say yes. Couldn't.

"I expect that woman 'th you has had enough time to cry by now. I'll go fix up the poultice. Maybe get her to do it while I plant that man you brought in."

"You don't have to do that, Parshann," Falc said, realizing that any man who misjudged Parshann as unwise was worse than unwise.

"Uh-huh," Parshann said. "Lay quiet!"

He left the room to find Jinnery in the kitchen, sweeping, while four cackoni watched. Jinnery's eyes were bloodshot and all dark and puffy under.

"He's going to do all right," Parshann told her. "Hard part's going to keep a man like that layin' still. Might be better if I *didn't* tape his rib! Know anything about making poultices?"

"Uh . . . yes . . . but not for a wound like that."

Still wearing his hat, he was gathering this and that from a cupboard. "Well, listen. You can be cookin' it while I go bury that man you brought in."

"Burn the swine!"

Parshann shook his head, still hatted. "Can't stand the stink," he said, and gave her instructions, and went for a shovel.

3

They could not stay here, Falc told Jinnery. They damned well were going to stay here, Jinnery told Falc. Parshann had forced upon her a tunic and leggings. Both were too large, but they were clean and they were female, and the nice soft gold-colored cord tied the pale green tunic well.

"It is not going to be easy on us, Falc; either of us, having to lie there and be tended by me. But we have to stay, and Parshann's got things he has to do. Just set your mind to it, cousin: staying here and being tended by me is what you have to do."

Powdered, poulticed, taped and on his back in the bed that had been Parshann's son's, Falc turned his face away. "No, and it is not easy living with knowledge that a—that you saved my live. A Son of Ashah does not have to have his life saved."

"By a woman, especially. That's what you were going to say, wasn't it."

"N—" Falc broke off and turned his head back her way as if it were an effort. He met her eyes. "Yes."

She nodded, aware of having gained a lot from him, in that single word of admission so difficult for such a man. She was pleased, but without the feeling of triumph she would have expected.

"I shall not call you Deathknight again, Falc. We both know I haven't been, but I want you to know that isn't by accident. Uh . . . perhap my darg were bettter named Tay? I had a cack named that once and it was a good loving cack. Got killed under a cart wheel. I think my darg will recognize Tay as well as Tain, don't you?''

Falc's face showed nothing. "Probably."

Abruptly she half turned, almost in a jerk, to send a sharp glance about the nice little room. Parshann had made the house himself, and he had done well. It was just that apparently he cleaned house even less often than he took off his big hat.

"This place is filthy and you need nourishment! Oh, the situations I get myself into! Sleep if you can, Falc. I'll wake you when I have some soup or stew or whatever can be gleaned here. Old Parshann's going to have the first decent meal he's had in over a year!"

Falc understood the sudden embarrassment and discomfort that made her return to her critical manner in an abrupt explosion of act and speech and exaggerated industriousness. He wondered about that last braggadocious part, though, until Parshann told him later that he'd just had the best meal he'd had in over a year. Falc tried not to chuckle. It would only hurt his cracked rib.

4

Falc was brought out of a drifty sleep late that night by the sudden illumination that entered the room.

He swallowed. He got himself up in the bed in time to see the *Manifestation* coalese out of the familiar ethereal luminosity: a wavery silvery-gray figure, robed and faceless in the helm and war-mask of Sath Firedrake. At once came from it that hollow, echoic voice Falc knew.

"Say to me the Credo of the Order."

"The purpose . . . of the Order Most Old is to preserve the social order," Falc said. "Thus the purpose of the Order Most Old is to hold and cherish knowledge; to hold ever foremost its duty to the social order; to dispense it with love and great care for its value and its danger to the social order; to assist commic—communication among its leaders; and to strive ever to maintain that social order." He broke the ritual then: "I am indeed Falc, and I am wounded."

The Messenger accepted the sundering of tradition and recognition phrases. "What happened?"

Falc explained, denigrating himself for being taken by surprise and naming his embarrassment and loss of face because it was a woman who saved him. Too, he had been helpless not to accept her aid, even in mounting.

"Cease these unseemly noises that question the word of Ashah, Falc. Ashah did indeed have purpose in guiding your paths to cross, and in guiding her into such tenacity. As to her prowess—we both know that she was trained by a master."

How gentle you are tonight, O spirit of the Firedrake, Falc thought in considerable surprise.

The voice from far down in a well came again: "What are your thoughts about them?"

"They wore no city's colors and the colors of no individual I know," Falc said. "Yet it seemed that they came expressly to kill me, and—"

"And were smarter and more cautious than those who tried previously. As if they knew about those attempts, perhap, and had been warned and taken counsel?"

"Ah, your wisdom transcends mine, as always."

"Of course. I may be right and I may be wrong, Brother Falc. I but name what seems to be a possibility. It is too bad that he who did not escape is beyond ability to talk."

"Yes. For that I am most sorry."

"Tell me where you are."

Falc tried.

"You are near the estate Holding of Daviloran. He is Contractor to our brother Kaherevan. Assuming that he is alone and can be contacted, Sir Kaherevan will soon come for you. Daviloran will house you until you recuperate. You must do that, Falc. You must not fare forth again until you are as well as you were yesterday, lest you meet others who will find you easy prey."

O Ashah, how Falc hated those words, that thought! Yet he realized that the Messenger spoke truth, and Falc had to admit it to himself. Even when he was less helpless, he would be no match for another attack. Even those four from Lango would have had no trouble with a Falc of one arm and a stiffened side! He must be well beyond a mere "less helpless."

"My news to you tonight was to be that Brother Kaherevan has been uncontactable these past three nights. At last contact, five nights ago, he was on his way to Lock on his Holder's business."

Damn!

"Thus, if he does not arrive in a few days and you can travel, do so by night. Go to Holder Daviloran."

Falc nodded, wondering if the Manifestation could see him, and thinking that it was so. On the point of asking in what direction, he curbed himself from showing the Messenger stupidity and a self-willed tongue: Certainly Parshann would know where lay the house of a nearby estatemaster!

"Falc: Have great care. You cannot be done without. The Master and the High Temple abide well. On those occasions when you despair that you are only a chesspiece of the cosmos, consider the despair of the player! May you be granted a morrow no worse than this day."

"And thou," Falc said, hoping that the morrow and several more to come would be beyond merely no worse than this day.

5

Once Parshann and his ever-present hat were out of the house on that better morrow, Falc suggested that Jinnery fetch the saddlebags off the dead attacker's darg.

"Perhaps it contains a clue as to who they were or who sent them."

Jinnery stared. "*Sent* them?"

'I believe those three were sent to kill me. Me, specifically, Jinn. And now you will ask no more about it."

"Hmp. Same Falc, vertical or horizontal! But come to think, that knapsack may hold something of value, too."

"That would be good. Something to give our host."

She snorted at that. "What Parshann is getting is a clean house, as fast as I can wade through the mess! Doubtless that will be for the first time in over a year, too, the filthy barga!"

She glanced around. "Falc . . . do you own anything? Do omos carry melts?"

"No. Sometimes I have some. Something always turns up."

"Yes, doesn't it! Someone who insists on being slain and leaving you his darg and possessions! And you refused to tell tales of blood-violence to Chalis! Oh, Mother Avmer, what a man!"

She waited, looking expectantly at him, but Falc disappointed her. He said nothing and his expression did not change. With a sigh Jinnery went to fetch in the pair of saddlebags from their mutual victim's darg. When she returned, he had succeeded in sitting up and propping himself in that position. She forewent comment on that, knowing it would avail her nothing.

They were disappointed. The leathern sacks contained no clues.

"I'm sure this bracelet was crafted in Lock," Falc said, turning the pretty trinket over in his good hand. "But that means nothing."

"Parshann won't have any use for a bracelet, either."

"True. We will give him the sacks themselves and the dried food they contain. Also the extra tunic and that blanket, thin as it is, and the knife and spoon."

"*Falc—I* can use the tunic, and the knife and spoon! I can *not* use another darg, but Parshann can. Falc? Falc? Hmp. Asleep. All right, Esphy m'girl, let's get at playing woman again. Two big brutes are as needful and dependent as children . . . on the good mother you'll never be!"

She left the room quietly and went into Parshann's surprisingly spacious kitchen. With moisture-sparkling eyes, she began work on another better dinner than the farmer had eaten (while wearing his hat) in over a year. Meanwhile she glanced disgusted about the messy hut.

By night Sir Kaherevan had not come. The Messenger did not appear. Falc fell asleep while trying to give serious thought to the indications that someone had actually formed and was implementing a plot against the very men who were dedicated to preserving them and all Sij from renewed Empire; from a repetition of disaster: the Order Most Old.

NINE

. . . for no one can know what is in the mind of
another. It is the way of some not to care. Of
others, to demand to know. Of others, to attempt to listen and to think, and so surmise
what is there that one did not hear—or heard
without hearing. None of these is "right" at all
times, as each is "wrong" at *some* time. Circumstances and sometimes opportunity dictate
method, as in nearly all else.

—the fifth Master

"Sometimes it seemed to me when I was teaching you," Falc
said, "that you were already familiar with knives and knife-
fighting. Now I'm sure. In that attack on us you surely
displayed more knowledge and skill than I've taught you."

She shrugged and avoided looking at him while she made a
show of tidying his chamber, which she had thoroughly cleaned
only yesterday afternoon. Falc sat silently regarding her. He
realized that her face had changed, so gradually that he had
not noticed. He remembered his first impression: that Jinnery
held her thin-lipped mouth neither attractively nor even very
pleasantly. The tight set of those lips had eased, although she
still chewed her nails. Her grim face and bitter mouth had
loosened up, with the new appearance heightened by her
wearing her hair down and loose. Only now did he realize
that change, as he saw it reverse: how tight her mouth had
just become and how her jawbone stood out!

We've grown comfortable with each other, he thought.
*Now I've jolted her back to the old Jinnery. I have hit a
nerve.*

171

At last the silence and his steady stare became unendurable. She straightened and faced him from across the room, eight or so steps away. Medium blue hair flowing loose and long. The clothing of a larger woman, blousing so that it merely emphasized her thinness. Eyes like almonds staring back at his.

'You're right again, Falc,'' she said, and added in a mildly exasperated way, ''*of course*. I lied to you. My father may have been slain in Morazain, and maybe he wasn't.''

He said nothing, but continued to gaze at her. Neither expectantly nor questioningly; he merely gazed with that open, rather ascetic and often dour face that could make her so uncomfortable.

''All right, all right,'' she said, as if he had been badgering her. ''And Querry was not my uncle. I never knew who my father was and my mother hardly knew him. She was killed when I was twelve. Murdered by . . . by one of her customers. Nothing came of it. I mean, he was fined, that's all. That's how the city gets money. It doesn't go to twelve-year-old orphans.'' She looked away. ''And girls out on the streets after dusk—they're thick as crellies and worth no more attention.''

Falc said nothing. He heard her. He had no need of asking what sort of customer, or what her mother was in the business of selling. That was implicit in Jinnery's words and stance and tone, and her attitude of resignation, as well as by her previously choosing to lie.

''My name was Esphodine,'' she told him, looking away as she pronounced the word, then returning her gaze to the steady stare of midnight eyes and that dark face that showed nothing. No disapproval, no querying or expectancy, no surprise. Just Falc, in bed and looking at her, listening.

''I said was, Falc,'' she warned him. ''Esphodine. My mother thought it sounded just so fine! I hated it. Hate it. I'd as soon be called Flunderpuff! I took her name after she died, and I . . . I took her profession, too. I went out on the streets. I did not do that well, but I survived. Not every man was so choosy as not to accept a skinny youngster with an ugly voice, at bargain rates. Some men like such a woman—or such a girl, anyhow.''

She said that defensively and as if challengingly in that

unfortunate voice that was more brass than silver bells or gold, and Falc nodded. That was all. His face didn't change, or his eyes. He merely nodded an acknowledgment that said nothing.

Suddenly she burst out,. "Don't you even *judge*, monk?"

"Too often. I am nearly always wrong when I do. I know that I will again, and I will know again that it is wrong and unworthy. I judged you awrong, Cousin Jinnery, long ago." His voice laid the slightest stress on her name and the word "cousin."

"The first day and night ever we saw each other! I suppose you did, as I judged you! Hmmp!" She turned away to pick a bit of lint off the flowered partial covering of the room's only chair; Parshann's work. Leaning one hand on its back, she looked at Falc. "That's where I was and that's what I was doing when a farmer named Querry found me, four years ago. He had a son and no woman. He needed help on the farm, and he needed the kind of release a woman provides. Even one as hard as I'd become. In me he fancied that he found both. Ah, how I leaped at the opportunity to escape the city and all those men! How I romanticized the peace and the idyllic pastoral life! It turned out not to be so idyllic, and not my pot of hax either. So . . . I became harder, and wore my dissatisfaction and bitterness like a cloak. I had much bitterness in me. That's why I was so cruel to you when you came, free and on the move, seeing the world. I envied you, you see, and so I was cruel! I had told myself Querry was getting plenty from me, and you had everything, and I had a right to be unpleasant. To nag.

"That's what I told myself when I thought at all, I mean."

At last Falc took his gaze from her. He looked at the wall beyond the foot of the bed and sighed. Without intending to, he spoke. Dull and quiet of voice, to the wall.

"I know. I fled too, Jinn. I fled my own Risskor. No normal man chooses to give his life to the Order Most Old."

More than surprised, she could only nod. Each of them had just told the other more than they had ever admitted or shared. They knew each other a bit better, and a bond deepened. They had made admissions each to the other, and understood without knowing details that did not matter.

"Falc . . ."

"I need to be alone now, Jinnery."

"Alone! You mean 'Jinn,' don't you?"

He looked at her. He nodded. "I need to be alone, Jinn."

"But we were just—you're closing me out again."

"Confound and damn it, woman, I have to increase the rainfall."

"Oh." She hurried out of the room, and shut the door.

Falc made noises with the bed, in the event she was listening, and reached under to move the chamberpot under the bed a couple of times, so that it made scraping sounds and she would think he was urinating, as he'd said. Then he resumed staring at the wall, thinking.

"It isn't right," Falc said with some heat. "It's embarrassing . . . demeaning!"

"Demeaning!"

"I mean to both of us, Jinnery!"

"You mean Jinn, don't you?"

"I mean it isn't right and it's embarrassing to have you come in here and carry that pot out and empty it."

"What, you think I'm such a weak *girl* and Parshann should do it?"

"No, I think I should." He gestured, and she noticed how short and slow the movement was. "I can throw it out the window, there."

She set the chamberpot down beside the bed, then pushed it under. She straightened and stepped back.

"All right then, Sir Knight of the Order, you do it."

Dark, dark eyes stared, and blinked. "Leave me alone, then."

"I will not! When you get out of that bed and fall down, I'm going to be here to catch you!"

"I will not f—I'm not wearing anything."

"That's a lie. For shame, Son of Ashah!"

"Damn you, woman!"

"Damn you too. Damn us both! Just go on and empty that pot, so I can get back to Parshann's bedroom. He doesn't want me in there but it looks as if thirty half-wits have been partying in that room for a month. He's 'way out in the field right now, and now's my chance. Move, Falc, move!"

He looked lances and throwing stars and knives at her. Then he spent about a minute getting himself into a sitting position. He kept the sheet over him, slung across one shoulder. He swung his legs over the side of the bed, and for the first time she saw their hairiness, their muscular calves and the thickness of his ankles. He sat gazing at the floor. Then at her. His face took on a look of resolution again, and he stood.

Fortunately, he fell backward onto the bed and she did not have to catch him after all.

Stalking over to the bed, she retrieved the blue chamberpot and started, stiff-backed, out of the room. Suddenly she turned, half-squatted to set down the pot, and strode to the bed with a rustle of a dead woman's long, pale green skirt. That was a surprise; so was her dropping to her knees beside the bed.

"Falc, Falc! We are not judging, remember? I must help you, for now. You lost about a third of your blood just three days ago, and you're barely strong enough to sit up in bed, much less stand and walk! Admit it—to you, I mean; you don't have to say anything. Just accept it, Falc, and let us both be glad I'm here. I—am—glad, Falc."

Then she rose with a new rustle and hurried out of the room.

Well, Falc, a proud and vehemently independent man told himself fully forty-five minutes of reflection later, *you can be a man or you can let her be* the *man. A man knows when he has to admit that he is dependent. Damn!*

Falc looked at the two savory bowls she had brought to him, and the mug of steaming hax.

"Thank you, Jinn," he said, and squeezed her arm.

"Here, careful with that touching now, you might break an oath or something!"

She was feeling guilty about that cut before she reached the door. She felt guilty right up until bedtime and past, but avoided letting Falc know. It was Parshann who went in and took away the empty bowls and mug.

"Good! You keep eatin' this way an' you'll be up on the roof doin' handstands 'fore you know it!"

"I keep eating this way and I'll have the belly you wear," Falc said, and that way everyone went to sleep feeling bad.

2

Leaning only a little on Parshann, Sir Falc of Risskor walked
with measured paces out of his house of convalescence. The
sun was only just up, but hardly showed; the day promised to
continue gray and probably promised rain. No matter. This
was the day. Neither Sir Kaherevan nor the Messenger had
made an appearance. Jinnery and Parshann had hitched the
dead assailant's darg to the old wagon, and loaded in her
things and the omo's. He insisted on wearing mailcoat and
weapons, but had been unable to get into his mail, even with
help. They did get the derlin on him, and Parshann's great big
hat. The farmer wore the one Falc had from Baysh. Overly
warm or no, Jinnery wore Parshann's coat under her derlin,
with its hood up. That way she looked larger, like a third man
on the wagon.

With help, Falc mounted into the wagon and sat facing
rearward. His back was against the front end just under the
seat where Parshann and Jinnery rode.

"Let's go, boy," the omo said. "Harr come."

The wagon started forward and Harr followed hurriedly. As
ever, Tay was happy to follow the leader. Rattling a little, the
wagon rolled along the dust-road that led to the back of
Parshann's holding. There it abutted Cragview, which was
the estate of Holder Karath Daviloran. The mansion of
Daviloran was just under a day away. Both the Temple and
Lock were too far. Falc rode, thinking. Eventually, despite
the rocking and rattling of the wagon—and worse, when a
wheel hit a rut or a weal or stone in the ground—he napped.
After six days, he was still disgustingly weak.

3

It did not rain and the disguises were unnecessary; they saw
no one and no one saw them until they reached the sprawling
manse of Daviloran, who was friend to Falc's Contract-
Holder in Lock. He took in the omo and Jinnery happily and
jovially. He embarrassed the well-rewarded Parshann by forc-
ing on him a good winter cloak and insisting that he partake
of "neighborly food" before he departed. Eventually Parshann

rode off. He had a new darg, a fine new cloak, and a new hat.

Falc was sure that the glances the bespectacled man cast back at Jinnery were of the longing variety.

Then Parshann was gone, and it was Daviloran himself who took the wounded Son of Ashah to a large and well-appointed guest chamber. The Holder apologized for a closeness in the room that was purely imaginary, and went about opening windows as if he were Housechief rather than lord and master of House, Holding and estate. The master of Cragview Holding was a man of average height whose face and body were the opposite of Falc's in every way: pale of skin, azure of eye, sparse of grizzled hair, slight of frame and yet fat both before and behind. Several chins wobbled under a roundish, jovial face that looked at least ten years younger than Daviloran's middle age. His skin was smooth as a boy's and devoid of hair below short sideburns.

"There, Sir Falc. You are both more than welcome in this House. And that's a good big bed for two, you'll find. And firm. I do like them firm."

"We will not be occupying the same bed, Holder," Falc told him.

"Or room," Jinnery added.

"We are cousins and accidental companions," Falc said to a face gone from jovial to confused, "not lovers."

Daviloran said, "Oh." He recovered only after a few seconds: "Well it's a big House, and plenty of rooms are available to guests. As a matter of fact, my lady—"

"Oh please, my lord, that title does not fit me!"

Falc was amused to see that Jinnery was indeed capable of being truly embarrassed.

"Well, perhap I know that, but saying the words doesn't hurt either of us, does it!" Daviloran's smile was huge and wide open, as if he were the most ingenuous man on the planet. He was a man who smiled easily, with the face almost of an angel. "What I was about to say, Jinnery, is why not take the room just next this one."

"Please, Holder, do not put yourself or anyone else out for me."

"All right," Daviloran said equably, bobbing his head and

chins. "The chamber beside and adjoining this one is entirely
empty. Would you like to call it yours, while you are here?"

She smiled and her nod was a little bow. "Yes thank you,
Holder."

"Lord Holder, may I inquire after Sir Kaherevan?"

Daviloran's face clouded. "Sir Falc, your brother omo
went over to Lock on my business, and is days overdue."

Falc's face was dour and midnight eyes stared. "Pardon
please, Holder, but was his mission to my lord Kinneven?"

Daviloran's smile was boyish. "No, to Stavishen," he
said, naming the Holder who was Kinneven's prime rival.

"Again, I beg pardon for inquiring into my lord's business.
And for coming here this way; infirm. I lost too much blood,
and while the arm is knitting well, thanks to Jinnery here and
the medical genius of your neighbor, I am slow in regaining
my strength. That fact chafes me sore, believe me."

"I do, honored Falc, but blood does not replace itself
overnight," Daviloran said, in one of those obviously non-
sense statements uttered merely to be making encouraging
noises.

"I am not incapable of movement, and will be exercising
daily—"

"A little," Jinnery put in.

"—in private," Falc finished, without glancing at her.

"O'course, Sir Falc. 'Course. I'll see to it that you have
attendants when you desire and an omo's privacy when you
desire. I'll tell you this: I have an ajmil who is more than
skilled at shaving a man, and trimming his hair. Perhap your
hair and beard—"

"I would appreciate a more kempt appearance to my beard,
lord Holder," Falc said, a bit stiffly. "Has not Kaherevan
imparted that no one sees an omo without his coif, ever?"

Daviloran sighed. "Oh yes. You'll find that I cannot seem
to help making little jokes, Sir Falc."

Next morning Jinnery told Falc that Parshann had pro-
posed. Awkwardly.

"Marriage?"

"Legal marriage, yes. And you know, I never saw that
man without his hat and he never so much as touched me!"

"A good man," Falc said. "Any woman could do a lot worse."

"Oh Falc, don't be silly!"

As it turned out, Daviloran's promise to respect an omo's privacy came close to being a joke. Perhaps he had intended it as such. The problem was that he assigned Falc's care to most attractive twins, Sulah and Salih. From the way they walked when they entered that first time, Falc saw that they were not long away from their native Mersarl. Why they claimed to be of Ryar he never learned. They were painfully shapely, woefully underdressed, and lamentably youthful. They were also loath to leave the bed-bound Son of Ashah alone. Who had ever seen an omo bare-armed before? Besides, there was the added thrill of hoping—trying—to catch glimpses of chest! Falc was sure they hoped to see even more of him; from the way they popped in and out so frequently he suspected that they were trying to catch him exercising or worse still, using the chamberpot. They were also flirtatious unto seductive. Obviously both wanted to share his bed, singly or in tandem. On the second night they feigned far too much terror at a relatively mild quake followed by a violent storm of wind and rain. Their impatient patient all but had to hurl them out of his room.

His special request of his host next day gained him an apology for Daviloran's failure to think of loaning his guest a robe. The desired garment was hurriedly fetched and delivered. Now Falc ceased bothering with trying to keep himself covered with bedclothes. He wore the robe night and day and made sure that it gaped nowhere. Sulah and Salih were disappointed. They were also bothersome; far, far too solicitous and ubiquitous. Jinnery reacted by becoming possessive and jealous. She complained of headaches. Falc's convalescence became more of a trial than when he had been feeling worse. He met a visitor: Daviloran's young nephew, whose name was Daviloran and was usually called Davilo. Falc actually heard himself suggest that the young man take "those darling twins and use them as they desire until they can't stand up." For that he assigned himself the full litany, twice, He never knew whether Davilo had taken his embarrassingly salacious advice.

On that third night in this maddening manse, he stopped
Salih and Sulah as, artfully loose of halter and shamefully
swervy-swingy of hip, they were departing with his dinner
things.

Both halted at once and swung back, and O Ashah but their
faces were happy and anticipatory! They also blinked surprise, for Falc had stood the moment they turned their backs,
in order to present a more commanding appearance in
Daviloran's long robe of maroon.

"Oh how tall my lord Falc is when he stands!"

"And how broad!"

Strength, O Ashah, please *loan me strength!* He spoke
quietly and sternly. "I am a knight of the Order Most Old
who is being punished for my sins by being rendered invalid,
left at your mercy while I convalesce. I am a man accustomed
to privacy, and I want and need it. You will knock and wait
until you hear me say come, and you will not even knock for
the rest of this night. Do you hear and understand me?"

Looking sad unto morose, the girls nodded almost in unison.

Then Falc máde his mistake. "Good. Fail to cooperate and
obey me in this and I shall prove that I am strong enough to
beat you."

Their darling little faces went from fearful dolorousness to
bright smiles.

Falc stared. *O Ashah what have I done? Ashah help and
guide me, but their faces are all happy and anticipatory
again!*

"No. Come to think, I am not strong enough. I shall have
Jinnery beat you. A woman knows better how to hurt a
woman, anyhow."

Bright smiles faded to be replaced by almost comical dolor.

Falc did not show his sigh of relief. "Go."

They went, and for once they forgot or forbore to wag their
hips.

Thus Falc of Risskor gained a bit of privacy—until a gentle
knock and a familiar voice persuaded him not to bellow but to
bid Jinnery come in. She did, but remained by the door.

"I will not apologize for having overheard you, Falc. I
must apologize, however, for thoughts I have had. I have
seen those two *girls* behave, and even heard them talking and

giggling. I had supposed you were enjoying the attention of two such—"

"Children."

"Well, that isn't what I was going to say," she told him with a smile, "but I like it well enough and besides it's nicer than crelly-brained cacks in heat."

"Not to their ears, likely. What they want above all is to be seductive."

"What they want above all is to seduce!"

Falc shrugged; one-sidedly because of his arm. "It is possible that I am not sorry you heard, respected Cousin Jinnery."

She smiled in a different way, and nodded. "Well, now it's my turn to respect your need for privacy, respected Cousin Falc."

She left him no time for reply but turned and hurried away. She closed the door behind her and he sat on the bed gazing at it, wondering whether he would have said anything more.

It's true, he mused. *Somehow we have achieved mutual respect. How strange for Falc of Risskor!*

Hmm. Now to block that door with the big chair!

He did, and within an hour it happened as he had hoped: the Manifestation appeared.

The Messenger sounded hurried. He bore no good news. He advised that the corpse of Sir Kaherevan had washed up in the reeds along the river below Lock. The body was unmistakably Kaherevan's, despite his nudity and some decay. He had been stabbed repeatedly as well as beaten and kicked. Another omo was missing; "uncontactable." Two, including Falc, had been attacked but had escaped murder. Saying that every Son of Ashah must be double warned, the Messenger vanished at once.

Falc sat abed staring at the place where the Manifestation had been, and knew that he could not consider sleep. Not only was it time for real thinking, he had no choice: his brain was spinning. Delving; working.

Simply put, someone was murdering the Sons of Ashah and stealing their arms, armor and clothing. At least four uniforms and sets of weapons were missing now, and the Order reduced by as many men.

Without even thinking about it, Falc rose to pace the nighted chamber.

This had to be a plot, a concerted effort. Throughout
history, no one had attempted to *murder* an omo. Now someone was doing so. Rather, some*ones were*, since this had the
look of a concerted effort. That tended to indicate an unheard-
of-unity with one instigator, a cabal. But—a plot against the
Order Most Old? Why? Many men were involved; he had
accounted for several, and more had come to try again. This
bespoke organization, a master mind or council.

Why?

Falc could not imagine. He pushed his mental exploration
further. Roaming the room that should have been darker but
for moonlight, he paced to the window and stared out at
nothing save trees silhouetted against the moons' light. He
stared at nothing, frowning in thought, eyes slitted.

Suppose that back in Lango Faradox had meant *Falc*'s
death only, in a way that would put the blame on Chasmal—
and there was no plot against Chasmal at all? *All to slay me,
with Chasmal to blame? How elaborate!*

Such a concept at least lent some sense to the murder of
"Falc's cousin" Querry, and this recent attempt. Falc of
Risskor had long since come to terms with the painful admission of a fact he would never have dreamed possible—or
admissible: but for Jinn, the attempt by those three just over a
week ago would have succeeded and he too would be a naked
victim of murder.

Since Sath Firedrake ended the imperial tyranny and founded
the Order, it had provided the communication link among a
loose continental "society" of autonomous citystates. Only
by a sort of myth-theory could they be called other than
autonomous: the position and person of emperor, after all,
still existed. Yet no empire existed and the emperor had been
only a convenient figurehead for many, many years. The
citystates were in turn full of autonomous, independent,
wealth-motivated, often envious and ever-competing Holders:
slaveholders who were the backbone of an economy based on
trade and slavery.

The Sons of Ashah maintained their communication lines
and provided a sort of bond among them. They also bound
various such "lords" to themselves and thus to the Order and
to various other Holders in various other citystates, along
with ardoms and keeps such as this huge estate of Daviloran's.

Thus no longer were the annual Fairs as marred by plots, assassinations, and riots as once they were.

We omos prevent renewal of that unity leading to Empire. We menace only chaos. We menace no one.

Suddenly feeling weary, Falc, returned to his bed. He stretched out and remembered to arrange Daviloran's robe carefully over his legs before he closed his eyes. That last thought wanted to lead to others. Still Falc was staring at nothing, even behind his eyelids, while he sought sleep. His mind continued trying to push, but at last gave up.

4

Doubtless he slept restlessly. He awoke next morning with the thought that logically followed his last one before sleep:

We of the Order do menace someone! Someone or some-ones who want more dissension and mistrust among the Hold-ers and thus among the citystates!

But—why?

Perhaps more importantly: who?

He sat up. Who would profit by—

He was interrupted. The knock at his door came not from the confounded twins or even Jinnery, but his host. At once Falc bade them enter, and was surprised: although the man who accompanied Karath Daviloran was unknown to Falc, he was manifestly a Knight of the Order!

"Morning, Sir Falc! Sorry to pop in so early, but we have a visitor, another of your Order. I thought you'd want to see Sir Mandehal."

Falc nodded a greeting. "Sir Mandehal."

Mandehal pushed back his long crawk-wing cloak. "Sir Falc! How sorry I am to see you brought so low!"

"My time abed is temporary, brother."

"Sir Mandehal is here seeking Contract, Sir Falc."

Falc blinked in new surprise. "You have not heard from Kaherevan, Holder?"

Daviloran shook his head, and Falc was aware that Mandehal was staring at him.

"Holder," Falc said, "I learned only last night that my

brother Kaherevan was murdered in Lock and hurled into the river, days ago.''

"You—know this, Falc?'' For once, Daviloran's face was not jovial. "Ah, good Kaherevan, poor Sir K—but how could you know this, Sir Falc? Surely you have not left this room, and we've had no visitors until now.''

Falc only looked at that ingenuous, almost angelic face of the Holder. Beyond him, he saw Jinnery just outside the doorway. She bore a little tray. More undercooked red meat, no doubt.

"I . . . have heard that you . . . can exchange information among yourselves, but always discounted such . . . such. . . ?'' Floundering painfully, Daviloran broke off.

Falc nodded. "It's easiest to say that in a way Sath Fire-drake is dead but his spirit has never truly died, eh Brother Mandehal? At any rate, my lord is indeed bereft of his Contracted omo. It would appear that Sir Mandehal's arrival is fortuitous. Brother, I have to admit that I have never heard your name aforenow.''

Mandehal smiled and made a modest gesture with a black-gauntleted hand. "I am not surprised, Brother. I assure Falc of Risskor, however, that *I* have heard of *him*! My career has been none so illustrious as your own. Nor perhap as distinguished as that of our departed brother Kaherevan; of course I too learned of his demise last night. It is sadness on us all. I was near here, and—'' He gestured with a shrug. "It is sadness too for me to find the foremost of all Deathknights of the Order abed with a wound. It is not, I hope, serious?''

"I was near slain, Brother Mandehal. But I shall recover, with another few weeks of rest and that dreadful medicine Cousin Jinnery forces on me.''

"Holder?''

Daviloran turned at that voice; Jinnery's. Wearing a little frown, she was gazing past him at the dark man in the bed. "Our patient needs medication and a rewrapping of his wounds, Holder. Holder, Sir Mandehal, I beg you . . . may I be so rude. . . ? He needs these things *now*.''

"In the name of Ashah, aye!''

"Oh, 'fcourse,'' Daviloran exclaimed.

The two departed. Jinnery stepped aside for them, looking most respectful. Ridiculously overdonely respectful, Falc thought. Then she entered and closed the door before wheeling on him.

"Why in . . . in . . . why *ever* did you tell them you have decided you will need 'a few weeks' to recover? And *what* 'dreadful medicine'? I force nothing on you, ungrateful *cousin!*"

He spoke briskly. "I commend your swift comprehension and devising a way to get them out of here, Jinn. Please find a way now to bring the Holder back, alone. Perhap you might say to Sir Mandehal that as he knows, only a man may—oh, see my head. Then talk with him while the Holder comes."

Jinnery put her head on one side and stared at his coif-covered pate. "Only a man! But you said before that—"

"Yes, Jinn, and that was true; no one sees the head of a Son of Ashah, no one at all. But you see I think Mandehal will not know that. Please—go and send in Daviloran. This is most important."

"Falc?"

He thrust out an arm with extended finger pointed at her and gave her pomposity: "These things are good in little measure and evil in large: yeast, salt, and hesitation!" Then he relented: "Please, Jinn. Now."

She sent a loud breath gusting through her nostrils. "I didn't know you knew that word," she muttered.

She hurried over to set down the tray before leaving him with swift steps. Falc didn't even think to check the contents of the tray. Moving as rapidly as he could, he fetched his weapons belt into the bed with him, and covered it and the sheathed blades. He sat up in the bed, staring at the door.

Ashah be with and guide me now, for I may have found it!

Suddenly it occurred to him that in his situation undercooked red meat would be as much value to him as the presence and guidance of his god. He snatched up the tray and began a most unmannerly eating.

He had just gotten rid of the grease on his hands and swallowed the last wolfed bite when Daviloran appeared. Falc was on his feet, staring darkly.

"My lord Holder, that man may be Mandehal, but he is not *Sir* Mandehal and he is not of the Order Most Old. He is an impostor and likely the murderer of Kaherevan; that is, one of them, for it would take more than one such as Mandehal to slay one of us."

Staring open-mouthed, Daviloran took advantage of his first opportunity to speak: *"What?!"*

"Holder Daviloran: In the event that he *might* be *nearly* as good as an omo, I suggest that my lord send household peacekeepers for him, numbering four. Bid them take care not to endanger my cousin Jinnery. I further urge my lord to have them bind his hands behind him and bring him here—where you, too, will be. I shall prove that he is an impostor, and we shall try to learn a few little things together. All this I beg, Holder Daviloran, for the good of the Order and society—and my lord Holder's estimable self."

"Sir Falc—oh, certainly, esteemed Falc, of course. May I ask how you are so sure that he is not of the Order Most Old? Do you know the name of every member?"

Falc nodded, mouth tight and grim. "I believe I do. He must be wary right now, for certainly he never intended to meet a real omo here! Thus care had better be taken in the manner of his detaining. Doubtless he does know considerable; and yet he was so stupid as to make the simplest mistake. It's a natural one to anyone not of the Order, I suppose, particularly its enemies. Aside from the matter of his accent: it is Darsinian, and through what I've been assured is mere coincidence, no Son of Ashah is Darsin-born. More definitively, he referred to me as a Deathknight. We do not call ourselves that, Holder, ever. We do not think of ourselves so. Understandably, we dislike the term."

"Uh, as you say, Sir Falc: understandably."

Falc continued to gaze at him until the fat man nodded, swallowed, nodded again, and bethought him to turn and quit the chamber. Immediately Falc of Risskor returned to the bed and hurriedly muttered the Words of the Blades while he buckled on his weapons over the robe. He listened to untoward noises from below, and on the steps. He heard no ring of weapons, and no cry of pain. He was standing before the window, weapon belt girding the maroon robe, when a man in Daviloran's colors bustled through the open doorway. Stepping to one side in an attitude of readiness, he joined Falc in watching two others hustle in the supposed omo.

Mandehal's hands were bound behind his back. He glared at Falc. Daviloran followed the others, and then Jinnery. She looked at once pale and yet satisfied. Jinnery had been given a mission and she had carried it out.

So had the lightedhearted and usually jovial master of Cragview, to whom it had not occurred that a knight of the Order Most Old had taken control of him and his household.

"He had to be taken physically, Sir Falc, but no one is wounded."

"Brother! What means this!"

Falc's gaze was on Daviloran, ignoring Mandehal. "Understandable, Holder. He is hardly so dangerous as a trained omo." Moving slowly, he used his left hand to push up the right sleeve of his robe. He held that hand out, palm up.

"See the scar on my wrist? Who knows what it is?"

"I know," two voices said; Jinnery and one of Daviloran's peacekeepers.

Falc looked at the man. "Say it."

"It's the scar of Sath," the fellow said, glancing around in embarrassment at being the center of attention of six people. He was close to middle-aged, but his cleanshaven face was open and youthful. "It is a part of the ritual of the Order Most Old. All omos have one, right there. My wife's cousin Sench of Southradd is a knight of the Order."

"Indeed he is," Falc said, realizing that this man and his wife did not yet know of the murder of her cousin. "Would you—excuse me. Lord Holder, would you please have this man show me the scar on Mandehal's wrist?"

"*Damn* you, Deathknight!" Mandehal struggled violently. He was held. The man he kicked kicked him back.

Daviloran's eyebrows were up. "Hmm! After that outburst, I s'pose we needn't bother. But do show us that wrist, Chalan."

The household guardsman did. Mandehal had to be held, and forcibly turned. Everyone present saw his scarless left wrist.

"He's a damned rotten impostor!" Chalan burst out, obviously scandalized.

"I'd say you know better than anyone that no Son of Ashah is going to refer to self or anyone else as 'Deathknight,' Chalan," Falc said quietly.

" 'Ndeed! Cousin Sen—that is, Sir Sench sure let us know that, Sir Knight of the Order!"

"We do indeed have an impostor," Falc said quietly, "and I'd say he is one of those who murdered Sir Kaherevan in Lock, and kicked and beat him, and stripped him, and dumped his naked body into the river with the sewage." He paused, noting how that grim catalogue stirred up everyone just as he wished. The dark glances and glowers Mandehal received were nothing compared to what these people would obviously love to give him. "My lord Holder?"

"Uh—the Query Chamber I maintain below the House, Sir Falc?"

"Just the place, I'm sure. Please, my fellow men of weapons, please don't rough him *too* much. Your lord and I shall want to hear a number of things he has to tell."

One of the two holding Mandehal chuckled.

"I'll tell you nothing, you grim-faced swine!"

This time all three peacekeepers chuckled.

"Out," Daviloran said. "To the Query Room with—that."

"My lord Holder," Falc said, "I need a brief conference with my cousin, and then I shall join you to visit with that source of sausage."

At last a smile returned to Daviloran's face. Then it fled, replaced by a look of concern. "You sure you're strong enough, esteemed Falc?"

"Holder, I have just grown immensely stronger," Falc assured him.

Over her objections, Falc had Jinnery tape him tightly so that he could move about and dress.

"Thanks, Jinn. Now you must wait outside."

"Oh, Falc! I can help you—think how often I've seen you with much less than your full . . . uh, habit."

"I know, cousin. But an omo must dress ritually, and that you must not see."

She gave him a look, but left the chamber. Falc locked the door. Then, for the first time in many days, he began the ritual and the words of attiring himself.

When at last he emerged, Jinnery and Daviloran were both impressed and shaken by how *sinister* he looked, the poor invalid in bed suddenly become the tall grim omo, all in black. This was no patient. This was Sir Falc of Risskor, O.M.O. Long jet cloak fluttering about his ankles, he paced to Jinnery and surprised her anew by gripping both her shoulders fondly. Then he turned to Holder Daviloran.

"Holder, this man must be questioned on behalf of the Order and I think all Sij. If you accompany me you may see things you would prefer to have missed, and hear things you will wish you did not know."

Daviloran put his head on one side. "We're going to question him, aren't we?"

"Yes."

"Do you think he'll speak up right away?"

"No."

Holder Daviloran smiled. "Good."

Jinnery put her hands over her mouth. The crinkles at the edges of her eyes showed that what she was concealing was not shock.

"May I try to extract Holder's promise that if after a time I ask to be alone with the prisoner, you will humor me?"

"So long as it isn't too soon, Sir Falc. Don't think you're going to be rid of me if you're going to whip or burn that swine a bit! The only thing I might see that I'd wish I hadn't," their ever jovial and almost cherub-faced host said, "is if the murdering turd-pile speaks up right away."

It proved to be Falc of Risskor who was shocked: Jinnery's laugh burst through her hands.

5

Holder Daviloran's gently-named Query Chamber lay beneath the rear of his manse. There he and Falc stood by while two uniformed men happily relieved Mandehal of the uniform of an omo. When the prisoner sought to resist, an unfriendly knee shot upward to come to a jolting halt at the apex of his thighs. Mandehal went delightfully pale, and sagged. He was swiftly stripped.

"Leave the coif," Falc said.

He received a couple of glances, but his face remained immobile and Daviloran's peacekeepers obeyed him. When Mandehal wore only the black skullcap, they swiftly chained him upright to a thick wooden slab, a broad door-like surface. A horizontally attached cylindrical projection across the small of his back forced him to arch his naked body away from the frame. The guardsmen stepped back, shooting hopeful looks at their employer and the omo who had risen from bed to become a dark and sinister questioner with a face of cold iron.

"Afraid not, lads," Daviloran said cheerfully. "Go along, now. Take those clothes to the seamstress. Remember that patch she put in Sir K's leggings last month? Ask her to look for it. When you have her words, come back and knock twice-then-once. We won't be responding to anyone else. Sir Falc and I believe this source of sausage knows things no one should, but we'll try to be heroic about it."

"Whoremongering son of a *guhh!*"

"Hope it was all right, me denting his gut that way, my lord Holder sir."

"It's all right, Sarminen, all right. If we learn what a son of a guk-k-hh is, we'll be sure to tell you."

Sarminen and Chalan left chuckling. While Daviloran secured the door against needless interruption, Falc stepped before the prisoner. Before he could speak, Daviloran did.

"Falc."

The omo replied by turning a questioning face toward the Holder.

"Everyone here liked Sir K, Falc. That's nearly all we called him. We were *friends.*"

Falc saw no reason to say anything. With a nod, he turned back to the impostor.

"You appeared here in a stolen uniform and arms of the Order Most Old, seeking the post of a man few people know is dead. You did not learn of his death the way I did, but you did know. It isn't possible not to believe you guilty. We will soon know from this Holding's seamstress whether you wore the uniform of Sir Kaherevan. It doesn't much matter. What we want to know is the name of your employer. You can tell us now or you can make us work for it."

Mandehal said, "Shi-i-it."

Falc's calm nod showed no emotion.

"Touch of the whip?" That cheerily spoken suggestion came from behind him.

Falc spoke without turning from Mandehal. "I'm just out of bed, Holder. I doubt whether I'm up to whipping."

"I am!"

"It's dramatic and a good enough punishment," Falc said, looking into Mandehal's eyes, "but usually a waste of time in getting a man to talk. Burning usually brings swift results, but I see no brazier aheating. Are we equipped with a lobster?"

"Right here." Quickly Daviloran produced that device called the Lobster's Foot. Merely a pair of pliers whose business end consisted of two iron blades some seven centimeters long. The sharpened blades were serrated. The resemblance to a lobster's claw was apparent.

"Of good Silkevare manufacture, too," Falc observed at a glance, and gave the prisoner all his attention. "Mandehal, you can answer me before or after you spend the rest of your life branded with notched earlobes. Understand that once I've started, it will be both ears before I take time to listen again."

"Going to enjoy it, aren't you, you black-winged vulture."

"Oh yes," Falc said calmly, and reached for Mandehal's left ear.

Mandehal rolled his eyes to see Falc's immobile face and steady stare. The prisoner's dull eyes shifted their gaze to Daviloran. Very bright of eye, the Holder was smiling.

"I'd say this is both stupid and wasteful," Falc said quietly, pinching up an earlobe. "We'll snip your septum next, whatever your name is from Darsin. You will embarrass and dishonor yourself by weeping and urinating. Then you will either tell us somewhat or we'll try something that doesn't merely hurt, but debilitates."

"You have all the emotions of a dragonel, haven't you!"

"I'm not doing this merely for pleasure, Mandehal. I know of the plot. The Master of the Order knows of the plot, and as of last night every omo does. Your fellow murderers are going to go down and then your employer will. You, meanwhile, will have suffered not for honor but for your own ego . . . and you will be an ugly cripple."

"You're right; this is stupid and wasteful," Mandehal said, and Daviloran looked disappointed when Falc paused, without taking the lobster away from the prisoner's lobe. "I was given the uniform in Lock and sent here from there. The man who gave it me and told me what to do and say is Holder Stavishen."

"Stavishen!" Daviloran said, not quite in a gasp. "The very man into whose bloody hands I sent poor Sir K! Ah, damn, damn. It fits, too. That devil Stavishen lusts after more than one slave and facility of mine and my rental property in Lock, too. He murdered poor Kaherevan and tried to put this spy here in his place . . . and might well have succeeded but for you, esteemed Falc!"

Looking thoughtfully at their prisoner, Falc nodded. "One thing does seem to follow the other, doesn't it. Now I make my special request, Lord Holder." He turned to face his host. "Please leave me with this man, just for a time. I assure you I don't intend to kill him."

The master of Cragview showed his reluctance and disappointment with a sour look, but went along because he had promised earlier.

When the huge door was closed behind him, Falc hesitated, but would not lock a man's door against him. He turned, removing his gauntlet. He drew off Mandehal's coif and ran his hand over the bald head. He found stubble.

"Many probably know that a Son of Ashah has no hair on his pate, murderer. What few know is that hair does not grow on our heads. It can't; it is permanently eradicated and further growth inhibited. The method is a secret of the Order. I tell you because you will never report to your master, whoever he is. Not young Holder Stavishen, I think, else you'd not have babbled it so fast. No, pitiful tool, I believe someone else charged you to submit to a little pain if you were caught out, and then to pass on that lie. Falc of Risskor tells you this, and you had best heed. Tell me who really hired you, and I guarantee you incarceration, which you may prefer to death. If you do not, spy and assassin, I guarantee you pain worse than you can presently conceive. Believe that, murderer."

That statement was the more chilling for being so calmly delivered, but the impostor was strong enough or stupid enough to say the wrong words.

"It was Stavishen damn you, Stavishen!"

"I think not. You have become far too anxious that I believe the Stavishen story. Heed me, Mandehal or whatever your slime-born name is. I am going to run this needle up your nose. See it twinkle? Either tell me right now, or don't

seek to stop me before the needle has come out the side of
your nostril.''

"Gods, Falc! Torture is torture and part of life, but do you
have to *mark* me?''

"I have never murdered, or stolen, or hurt the innocent.
How can I be concerned with your appearance when your
people are murdering men and you can help me stop it? All I
seek is the swiftest route to any destination without going
over or through anyone innocent. With you I don't need to
worry about that, do I.''

"You pompous son of a syphilitic she-barga!''

Falc sighed. "I will admit to pompous. It has long been a
fault. I try to fight it. Usually I'm successful. Usually I'm
successful at holding in check my pleasure in giving pain,
too. You don't try to help much, do you?''

The prisoner surprised him then; he yelled for the Holder.
On the instant, Falc clamped his chin with his right hand.
With his left, the omo did as he had promised.

Daviloran came rushing in. He saw the blood, and the
needle still in place. Blurting boyishly, he accused Falc of
high-handedness.

Falc showed no offense. "Yes. I have acted high-handedly,
Holder. Someone ordered the murder of Sir Kaherevan and
others, and I am convinced it was not Holder Stavishen. I'm
also convinced that it's part of a plot against the Order, the
very Order itself. I am high-handed, superior and egoistic
about it, and arrogant. This in addition to being religious and
dedicated to my Order and the society we are sworn to
maintain.''

Daviloran stared. Slowly his eyes narrowed. At last he
smiled. "And *truthful*, Falc! Don't forget truthful!'' He
chuckled.

"To a fault.'' Falc shrugged. "It would never occur to me
that you might question that, so I did not mention it. Might
my cousin join me—assist me?''

"In here? With that mess?'' Daviloran's angelic face took
on an expression of shock. "Of that I can hardly approve!
Nor will I leave again. I have seen men tortured, Sir Falc,
and women as well. I've taken a hand. My sensibilities will
not be offended, nor my corota gland either.''

"You both enjoy it!''

Falc and Daviloran exchanged a look at that outburst from
their prisoner. What a stupid thing for Mandehal to say, even
in his distress! Of course they enjoyed it. They were hardly
fergs or butterflies; they were men of Sij.

Falc glanced around. "I promise not to be so disrespectful
as to kick your corpse as was done to Sir Kaherevan's body,
murderer."

He held his stare until the impostor proved unable to meet
that steady gaze, and looked away. It was then Falc knew that
what he had suggested was true. Kaherevan and almost un-
doubtedly the other omos as well had been kicked *after* they
had been stabbed and sliced, and even after they had died. He
swallowed hard. Neither of the others saw the quiver of his
hands. He turned from a man he wanted to strangle, slowly,
but would not.

"Holder Daviloran: Are you sure you're prepared to know
who *really* ordered the murder of your Contracted omo—and
at least four others?"

Daviloran blinked, wondering. He nodded. "Of course I
am."

A Son of Ashah surprised both the others then, by actually
laying hands on a lord Holder. In astonishment the prisoner
watched the incredible monkish fanatic wrest an oath from the
shocked lord of lands and wealth, his own host who dared not
resist. Falc dictated the oath in the names of Ashah and
Markcun, holding the other man's hand to his head in the
swearing pose: that Daviloran would not tell anyone, or take
any action on what they would soon learn, until Falc had
reported to "my Order's Master, and to my Contractor whose
name you know. *Swear,* my lord."

The face of the master of Cragview was darkened by
congesting blood and his voice trembled in outrage, but he
swore. He also bestowed dark looks on Falc, who thanked
him and bowed respectfully before returning his attentions to
the prisoner. Even on the heels of that impassioned scene he
spoke quietly and seemingly without emotion:

"I hope you are convinced that I am a man of my word.
When I tell you that I shall not stop before I have finished
what I set out to do, it is so. No amount of babble will
persuade me to stop before I am utterly finished. So, whatever your name: speak."

Falc took up another needle. The prisoner gasped. He cringed, but would not speak.

"Man, man! This time the needle goes directly into your eyeball. You will suffer more than pain; think of the unfortunate aftereffect! It will last so long as you live, which will be longer than you will prefer. *Who employed you and others to murder Kaherevan and others of the Order Most Old? I know the plot,* you poor tool! Your employer seeks to create dissension among the Holders and thus the citystates all over the continent. He chose to accomplish this by weakening the Order Most Old by the deaths of its members, at the same time creating mistrust of the Order. For who can trust an omo, when he may be an impostor? Your master is an enemy of civilization! I believe you came here to *prove* yourself an impostor, though not by this means, for you had no reason to expect me here!"

Suddenly Falc paused, cocking his head in thought. "Hmm . . . probably by murdering Daviloran and escaping, hmm? All would know that a false omo had done it." He glanced significantly at the Holder, who looked no longer angry but shocked. This was the first he had heard of a plot. "Yet some would suspect that it was a true Son of Ashah, which is worse. Now, slime-born. The . . . left eye, I think. Speak, tool! Your employer cannot do as much to you for confessing as we can for refusing! We are here now, and he is . . . where?"

The prisoner refused to speak.

Amid the shrieks that resounded through the underground chamber and back from its padded, reinforced walls of stone was . . . a name. That name was so staggering to Falc of Risskor that he broke his pledge and stopped what he was doing before he had finished. While he and an open-mouthed Holder Daviloran listened, staring, the weeping prisoner babbled all he knew.

6

Omo and Holder were in agreement that no one else must know what they did; not yet. They made the search of the impostor omo's darg and bags themselves, in private. Daviloran brought forth an indication that the prisoner must have been something of a poet. He handed the verse to the man in black, who read it aloud.

> Lords rise like grain, men fall as rain,
>   And O the shume, with his purple plume
> Withstands them all; blooms ever till fall.
>   Impervious to pain its imperial stain!
>
> The crawk flies high, sends down its cry
>   From woodland glen to homes of men;
> Purple shume heeds not but rises from rot
>   When the crawks die and vacate the sky.
>
> Seek ye in vain to challenge the rain;
>   Think not to rise, O creature that dies—
> For rint and hawks, longbean and crawks
>   Strive on in pain with nought to gain!
>
> They fly in speed but drop no seed
>   Whilst ever they seem to chase sun's beam;
> Never dies the shume of purpling bloom!
>   It sheds its seed and spreads its breed.

Falc finished reading and looked at the other side of the paper. It was blank. There was only the poem. The master of Cragview Holding gazed at the black-clad man who stood reflectively staring at nothing. He was silently recollecting the message he had delivered to Chasmal, from his own Contracted Holder:

Here is something no one knows about the purple shume. Not only does it stand tall and its main stem grow ever thicker, but it puts forth aerial roots.

"Quite the poet," Daviloran said at last—quietly.

Falc looked at him as if he had forgotten the man's presence. "No. Mandeh—that man did not write this," he said, immediately realizing that the prisoner had spoken truth that last time. And now Falc of Risskor was sure that he understood the entire plot—and it was enormous indeed!

TEN

Fear is the parent of foresight.
                              —Sath Firedrake

Aye, there is indeed a magic place beyond the
twinkle of the stars, beyond the moonbeams.
It is called Darkness.
                              —the second Master

A billowing cloud of dust rode the wake of the six riders in
the brown-trimmed grass-blue and yellow of Holder Daviloran
of Cragview. They slowed only when they reached the pink
walls of Lango-by-the-Sea on slobbering dargoni whose tongues
dangled. The people of Lango got out of the way of that
sextet with the determined look, although even in their obvious haste the riders were mindful of the people on the streets
they traversed. They arrived swiftly before the sunburst gate
of the Holding they sought. Nervous guards, all placket-
armored in green and yellow with strong black piping, held
the dangerous-looking group before the gate while they sent
word to their employer.

After a time he appeared on the wall, a nigh-bald man in a
long singlet of black-piped green and yellow over clothing of
azure and gray. Faradox of Lango stared down at the visitors
seeking admittance. He recognized their colors. One of them
swiftly uncovered and the Langoman recognized that round
face and its features, too: his fellow Holder Daviloran, he
who chose to dwell outside city walls without being arlord.

"A greeting, Lord Daviloran, and I hope your blood runs swift and warm. You will pardon my concern, but you look quite the war party. . . ."

"That because we feared attack on the long ride here, my lord, whose blood I hope runs swift and warm. Apprehension is understandable. If it soars in you, admit only one of us then, under guard. Five of us, at least, will hand over our arms. We have ridden long and hard, and we absolutely must talk with you."

That decided Faradox of Lango. "Open the gate for the lord Holder Daviloran of Cragview!"

"Their weapons, my lord?" a sentinel asked, even as the great gate was unbarred.

"Don't anticipate me, man," the Langoman Holder said, and smiled a tight smile.

Even after they had been admitted and their dargs taken to be fed and watered, their host was reluctant to dismiss the several peacekeepers he kept in his private audience chamber. They stood here and there about the high-ceiled hall hung with the colors of Lango and this Holding. A tapestry of six colors and many hues covered one wall, depicting the city-god Ro wresting arms and Lango's banner from demons with the look of First Civilization men. Warm brown-and-red chairs ranged along two sides of a heavy table of polished brown wood. The chair at its head was larger, and beautifully carven, and provided with a cushioned back and seat.

"That is well with us, so long as my lord Faradox absolutely trusts these men and they are sworn to secrecy about our identity and business here."

The Langoman blinked richly blue eyes under handsomely arched brows. He was a man of average height past middle age, with some girth he carried well. His chin was unusually square below a blue-and-gray mustache that covered a mouth apparently short and straight and sparse of lip. His nod was a single jerk of his nearly hairless head.

"I speak for them in that, on pain of their heads and tongues."

Immediately the tallest of his visitors removed his wide-brimmed hat and thrust back his cloak.

"Wh—Sir Knight, never have I seen one of you in disguise!"

"Nor do I like it, Holder Faradox. I am Falc of Risskor,

Contracted to Holder Kinneven of Lock. With the hope that
Holder Faradox's blood runs swift and warm, I have a question. Before my lord answers, I beg that he dismiss these
guards and speak with us in private on a matter more important than my lord Faradox could believe. My question is
whether four weapon-men of this Holding have recently been
slain and beheaded.''

Faradox could not conceal his surprise. ''No! But a darg
with my colors was brought me just at the beginning of this
month of Vorn, bearing four heads in saddle-bags . . . Sir
Falc. They were not, however, of my men. Shar, take your
boys and depart. I am quite safe with these guests. Leave the
door open. Post two men ten paces from it and let no one
closer. Except Mellil; send her hither posthaste, with her
pipes.

All of them watched Faradox's peacekeepers leave, and he
spoke again only when they had gone:

''An open door preserves secrets better than a closed one.
The sound of Mellil's pipes will entertain, but more importantly prevent even the two nearby guards from being able to
distinguish our words. Sir Falc: my Housechief did recognize
one of those heads as a peacekeeper of another Langoman
Holder. . . .''

''Lord Holder Chasmal?''

''Wh-why . . . yes . . .'' The face of Faradox renewed its
look of surprise.

''Please pardon my interruption, my lord; you needed to
know that I knew. Wearing your colors, those four lay in wait
and attacked me. In my ignorance I sent you those heads to
let you know that your attempt had failed.''

''Name of Ashah, Ro, and Markcun—I made no such
attempt!''

''We all know that,'' Falc said, ''now.''

He went silent when she entered; surprisingly not the young
ajmil he had expected, but a well-dressed and far from pretty
young woman he knew and recognized. A little surprised and
showing nothing, he bowed to Faradox's daughter.

Her father said, ''Privacy sounds, Mellil, please.''

She nodded and sat in the chair near the door, where she
commenced a slow, quiet playing of her twin-piped instru-
ment. Noting without thinking about it that it was of Kemite

making, Falc returned his attention to the square-jawed man
gazing expectantly at him.

"Uncover," Daviloran said, and the other four revealed
new surprises. Three others wore his colors but had left their
weapon-belts outside. The fourth, incredibly, was a woman
even less attractive than Mellil. She bowed a head whose
medium blue hair had been gathered carefully under a
peacekeeper's helmet of Cragview.

"My cousin Jinnery," Falc said. "She only just managed
to escape when those same four men murdered her uncle and
his son and burned their farmhouse. I assumed her protection,
near Morazain."

"Your . . . cousin," Faradox said, sinking his azure-and-
gray-clad form slowly into the beautifully carven chair at the
head of his conference table.

Falc glanced at Daviloran. "Nothing but truth must be
spoken in this room. I have merely called her my cousin. Our
relationship has been brother and sister . . . and we have
frequently gotten on no better with each other."

Faradox nodded, waiting.

"I'm glad you chose to sit, my lord," Daviloran said.
"Esteemed Falc?"

He had not intended to remind Faradox of his manners, but
his words served that purpose. Faradox gestured. "Be welcome in this house, all of you, and do seat yourselves, all."

They did, in good chairs without the padding of the Holder's. Falc spoke at once.

"My lord Faradox, the Holder Chasmal is part of a continent-
wide plot. Its purpose is to weaken the citystates of Sij by
destroying the Order Most Old and thus trust and confidence
among the citystates. They have already attacked me twice,
and slain six omos."

Faradox sat up very straight. "By all gods! I'm glad I
seated myself! Is this possible? Man, you speak enormity!"

"I know."

Faradox rapped two fists on the long table and thrust
himself to his feet. His hands were as pale as his face was
dark with infusing blood. "Your count is wrong, Sir Falc.
My newly-Contracted omo was ambushed, trapped, and slain
only two nights ago—less than three weeks after I employed
him! Fortunately I was approached by another only today—"

"What is his name?" someone asked in a strange voice, and the lord Holder Faradox would have sworn that it was none of these six.

"Sir Sench," Faradox said, his eyes casting glances among the six, "of—"

He broke off as a strange illumination came into the room. It brightened, shimmering. It was coalescing into something; an image. . . . Men reached for weapons that were not there, and previously unseen daggers appeared in Faradox's fists as if they had grown there. Mellil's playing broke off on a dreadful note. Eight people stared at an image that only Falc recognized. That did not save him from being more than surprised. No such appearance had been mentioned when he had reported to the Messenger, three nights ago.

The Messenger spoke to them all in that eerie voice out of the depths of a stone well:

"None but the knights of my Order have ever seen me thus. Circumstances dictate extraordinary measures. Sench of Southradd is dead, murdered by the plot-cabal of which Holder Chasmal is a part. Their recognition code-phrase is the plant you call purple shume.

"The supposed Son of Ashah who approached you today is an impostor," the Messenger went on, indicating to their further shock that he must have overheard their very words. "Doubtless he is wearing the true habit of a Son of Ashah . . . stolen from a murdered corpse. Faradox of Lango will be uplifted among men if he allows his visitors to convey that impostor to the High Temple of the Order of Ashah."

Faradox sagged. His daggers were forgotten in pale-knuckled fists. His fear of treachery had faded when he saw that the others were surprised and shaken, too—except for the renowned Falc. Somehow that eased Faradox's apprehension, if not his comprehension. How possibly could this be? He started to speak, had to stop and clear his throat, and tried again in better voice:

"Who—what—"

"I am Ashah, patron of the Order Most Old, Faradox of Lango. Only the most monumental threat to your entire society prompts me to reveal myself thus to anyone not of the Order founded in my name, who are my chosen men. If others do not know that I have thus appeared to you, all will benefit. Faradox of Lango, this threat to your civilization must be removed.''

A visibly shaky Faradox agreed.

"Mellil," he said quietly, "hurry and fetch Prefect Shar to the door. My lord Daviloran, will you loan me your three guardsmen?"

He followed the shaky young woman to the door, with the shaky men of Daviloran following him. Faradox spoke to his peacekeeper chief just outside the audience room, that the fellow might not see the impossible *manifestation* inside.

"Give these three men of our very good friend Holder Daviloran their weapons, Shar. Take them to that fellow Sench who came today, and arrest him. He is not an omo at all, but wearing the garb of a murdered one."

Leaving Shar to handle his shock in his own way, Faradox paced back to his chair. He kept his gaze on the wavering manifestation all the while. He could not *quite* see through it. Was it watching him, too, or merely moving its eyes at will? It? Ashah! After this, should a man perhap cease swearing by the demigod Markcun and Lango's divine protector, Ro?

"Faradox," that hollow voice said, "I shall send you a true knight of my Order before the nearer sun has completed a full circuit of Sij. May the blood of all of you run swift and . . . *hot*."

The Messenger vanished, and the outré light left the chamber more rapidly than it had come. Sighs gusted out, and the other three stared at Falc.

"You have seen—experienced this afore," Faradox said.

"Yes."

"Sir Knight, that is not enough answer!"

Falc nodded. "He appears to all of us, but nearly always at night and only when we are alone. We often are."

Jinnery sat back, releasing a sigh of revelation. Now she understood a thing or three!

"He . . . He *sees*," Faradox prompted. "He knows when you are alone."

"Yes."

"He knew what we'd said!"

Falc nodded.

"Well. His final promise is manifestly impossible. Thus it will be proof of the identity of this . . . apparition, if an omo—that is, when an omo arrives.'' Faradox glanced down then, and noticed that he was still making fists, and that each still sprouted a long dagger. He laid them on the table before him, careful of its finish and polish. "I can . . . I—with this appearance and your news, I can no longer be sure of anything I know to be—anything I have always *assumed* to be true.''

Falc saw no reason to say anything to that. He was at thought, marveling that he had never previously noticed: Ashah or no, the Messenger lent the same peculiar pronunciation to the word "hot"—so that it rhymed with "bought"—as did the Firedrake.

Faradox, Daviloran and Jinnery looked at Falc and at each other in silence. Perhaps their thoughts were similar to those of Faradox:

What meaning had all this?

Why did this fellow Falc of Risskor to whom he had tried to send word never come—oh.

Sir Falc had never received the word.

Why had Chasmal been so inimical these past few months—oh. But . . . *Chasmal!*

And how had this ghostly Appearance taken place? A *god?*

The false Sench put up a fight. They took him alive, but perforated.

A real knight of the Order Most Old arrived before dawn. Sent, he said, by Ashah Himself.

ELEVEN

Death exists that life may not become boring.
                              —the fourth Master

We must then seek the development of our po-
tential not as makers of things, but as discover-
ers of self. . . .
Men breed conflict and conflict breeds wars.
The thing called Nationalism makes for larger
wars, and the evil called technology makes that
untenable. The social system we have is best,
because it is safe. We do more than survive; we
abide. It is Change that must be feared.
                              —the second Master

At last, on the sixth day of the eighth month, called Belief,
Falc and Jinnery reached that place which Falc had for so
long called home: Lock.

Jinnery saw nothing magical about it. On the other hand,
Falc had never indicated that he thought of it so. Still, she
had expected more than walls of cut pinkstone and buildings
mostly of wood rather than stone. She made no comment.
Riding through the sovereign city that was as dirty and crowded
and noisy as them all, she did notice how well-known he was,
and how liked. Respected, at least. It occurred to her that she
had long been in the company of a man who was genuinely
renowned. That led her to the realization that she was among
the few ever to have insulted him and lived. Probably she was
the only one living who had insulted him several times!

Jinnery swallowed, and none who watched them pass could
guess why she was smiling.

He was hailed from within the roundhouse rising above and behind the glaring whitewashed walls as if he were Sath Firedrake himself. His responses were . . . Falcian.

"Welcome home, Sir Falc!" a rather aged stable "boy" said, with a big smile showing a tooth containing metal, and he took their dargs. He led them away talking fondly to Harr, Jinnery noted.

Then they were mounting three steps to a big thick front door. Suddenly it was opened from within and a smiling man came hurrying out to them. He was fully as tall as Falc, and a good-looking man of about fifty. His big smile looked genuine, and became him. Falc had told her his age, for this was his lord by Contract. Good-looking legs, too, Jinnery naturally noticed, for the broad-shouldered man wore no leggings under his ultramarine, gold-bordered tunic. Sandals on his feet, too, rather than boots.

"Falc!" his big voice boomed, and he shocked Jinnery then: he embraced his omo, whose arms went round him as well, perhaps with less enthusiasm of clasp. "Long and long you've been gone this time, old smiley one! And who's this you've brought?"

"My lord Holder Kinneven of Lock, this is Jinnery of Morazain Road, whom I call cousin and is the first woman ever to have been to the High Temple. Also," Falc bravely added, "the only woman ever to have saved my life."

"Indeed? Lady, I am honored. The first *person* to've saved your life, I'd say, Falc. Come in, come in both. Ashah and Vier, obviously you have tales to tell!"

As they entered Falc said, "Well my lord knows that he once saved my life."

"And he mine, more'n once I'd say! But let us stop confessing past sins! Lady Jinnery, that is a most beautiful tunic and cloak. If Falc has taught me well over the years, I'd hazard that it is of Langoman making."

"Thank you, lord Holder; and I am no lady."

"Hmp! I'd never've known *that*! Sometimes it's in the person rather than in the birth or station—or marriage, isn't it!"

She smiled and looked down. She was self-conscious in the short tunic of tricolor paisley Faradox had presented her. She felt hardly worthy of the long, billowy cloak of scarlet silk.

An hour ago Falc had caused her to take off her leggings—soft leather beauties, forced upon her by Millel of Lango—and exchange boots for sandals. The women of Lock, he told her, wore no leggings and no boots and she would not care to be stared at. It had not occurred to her that she would be stared at anyhow, because she was with Falc of Risskor whom they considered their own.

And this man and Falc had embraced, she marveled. Falc! And he'd called him what?—old smiley? Ashah, what a relationship!

"Calling her 'cousin,' is it? And what d'you call him, Jinnery?"

"Cousin."

"Hmp! Probably beat you if you dared use his name, and remove this or that portion of your anatomy if you tried 'old smiley one,' is it? Your quarters here going to be big enough for two, Falc?"

"Yes. My lord has been most kind, despite my protests, as to the size of my accommodations."

Kinneven laughed. "Going to keep on My Lording me so long as Jinnery's about, Falc, or is this another new development?"

Falc sighed, looking around at cool halls whose walls were painted cerulean. "It has been long, Kinneven. And I had better return to the old habit. I had best tell you at once of the imminent arrival of visitors: Holder Daviloran and his nephew. They wish to discuss your daughter, and alliance . . ."

"Oh really. Old Cragview himself! How imminent, Falc?"

"I'd say tomorrow. Perhap, late. Perhap the next day. Soon."

"Um. We must prepare. How's this nephew look, Falc?"

"Like the heir to Cragview's many hectares, my lord."

Kinneven laughed and stretched an arm across his omo's back, to clap the far shoulder. "Damned good answer! Damned good answer! Have you seen him, Jinnery? How's he look to a woman?"

"Young, sturdy, nicely built. To most women, my lord, he looks like the heir to Cragview."

Kinneven of Lock laughed the more.

They walked, Kinneven talked and laughed, Falc replied. Jinnery met Kinneven's Housechief and immediately forgot his name; the Holder told the little fellow they were about to have guests, and to lay on a banquet or two and see that the guesting chambers were well-aired and the ajmini instructed. She met Jorgen, an inordinately chesty man who was Prefect of Kinneven's household peacekeepers, and saw what friends the truly burly man and Falc were, and how glad to see each other.

"Ah, from Glabbleglabblenongo, I see; one can always recognize a woman from there by her left little fingernail," he said, and went off practically bellowing with laughter at his joke on Falc.

Falc looked almost ready to smile.

Kinneven mentioned wine and laughed when his omo said no. He thought to ask Jinnery, who accepted the offer.

This was difficult for her. It was difficult for all of them: Falc, Daviloran and the nephew named for him, and the Master and the Order, and of course now Faradox and the man she had not met: Kaladen. How messages had flown back and forth, omos contacted by the Messenger and reporting to this Holder and that; Holders sending communiqués by Holders through the Messenger. And now, here, meeting this fine and nice and nice-looking man . . . it was harder still.

Wine would be nice. Even from him.

As she and Falc had ridden here, he and the Messenger had not bothered to hide the Manifestation from her. All gods smile, but she had actually met the Master of the Order Most Old, and accepted his thanks for saving "our best, dear Jinnery my daughter, our very best!" The false Sench had known more than "Mandehal," and had been persuaded to share his knowledge. They had learned that the employers of the murderers in the biggest plot in the history of Sij were Holders Barakor of Missentia, Chasmal of Lango, and . . . this nice and nice-looking man, Kinneven of Lock. Only days ago they had become sure that this jovial man who had embraced his own Falc had plotted against the Order itself; and had plotted against Falc. He had sent his long-Contracted omo and *friend* to his fellow conspirator Chasmal, with a message whose meaning Falc would surely never have fathomed but for what they had learned.

Now he had interpreted the message, and even the Master agreed with him:

In a few words about the purple shume, Falc had unknowingly apprised Chasmal that the conspiracy was growing by the day and "aerially rooting"—that is, picking up peripheral aid or hired help; that the killing of omos had begun; and further that they durst not ask Faradox to join, and must consider him Enemy.

The long road leading to discovery of the plot had begun with Chasmal's Housechief: the fellow had slipped badly. Falc was supposed to die *after* he had reported to Chasmal. Poor Alazhar had been less than a tool. He really did believe that he had been employed by Faradox! As to the guards, Chasmal's peacemen were ancillary tools. It was Alazhar who had subverted them with coin and promises.

Now Falc understood why Chasmal had ruined the poor fool's mouth. Plotter Chasmal had wanted no more talking that might prove embarrassing and worse!

Now they were sure of Chasmal's cleverness and treachery. He had covered fast, and gone along. After thanking and congratulating and practically fawning over Falc, and presenting him with gifts, Chasmal had sent after the "estimable Falc" the four assassins in Faradox's colors. If they had succeeded, he who was probably the most dangerous omo would be gone forever. If they failed, Falc would believe as he had: that the attempt came from Faradox! Chasmal never knew what happened to the four, or whether Falc of Risskor was alive or dead. In a roundabout conference over distance three nights ago, via the Messenger, Falc had avowed that Chasmal's son Chazar knew nothing of any of this. Faradox, who knew Chazar, agreed; the Master and Daviloran and Kaladen of Missentia reserved judgment, saying that they would not trust Chazar until they were surer than sure.

Last night, for the first time and in Jinnery's presence as well, Falc had addressed the Messenger as "Master." That was one more ripple added to the tide roiling in the mind of a woman of twenty who had never known her father and had taken to the streets, an orphan, at twelve, and lived the almost newsless life of a farmer for the past four years.

Now she accepted wine from the hand of a smiling, nice and nice-looking deadly enemy, and was even able to look him in the face and smile as she thanked him.

*Ah, damn you, Falc! It was easier on the farm, being a
bitter nagging drudge!*

2

That first night of his arrival back in Lock and his Contract
lord's household, Falc waited behind a locked door with his
"cousin." They had decided that they could stand the inti-
macy in a single room as they had on the road, with more
care for each other's sensitivity. It was wiser to let Kinneven
make the natural assumption that they were bed companions.
For Jinnery was Falc's friend and his confidante if not his
cousin or his sister, and a member of the plot against the
plotters, and privy too to the appearances of the Messenger.
They had their answer now. The Messenger (the Master? But
how?) had reported last night, appearing to them among trees
in a canyon well off the road to Lock. It was all part of the
purple shume business, and the poem.

Who was the "main stem?"

Who, indeed, would profit by the end of the Order and lack
of trust and communication among the Holders and thus of
the citystates?

Emperor Shalderanis.

"Chasmal, Barakor—and yes, Falc—Kinneven are the promised high barons of the new empire," the Messenger had
reported, in a voice more sibilantly whispery than hollow.
"Satrap rulers without rival, of territories each to contain
more than one citystate; all under their 'employer': Shalderanis,
Emperor."

Boy or no, the plot was all his. He could even be said to be
acting rightly, or rightfully. All the too-clever youth wanted
to do was make his old title reality again. To return Sij to the
days before Sath Firedrake. To rule the continent as he had
never ceased feeling he was meant to do, as descendant of
Sarl Sarlis. Oh, some of it was doubtless the result of the old
tutor and advisor of his earliest years. But all persons were
partly the result of their early mentors, and the plot was
Shalderanis's.

And now Jinnery and Falc waited in his long-time quarters,
a large chamber in the keep of the enemy. They awaited the

growing illumination that would herald the Messenger, and more knowledge from several Holders and many omos in many places: their fellow plotters against the plotters.

In the small room adjoining, Falc had ritually divested himself of his garments and weapons. He returned to her in his clothes of ease: a long mossweave tunic of glittery black, snug black woolen leggings, and short boots of maroon felt. The chest of the high-collared tunic bore the Order's blazon in deep scarlet: a closed fist and enough forearm to show the scar of Ashah.

They waited.

"The Messenger is very, very busy these past days," Jinnery said, because the silence wanted filling. "He contacts us, reports and listens, contacts Holder Faradox and company, reports and listens, contacts Sir Somebody, and so on. Then he starts again, reporting to each the information the others gave him. But then other things have happened, and he gains new information. . . ." She trailed off, shaking her head. "It is magic and wonderful, but what a terrible strain on the Mas . . . the Messenger."

"Jinn . . . do not get the idea because I called him 'Master' that I believe the Messenger is the Firedrake. Obviously that is impossible. Whether he is Ashah or the spirit of Sath Firedrake, though, he *is* my master."

"Oh, *Falc*! I thought you'd given up lying to me, Old Stoneface."

"Just don't think too much for your small brain, Young Stoneface."

She smiled. "Falc . . . how old are you?"

"Years older than you, but not old enough to be called 'Old' Stoneface!" After a moment he came very close to making a joke: "It makes me think of the lovely name 'Esphodine. . . .' "

"You'll never hear Old Stoneface from me, Cousin Falc!" She glanced around. "This is a lovely chamber, Falc. And with that little room adjoining, too! After seeing the Temple and its quarters, this is exceptional luxury for an omo!"

"Too luxurious for an omo. Kinneven insisted. I think now that he was trying to subvert me."

"Hmm!" she said, and the Manifestation stopped their converse by beginning to illumine the room.

"Harr," Falc said, and "Tay," Jinnery said, for time was important and the recognition codes had been shortened and stripped of the trappings of the Order. In two words they had identified themselves to the Messenger's satisfaction.

"The Sons of Ashah are ascramble all over the continent. In Lango, *unknown assailants* have slain Holder Chasmal, but there is evidence that they were working for Barakor of Missentia. It has been established that Chazar knew absolutely nothing of his father's plans. However *Holder* Chazar will not have opportunity to take vengeance. By the morrow he will have been advised by Sir Ashox of news in Missentia: Holder Kaladen of that city has seized the Holding of Barakor, and is daring anyone to do anything about it."

"Two down," Jinnery murmured, knowing that Faradox and his new omo had planted the evidence against Barakor when they slew the plotter Chasmal. She marveled at the swiftness and efficacy of the Order and its allies. All because the Messenger kept them in contact. How wonderful knowledge and communication were!

"By sunrise the Temple of Missentia will have endorsed Holder Kaladen, and citizens will see four Sons of Ashah ride from the Temple to stand by Kaladen in Barakor's former Holding. Word of further support of Multiholder Kaladen will arrive with astonishing swiftness from Holders Daviloran of Cragview and Stavishen of Lock, since it was on its way minutes after Kaladen succeeded. So will word of what that wicked Barakor caused to be done in Lango: murder of a fellow Holder! Stavishen is awaiting the visit of Jinnery to advise him when Kinneven's guests have arrived and are in his House.

"They should arrive late on the morrow, with things to tell you. You will have things to tell them?"

"Yes."

"May the morrow be better for you and for Sij than this day has been!"

Light and the manifestation of the Messenger left the room more suddenly than they had come, as usual.

Falc sat staring at the place where the silvery image had been. It had begun, and more than begun. Two of the three main plotters were dead. Assassins would be scuttling for their holes and hoping no one ever traced them to the men whose money they had taken. It was the nature of citystates to remain aloofly apart and autonomous, and so did most of the Holders within them. They did not realize how entirely dependent they had become on the Order and its omos. Holders sent messages by the knight-Sons of Ashah; Holders learned and knew what omos told them. Kinneven's prime co-conspirators were dead and he knew nothing of it. Yet those they had made their enemies were in constant communication, receiving and exchanging each new piece of information daily and even oftener. As for the too-clever young man called Emperor: Shalderanis would learn of all this only by the normal means: the length of time it took his spies in Missentia and Lango to learn and confirm the news, and then ride to destroy the hopes of their young and ambitious lord. He might learn what had happened in those places within two days, Falc supposed.

As to events here in Lango; well, those had yet to happen. A ferg was not a meal until it was in the pot.

He looked at Jinnery. She sat hunched forward, staring at him from large eyes.

"Falc? It's . . . it's begun."

He nodded. He saw no reason to say anything, but did. "*We've* begun."

3

Daviloran of Cragview and his slender young nephew Daviloran arrived in style and panoply. Ten weapon-men rode before and six more behind them and their drovers, with the several dargs bearing supplies and gifts for Kinneven. The Cragview colors of grass-blue and yellow with brown trim were much in evidence. Helmets with cheek-protectors like stylized battle-axes and broad nasals gleamed in the late afternoon sunlight, along with the overdone harness on every darg. Only the heads of the two Davilorans were bare, with the hoods of their cloaks thrown back. Of the palest yellow, the cloaks of uncle and nephew spread out behind them over the rumps of their mounts, which were caparisoned in yellow trimmed with blue.

Because Holder Kinneven's man had long since apprised

the gatemen of this arrival and bidden them open after the briefest of challenges, the glittering procession was swiftly passed into the city.

The entire party rode erect, gazing straight ahead without seeming to note the stares of the people of Lock and their shouts to others to come and have a look. These foreign helms were fascinating! They were so covering with their ferocious barga-head visors that not a man of the escort had a face save for mouth and chin and, in most cases, mustache.

Kinneven had dressed for the occasion hours ago, in his own colors and best dress cloak. Word reached him well ahead of the visitors, for Lockman citizens of both sexes and all ages flocked to see the procession and gain glimpse of one of those country holders they had never seen. The foreigners must be careful of their dargs with the Lockmen crowding them close. Thus Kinneven in his white-lined scarlet cloak was waiting just outside his open gates when they reached his Holding.

Daviloran dismounted at once and in the view of many watchers unbuckled his melt-studded weapons belt. He proffered it and its sheathed blades to Kinneven. That Holder accepted the symbolic presentation and used all his voice to say loudly, "Be welcome in this House." Then he handed back the visitor's weapons. Daviloran passed them up to one of his armed escort in another gesture of trust and amicability.

Kinneven stepped back, mindful of the extra long hem of his cloak, and gestured broadly. Furling the cloak over one arm, Holder Daviloran remained afoot and led his mount. The visitors entered the courtyard. Servants and slaves took the animals away for food, water, and stabling. The drovers unloaded the pack-dargs. With the aid of the fiercely helmeted escort, they bore the packages into the House of Kinneven.

"My lord of Cragview," Kinneven said as he watched all those guest-gifts pass, "you travel with a goodly escort."

The round-faced man smiled. "Nor will I ever know whether it was worth the trouble, my lord. We were not molested—but might not have been had we left ten or so behind! One is not used to traveling, and I am sure those of you in cities hear tales of the countryside just as we do of cities! We had heard of some trouble in Lango, and I admit it made me overly cautious. Do you travel much, my lord?''

''No. What need has a man to leave his Holding's city, save to go to the occasional fair? I too am nervous when I go out into the world we know so little about.''

''Indeed. Lord Holder Kinneven, may I present the son of my brother, who named him for me. We have ever called him Davilo, to avoid confusion.''

''My lord Daviloran, Holder Daviloran: be welcome in my House. But what's this of trouble in Lango?''

Daviloran shrugged. ''I've really little idea. Some passages at arms between Holdings, as I have it. Lord Faradox was involved, but I forget the other name. An omo brought the news; he was on his way somewhere else, as they usually are. Does my lord have friends in Lango?''

''Not really. Do come inside.''

They went inside, all of them. Three of the supply bundles were borne by Daviloran's weapon-men to the quarters assigned them. There they took care to pile them in a corner beyond the pallets, making sure that the other two were atop the one containing crossbows, quarrels, and uniforms. Next they unhelmeted themselves. Only six of the escort were of Cragview. Four were Langomen: Holder Faradox's very best. Of the others, three were superbly skilled fighters his nephew had employed years ago. The proper uniforms of the other three were packed away. Under their helms, they wore the black skullcaps of the Order.

While Kinneven showed the Davilorans around his household, their escort waited opportunity for Falc to apprise them of the situation here and what he had learned of the traitor's men. Jinnery meanwhile slipped out to take a roundabout route to the Holding of Stavishen, to advise that the invasion force had been taken into the traitor's House.

Most privately indeed, Falc of Risskor, O.M.O., was gazing dourly at a pale Prefect Jorgen.

''It is all true, Jorgen. Both the other two are dead. I know it is a blow, man; it was to me. Would you like me to swear?''

Slowly, shaking his head, the big peacekeeper sank into a chair.

4

After last night's sumptuous feasting and the first meeting of Davilo and Kinneven's daughter Kinnemil, host and guests held a meeting in Kinneven's lovely rear garden. Also present were Falc, three of the escorts, several household peacekeepers and their prefect, and at Kinneven's whim, Jinnery. Indeed he held her arm as he ambled deep into his sprawling garden, all in white with a sash of his colors girding his waist and a short blue cape almost exactly the color of his eyes. About the backs of her ankles fluttered the yellow cloak that was his personal gift. A good color for her, the charming man had said.

They came to pause where several chairs and two large tables of white-painted stone rested in the sun-dappled shade beneath an enormous say tree of great age, garlanded with ghostvine like blue-gray strings of pearls and giant cobwebs. Just beyond was a prettily painted summerhouse. Kinneven paused, one hand resting on a stone sun-clock. He took his hand from the so-thin arm of Jinnery, who tarried there near him in his yellow gift-cloak, not knowing what to do.

"So, my lord," he said, smiling that handsome and so-open smile, "it would seem that your nephew and my daughter do not dislike each other. She is eighteen, the daughter of my second wife. I would know the lord Davilo's age."

"I am twenty-six and have been wed, Holder. I lost my wife two years ago to childbed fever."

"But their ages don't matter," Daviloran said. His usually open and ingenuous expression had become serious and boyish eyes were suddenly mannish indeed. Their stare pierced like crossbow quarrels. "He does not need my blessing, and may marry the orphan of a murderous traitor if he so desires."

Kinneven's reply was barely controlled: *"What?"*

"My lord," Falc said quietly, "I know who tried to have me killed, and who employed those men who murdered my brother omos and would have murdered more; and I know fully the meaning of your message to the late Holder Chasmal, including the identity of the 'main stem' you referred to when you sent me there to be slain."

"What? Falc, Falc!—what *ever* are you talking about?"

"About you, and the Emperor's plan, and the plot of his

barons-to-be, you and Chasmal and the late Barakor of Missentia. Chasmal was so misadvised as to entrust the matter of my slaying to his Housechief Alazhar, who thought the order came from Holder Faradox. At any rate, he and Chasmal's prefect felt that the prefect and three others were enough to take me. They were mistaken.''

Jinnery took a step back from the staring Kinneven. Accused and accusers, household peacekeepers and escort-guards stood in frozen tableau in the lovely garden of Kinneven, their faces and colorful clothing dappled in sun and shade filtered through the huge old say tree and its ornamental burden of ghostvine. All stared at Kinneven except Kinneven. His stare roved among them and he trembled.

Abruptly he smiled. "Now, treacherous swine, learn that I am none so trusting as you supposed. All of you are watched and menaced from my walls and that lovely little summer-house just behind me. Best surrender your arms. Jorgen! Take them!''

"Take them yourself, my lord. I'll have no part of your stinking plot.''

"What?" Holder Kinneven stared hard at his prefect. He let Jorgen see the curl of his lip before he turned his head partway to one side. "Garsh! Come out the summerhouse and show yourself! You on the walls—show yourselves and your crossbows.''

Smiling again, Kinneven confidently watched the men he faced shift their gazes past him, and was sure that armed men were emerging from the summerhouse. Still, he saw no alarm in the faces of his accusers, and heard nothing . . . and then he did. A voice called out, from behind him.

"They're all secure, my lords. Three of us were enough. I am happy to report that only one was so stupid as to get himself wounded.''

In his alarm Kinneven forgot the menace before and whirled to face the one behind. Beside the summerhouse, weapons sheathed, stood a man in helm, tunic and leggings of black. From his shoulders hung a long twin-pointed cloak black as the wing of a crawk.

When Kinneven spun back, one of the three men who had just stepped past Daviloran had removed his helmet, to reveal a skullcap identical to the one Kinneven had seen so many times on the head of his own Contract-omo. For an instant he stared. Then he looked about wildly.

No one stood on the walls. No one.

"My lord," Prefect Jorgen said, "once you had placed the men in the summerhouse, I summoned the rest of your peace-keepers to a special meeting in the barrack-room. Evidently they went. Since the walls are unmanned, they must have decided not to try to force their way past the leveled cross-bows held by Sir Ashalc of the Order and four of Holder Daviloran's men."

"I'd say that by now those five are backed up by a number of men from Stavishen-Holding," Daviloran said.

"STAVishen!" Pale and unsmiling at last, Kinneven looked about at them. Jinnery backed another pace from him. "So. I have been tried and found guilty. Well, by all the gods, the world were better off with some of that unity you omos mouthe about, Falc, rather than set all apart behind the guarded walls of little sovereign cities! Damn you all! With that malleable boy Shalderanis as a symbol, we could have created true unity, and started Sij again on the road to progress! Look at us! *Swords and cross*bows, indeed!"

No one spoke. Every eye gazed at Holder Kinneven of Lock.

"So. Found guilty and now guilty from my own mouth of the heinous crime of hoping to drag Sij back from this world of mutually mistrustful slaveholders inside mutually mistrustful walled enclaves we pretend are cities! Guilty, by the gods! Even by *Ashah,* you damned monks who hid under the fierce helmets of peacemen! Then what is the sentence, hmm? Has that too been decided?"

Yes, he saw that it had. He knew, looking at their implacable eyes. He knew, for he had heard the calm, unstressed words of Falc: "the late Holder Chasmal; the late Barakor of Missentia . . ." Dead then, both of them. Lost, all lost. Of course he had been sentenced. The sentence was death. Lost: an enormous plan; the promise of extraordinary power. All lost, lost. But *Death,* by all gods!

He nodded. "So. And who is to carry out this sentence. Daviloran? Or you, little Daviloran? Jorgen? Are you prepared to slay me as well as betray me, hmm?"

"You betrayed me, Holder."

Kinneven showed him only a sneer. He took a step toward Falc. "My own Contracted omo? You, Falc?"

"No man must slay a Holder he protects," Falc said quietly, dark eyes showing pain but meeting his Contractlord's all the while. "And yet no man has more right or so much reason to slay the honorless Kinneven of Lock."

Kinneven took another step toward him. "You, then! Deathknight indeed, eh?"

Falc said nothing. Falc gazed at him.

A frozen tableau, in the lovely and well-tended garden behind the House of Kinneven, under a sky-reaching old say strung with ghostvine.

But *Death*, by all gods!

It was Kinneven who moved, and in a lunge. Jinnery had backed but two paces from him; now he too had taken those two paces, supposedly toward her grim "cousin." He had to make only a short swift lunge to whirl her with an arm across her breast. His other hand was a fist, holding a dagger across her throat.

"You will all stand very still while the honorable Falc's cousin and I depart this boring meeting. If you charge you will have me, but she will have a second mouth. Well, Falc? Do you call yourself her protector still, or do you turn on her as you have me?"

Falc stood still, his cloak shifting in a gentle breeze that rustled through the dangling strands of ghostvine. He said nothing. The voice came from behind Kinneven:

"I can put a bolt through his cloak and between his shoulder blades from here, brother."

Falc shook his head. "No. In reflex he would gash her throat. I beg you all, lords and men of weapons: let this be. All is lost to this plotsome traitor. What use if he escapes us now?"

Kinneven chuckled and began to back away. Jinnery staggered. His hand shifted and blood appeared on her throat. She made a noise and he eased off hurriedly. She slammed herself back, then, and whirled as he staggered away. That movement made a further cut in her neck, but her right fist jerked up from low and drove into the plotter's belly a long and sharp gift from his fellow plotter Chasmal. She let go the dagger's hilt at once, and leaped away as his arm and indeed his entire body twitched.

Kinneven looked down at the jeweled hilt standing from his middle.

"Damn!" he said in a gasp. "Trust a damned woman not to do a thorough job!"

At the same time as he grasped the hilt and pushed with all his strength, his other hand drove the point of his own dagger into his throat.

They stared without speaking for many seconds after the fallen Holder's legs ceased jerking. Daviloran spoke first, and moved.

"Halllp! Assassins!" the fat man with the face of an angel shouted, and in two swift movements slashed his right forearm and stabbed himself in the left upper arm.

5

"In Lock," the Messenger said again and again and again, to man after man after man, "Holder Kinneven has been murdered and his guest the valiant Holder Daviloran wounded when two of Kinneven's own peacekeepers broke into the garden and tried to murder them both. Their motive is unknown, as they were slain by the noble Daviloran and Sir Falc of the Order, but the late Holder's Prefect of Peacekeepers states that he has evidence that both men were paid by the late Barakor of Missentia. The peacekeepers of Holder Vannashah of Lock are maintaining security in Kinneven-Holding, and Vannashah has called Lock's Council of Holders into an emergency meeting.

"And now . . . here is something we all know about the purple shume. It stands not tall, and though it puts forth aerial roots, its main stem is young and thin, and unsupported, and weak."

All over the continent, the Sons of Ashah and certain Holders smiled and expelled sighs of relief.

TWELVE

In each ending there is a beginning
—ancient Sijese saying

In the beginning is the seed of the end.
—Sath Firedrake's addition

The unprecedented *Manifestation* was shock and enormity throughout the continent, and so was the news it conveyed. Every Holder on the continent was alarmed by the sudden appearance of a strange light, and an image in shimmery silvery gray, and saw the ancient habiliments of the legendary Sath Firedrake. And they heard him speak.

Each was advised of the prodigious occurrences in Lango and in Lock and in Missentia, and each was told that investigation by the Order Most Old and nearby Holders proved that the assailants were the same as the murderers of no fewer than seven omos in the past two months: agents of Emperor Shalderanis!

2

The first time they had made this darg-back trek to the Mountain of God, they had been companions by circumstance, each striving to be tolerant and civil. Their success in

221

that was occasional. Now they came riding again, and they were friends. Once again Falc of Risskor journeyed to confer with his Order's Master. This time he sought not permission to err terribly, as he had before and had so fortunately been denied; this time he sought to counsel with the Firedrake about which offer of Contract he would accept.

Jinnery rode where he rode, for now. She was the first woman ever to enter the Mon-Ashah-re, the Order Most Old's High Temple of Ashah; the first woman ever to have met the Master after he was in that post; the first woman ever to have saved the life of an omo; the woman who had saved a Son of Ashah from breaking the solemn oath of omo and Contract agreement to do that which he knew he must: kill his own Contract-lord. She was also the first woman ever to have killed a Holder and been hailed as hero for it.

Only a couple of days ago she had learned something else. Until Falc told her, it had never occurred to her that she was the only woman he had ever thought of as friend.

"I am happy to call you cousin, and I would call you sister," he said in an extremely low tone, and she would always believe but would never, never say that she thought she had heard the quaver of emotion in that voice.

As for Jinnery, she had wept. Eventually she had had to explain to him who knew everything that her tears were of joy. Falc had looked thoughtful, and nodded his belief, if not understanding. Predictably, he saw no reason to say anything.

Today they had been riding in silence for a long while, which was far easier for Falc than for his companion. Jinnery was tired of it.

"I understand your wanting to talk with the Master, Falc— how tired he must be, that old man!—but is it necessary? I mean—haven't you made up your mind?"

"No."

"I'd have thought . . . well. Holder Daviloran offered you Contract, and so did his nephew, right?"

"Yes. I could not of course accept with the younger when the older had offered, and so I discounted Davilo's."

"Umm. And *our* friend Daviloran turned out to be no-where near as soft as he looks, didn't he! Anyhow, Holder Faradox of Lango also offered you Contract."

"Yes."

"And Holder Chazar, also of Lango, offered you Contract, too."

"Yes."

"And Holder Stavishen of Lock. He too offered Contract."

"Yes."

She gestured and white cloth rustled; she chose to wear Falc's derlin rather than the gift-cloak of the late Kinneven. "Since it's right in the same city where you have dwelt so long—when you're at, uh, home I mean—I should think that one would be the most attractive."

Falc rode gazing straight ahead. "That one is out of the question."

She said "oh," and they rode for a kilometer or so in silence. Then: "Falc? Why is Stavishen out of the question?"

"Because he is in the same city where I have dwelt so long, Contracted with Kinneven. I . . . liked Kinneven."

She sighed as she nodded. "I know. Liking him was easy." Suddenly she erupted a short burst of laughter. "A lot easier than liking either of us."

"Yes," he said, looking straight ahead.

She shot him a look.

After a time, she said, "Cousin? Why don't you try think-ing aloud, tell someone what *you* think for a change. Tell your cousin, Falc."

He looked over at her, blinking in surprise. She saw the light come into his eyes and knew that he was smiling, for she had learned to recognize that sign, even while the rest of his face showed nothing.

"What's funny?"

"I didn't laugh, Jinn. You said 'for a change.' I have spent most of my life bearing messages and giving advice. That means telling people what I think, precisely what I think. I think now that I should much like to Contract with Daviloran, whom I respect. I wronged him once, laid hands on him and *forced* him to take vow, and he is so mature, so much man, that he set it aside and offered Contract anyhow. Yet I feel that I can best serve by joining Chazar of Lango, who is painfully young and needs aid and guidance."

"I like the sound of that." She waved a hand, with a flash of the bracelet that was hers as spoils of combat won. "Perhap he could use a housekeeper or something. I am also painfully young and could use some aid and guidance.''

She smiled. Not until they reached the Mon-Ashah-re and she had cornered that old, old man called Master would she broach her real goal, and she was prepared to be just as persuasive and insistent as his reluctance might require. Yet Jinnery *knew* that she would gain her dream: the formation of an Order called the Daughters of Ashah.

Each of them was quiet amid separate thoughts as they wended a slow way around a gigantic outcrop of rock that was no smaller than Cragview manse. At last their mounts paced out of its shadow.

''Ah! Falc, look!'' She pointed at the long slope of a mountain ahead, and the tumbled rocks and rocky débris lying at its feet like broken offerings. ''We're almost there. The Mountain of God!''

''Yes,'' Falc said. ''Almost there.''

EPILOGUE

In the innermost chamber of the Mon-Ashah-re, the Master of the Order Most Old was on his knees, praying for guidance. Perhap it should be for forgiveness. He was weary and very, very glad that this crisis was over, and yet he felt that he owed his god apology and prayer for forgiveness. He had spent many hours, mostly at night, appearing as the Messenger to many men not of the Order, and even to a woman as well; and he had iterated and reiterated the awful lie that he was Ashah. Yet that way he had not revealed to anyone the secret of Secrets of the Mon-Ashah-re: the ''Magic'' of the Mechanists' monitoring and communications devices of the First Civilization that allowed him to send his voice and his image (however mottled and ghostly) anywhere his omos had been or were; and more importantly, to hear them.

The Master prayed also for guidance. He was old and he was tired, and he had not yet chosen his successor.